The Allentown Murders

by

Michael J Maccalupo

Website: http://mjmaccalupo.com
Email: michael@mjmaccalupo.com

Available in Hardcover, Paperback & eBook
[Audiobook coming soon]

ISBN-13: 978-0-9894340-2-7
ISBN-10: 0989434028

Write Beyond Publishing
PO Box 10778
Wilmington, NC 28404

Also by Michael J Maccalupo:

Where the Road Begins (2011)
Murder at Ravenswood Hall (2012)
The Almost Definitive Collection vol. 1 (2013)

~Coming Winter 2014~

The Umbrella [A Twisted Mystery]

All available in Paperback, Hardcover & eBook
Audiobooks coming soon

Dedication

This book is dedicated to my family, as I watch it grow — bigger, stronger and happier!

Acknowledgments

This, my fourth fictional work, like any book, is finished but never done. I hope it meets and surpasses the expectations of my readers.

I want to acknowledge my wife, Gigi, who continues to support me in my writing habit, as well as those family members and friends who have been cheerleaders for me along this rocky road.

I would also like to acknowledge all of those distractions that kept me from working on this for many months at a time. I had every intention to complete this book six months earlier; but, due to various impediments along the way, it has been the better for the delay. Oftentimes living life can bring things to light that may have been missed when pressured by the constraints of time itself. What seemed to some like idleness was, in reality, a story brewing. So thank you to all that distracted me!

Contents

Part III
The Murder   [Hap Pozner]   91

Part IV
The Convergence [Hap Pozner]   193

INTRODUCTION

It was the spring of 1986; a time of great promise. The cold war was virtually over, the Berlin Wall was soon to come down; and the promise of a bright future for Joanie and I lay just ahead within our sights.

Slick and Susie were still Slick and Susie, but with careers, and our families were healthy and happy. Who could ask for more?

But this was real life, not some storybook tale. And oftentimes in life when things seem to be going smoothly the bottom drops out.

This was the year when we all learned a great deal about life, about love, about hate and about nightmares.

But I'm getting ahead of myself. March of that year was only the beginning of what was to be a year to survive.

Michael J Maccalupo

"Beware the Ides of March!"

Part I
The Investigation
[Bob Griffin]

ONE
SATURDAY, MARCH 15, 1986

This seems all too unreal to me. Here I sit writing a letter to a complete stranger, sending him all of my research that could potentially destroy the lives of some very bad people who would in turn destroy me. *That's insane!* But as crazy as it may be, I *am* doing it; I *must.*

> *"Dear Hap,*
> *I address this note in a very informal fashion, not because we know each other personally or even in a business way..."*

Well, there it is; most likely my death warrant – and possibly his. I just hope he succeeds for both of our sakes. What have I forgotten? It seems like there is something critical that I've left out; some little clue that might help him. What could it be?

"Kate would you mind going over what you've found out once more. I'm trying to put it all together and there seems to be something important that I'm overlooking."

"Sure Bob, let me get my notes first. I'll meet you in your office in about 15 minutes. Is that okay?"

"Hey, you're the one helping me. Take whatever time you need, but hurry," I said with a laugh.

"All right, here are the cold case files we have on murders in the Allentown area over the past three years. And this pile over here is all the information that I found on that shifty union boss named Fitzpatrick. I know that he is involved in drugs and prostitution in the area. In fact, I believe he's now the number one player. He also has some shady dealings going on with several politicians in the area and has connections in the Buffalo Police Department. He must – "

"Hold it right there! You know these things; you believe these things; but can you prove these things?" I interrupted.

A bit squeamishly, "Not exactly. But isn't that *your* job? I'm just the gopher; you know, go for files, go for coffee, go for chocolate donuts, go for –"

"I got it, I got it. So let's lay it all out, go through it and see if we can connect the dots. Then maybe we can find proof. How's that," I said confidently.

"And that's why *you* get paid the big bucks," Kate said with a girlish smile.

"I'm exhausted boss, it seems like hours. Can we quit for today and pick it up again tomorrow? It's got to be late; look out your window. It's dark out there," Kate said, exasperated.

"You go home. I'm sorry to keep you out so late; it has been hours. In fact, it's well after ten p.m. Now go. I'll see you in the morning."

"And what about you? Will I find you still here when I get back at eight in the morning?" she remarked.

"No. I promise I'll be out of here in just a few hours. Okay? Now get going, you're slowing me down."

*   *   *

SUNDAY, MARCH 16

"Why am I not surprised? You *did* stay here all night."

I could hear Kate as I began to wake up. She was standing over me now curled up in a ball on the one old stuffed chair that I refused to get rid of. As I opened my eyes I could see her leaning over me with a stern look on her face and her hands on her hips letting me know of her disapproval.

"Okay, so I did stay all night; but before you get on your soapbox about my not taking care of myself, let me show you what I found out."

It looked like I had bought enough time to divert her attention to more important matters.

"Here, in this pile of news clippings and assorted police reports, I think I may have found just what we need to put these players away for a long time. And, as an added bonus, I may have found the identity of the man behind the scenes pulling the strings!"

"Well! That might just make it all worthwhile. I'm sorry I didn't stay to help," Kate said in a forgiving tone. "But I have some news that just might be of interest to you; and I didn't have to stay up all night to find it. It was right here in the morning paper."

She paused long enough to open the local section of the Buffalo News to find what she was looking for.

"Here, look at the police blotter. It says the body of a woman named Shelly Donlevy was found in an alley on Elmwood near Allen this morning hanged. Her death appears to be drug related and is being investigated as possibly the latest in a string of murders dating back to 1983. It says she was one of the regulars there, a hooker. She worked the corner of Allen and Elmwood, right near the Allendale Theater. It says here that her roommate, a rather large local exotic dancer who goes by the name of 'Tons of Fun' claimed that Shelly told her that some of the other girls had it in for her because of her popularity with the Johns. She said some of them were very powerful men in the community, but refused to divulge any names."

She could see that my curiosity was piqued. I interrupted her with, "Who could they be? Is one of her Johns the key to this whole thing?"

"Slow down a sec. The report doesn't say; but the police are investigating and will release names only when and if formal charges are brought. Do you think we need to go in and find out for ourselves?" Kate asked.

"Yes, but I'm afraid you're the one who can get the information, seeing as how I'm not too good looking in a mini-skirt and halter top. Right?"

I could see that Kate had caught on to what I was getting at.

She responded with, "Oh, I guess that means that I should be out on the streets doing my job instead of standing here talking to you."

"Exactly," I said with a smile.

"Now remember, don't get into any cars or go into any of the back alleys in Allentown," I reminded her.

"I know. I need to look like a hooker and talk like a hooker, but not act like a hooker."

"Yeh, and by the way, if you do – don't take any wooden nickels, ha!"

"Why, because I might quit this job 'cause someone else is willing to pay me more than you do!" she shot back.

*   *   *

MONDAY, MARCH 24

"Doctor, is she going to be all right?" I said standing just outside Kate's hospital room door.

"Yes, of course. She will be just fine, but it may take a month or so for her to heal completely. That is, from the physical injuries; the emotional trauma that she has gone through may take years."

"May I go in and see her now?" I said almost in tears for what I felt was entirely my fault.

"Yes, but don't wake her. She needs rest right now. You can sit with her and if she wakes on her own please keep the conversation light and pleasant," he cautioned.

"Of course. I understand."

As I slowly and quietly pushed open the door I couldn't help but feel the weight of this whole episode sit squarely on my shoulders. Why did I send her out there to do *my* work? I could have done this a hundred different ways. I should have thought this thing through better. Now, because of me, she's lying there taped up and plugged in with monitors and tubes.

"Bob, Bob; Bob are you dead or what?" Kate strained to get out while I lay sleeping in the armchair next to her bed.

As I slowly woke out of a well-needed rest, I could hear her calling out my name.

"What? Where am I? Kate, did I wake you?"

She just grinned through the swollen lips that had been stitched, "No I woke you. I've been awake for almost a half hour just watching you sleep there. You looked so comfortable and cute all curled up that I hated to wake you. I know that you haven't had much sleep these past few weeks during your investigation, but I had a feeling I'd better wake you. After all, what would your ex-wife think if she knew that you and I were sleeping together? Ha!" she said with a painful laugh.

"I suspect she would say that she knew it all along; and that's why she left me," I replied with a sheepish smile.

At this Kate lowered her eyes at the thought that she had in some way broken up an already failed marriage.

I quickly added, "I am so sorry for what I caused. If I could redo this whole thing and let it happen to me you know I would. I never meant for anything to happen..."

As I rambled on with my feeble apology she interrupted.

8

"I know, I know. We both regret what happened. I should have followed your advice, but the guy had a whole handful of wooden nickels. So what was a girl to do," she said trying not to laugh this time.

"Look it, the doctor told me I was supposed to have only pleasant conversation and not get you upset; so let's change the subject."

She added, "I think I'd be more upset if we didn't talk about what happened – and what I found out!"

With that she caught my attention. As bad as I felt for her this news brought me back to the matter at hand.

"At the risk of being insensitive; what did you find out?" I asked in a somewhat impatient tone.

"First, you have to know that the beating I got was not because I wouldn't put out, it was because the John I was pumping for information had gone too far – he told me some things that I was definitely not supposed to know. I guess he figured that it would impress me that he was so important in the 'organization' and that I was just a dumb hooker, so I might give him a freebee."

"Well? Did you?" I said kiddingly.

"Not funny! Do you see these tubes and bandages?" she came back with.

"Sorry, I couldn't help myself."

"And neither could he. He gave me names of some of the important people he knew up the food chain and what he did for them. When I asked him about some of my co-workers that have been killed the past couple of years he started to lay it all out for me; the who, the when and the why."

I was captivated by her story. I inquired, "Well, who did them in?"

"Let me finish. It was then that he began to suspect my motives, I guess since I wasn't laying there naked and spread-eagled."

"Just what were you doing and where were you? You know I told you to keep it out in public where you would be safe," I said.

"I know, but he insisted we go to a quiet place to talk. I didn't know he meant *his* place. It was a room just off of a back alley on Allen St. Really more like a converted storage room with a bed, hot plate and an old broken down sink and toilet."

"Sounds lovely. And he thought that this should impress the clothes off any woman; right?"

"Well I might have been impressed if he had a curtain hanging over the one window he had. Anyway, what got me there was the information he promised, not his good looks or incredible charm; and he was about to give me more details."

I had to ask, "What happened? Why did he stop?"

"He was about to name the head of it all when the door suddenly burst open. There was a very tall, muscular man in a blue pin-stripped suit standing in the doorway."

"Did you see who it was; can you describe what he looked like?" I began to ramble.

"No, the room was very dark and when the door opened he appeared to be a silhouette against the bright light from a flood light streaming through the alley behind him. It was then that I heard his voice for the first and only time. *That* I won't forget!"

"What did he say?" I said leaning forward in my chair as I got caught up in the moment.

"He said, 'It sounds like you want too much too soon. *You know Rome wasn't built in a day. Now was it?* That just cost one of you your life.' No sooner had he spoken these words then he grabbed me and threw me against the back wall of the room. As I slumped to the floor I could see him pull out a knife and slit the man's throat. He then came toward me. I knew I was next and the only hope I had was to try to escape. I got up and tried to evade him in an attempt to get to the door, but he grabbed my arm and held it tight as he struck me across the face and then into my ribs. Just before I lost consciousness he once again threw me against the wall. In a calm and disturbing voice I could hear him say, 'I guess you got lucky. This time it cost *him* his life; next time it will be yours.' And as he left the room it went black. The next thing I knew I was here in the hospital."

I slumped back in the chair and said, "Maybe we'd better call this whole thing off. I'm so sorry for what happened to you. I don't want anything else to, and I don't want anyone else to get hurt. We've come too close to very dangerous people that don't play. We are way out of our league. Let's just turn over what we have to the police and let them sort it all out. It's time for us to bail."

Kate struggled to sit up, and with a very determined look she said, "Look it; this is just the time to *not* quit! We've come this far and I have the bruises to prove it. They're scared; they're scared that someone has got them by the gonads. It's not the time to cut and run; it's time to squeeze them!"

"You are one crazy bitch – excuse me, I mean hooker!"

I could see a crazed look in her eyes as she responded, "Don't piss me off or you'll be ahead of the guy that beat me on my '*to-do-in list*'!"

I could see she was lapsing back into a well-needed sleep that would help her heal, so I sat quietly as she drifted away.

It's time to again work on my back-up plan. If Kate and I aren't able to see this through then it will all fall on that poor, unsuspecting writer I found to carry this thing through to the end.

"Now where was I with my letter; oh Yeh..." I said out loud while Kate slept peacefully in her bed next to me.

> *"...no, I do so because I have been following you (figuratively) for a while, looking for someone that I can trust to carry through with what I've started if something were to happen to me. The fact that you received this means that I am no longer alive and must rely on the person that I believe you are to finish the work I've begun.*
>
> *I must, here, warn you that, as I have met an untimely demise, there will not be the same threat to you unless you let the wrong people know what I am asking you to finish for me. I believe your character, intelligence, unswerving desire for truth, and your honesty and integrity are the backbone of what*

led me to you. But most importantly it was your inquisitive nature that led me to believe that my story, here enclosed, will find its way to fruition in your hands.

If, for some reason, you don't find it in your soul to right this wrong then simply destroy the contents of this message and the evidence that I have gathered and put me out of your mind. No one, with the exception of myself, knows anything about this information being in your hands. There are, however others whose lives are, or will be, in danger as you finish the task I have begun; that is, exposing the murderous greed and other crimes in the city that you and I both love – Buffalo."

Your brother-in-arms,
Bob Griffin

As I finished, I too began to slip away into that dream world we call sleep.

TWO
SATURDAY, MARCH 29

"No Kate, it's not called 'penetration', it's 'infiltration'; when you assume a false identity and try to get inside to find out what someone's up to."

"Well, isn't that what penetration is as well? You know, getting inside of something," she said with a slightly twisted smile.

I laughed as I finally got it, "I get it; you're just baiting me. Trying to get a rise out of me, heh."

"Now *who's* talking about penetration? Ha!" she said.

I had to concede, "All right. You made your point, but I'm still going to go through with it. Don't forget you were the one that said we needed to see this thing through. You were the one who took the licking – and apparently are still ticking. Right?"

"I'm ticking all right! I'm a damn ticking time bomb. You know what Shakespeare said about a woman scorned, well it applies to one beaten half to death as well!"

I replied, "I'm just glad I'm not the one that did it."

"Well, now I want you to be careful. These are not boy scouts; they mean business – as I found out. And they *will* kill you, you know."

"I'm well aware of that possibility, but we both know that this has to be done. Besides, once we find the evidence we need to put the boss away we can go back to our dull, boring and might I add, lucrative day job."

As I was about to leave her, still half incapacitated in the makeshift office I had put together for her in my cottage at Sunset Beach, she reminded me of something I once said to her.

"Listen, you be sure to stay in public areas with these guys. Don't give them the chance to harm you...oh, and don't take any wooden nickels," she said with a laugh.

I laughed as well, but mine was an uncomfortable one, remembering what happened to her after I said that to her just a few weeks ago.

*　　*　　*

SUNDAY, MARCH 30

"Excuse me, are you reading that paper?" I said as I sat at the counter in the Deco Restaurant at the corner of Allen and Elmwood.

The man seated to my right was turned to his right talking business with the guy sitting next to him. The two were drinking coffee and eating pie. They looked to be engaged in this conversation for quite some time as their coats appeared to be dry and it had been raining outside for the past hour.

The man I addressed had his elbow resting on the Buffalo News newspaper and didn't appear to be moving it any time soon.

I asked again, a little louder this time, "Excuse me, but could I see part of the paper?"

I must have broken his concentration because the two men stopped talking and both turned in my direction.

He responded, "What was that Mac?"

I squirmed a little at this intimidation and then, taking a deep breath, shot back, "The paper, the paper. Can I take a look at the sports section of the newspaper? I wanted to see what the ponies did last night at the raceway."

I could see I had caught both of their attention at that. The man sitting farthest from me replied, "You're a gambling man, eh? You know betting at the track is fine, but you can't make any real money that way, Right Jimmy?" He poked his friend as he said this.

The other man was not as willing to interact with me. In fact, I sensed he didn't want his friend getting too chummy with me either.

At last the man with his elbow on the paper spoke up. Lifting his elbow and picking up the paper he gestured for me to take it and then he said, "You want this? Sure. Take the whole thing. We're done with it, ain't we Tony?"

The other man replied, "Yeh, sure. We're done reading it. Besides, I only read the society page – "

His friend interrupted, "...and the obituaries. You know, in case one of our friends accidently passed away."

They laughed as he said this. I joined in, but mine was an uncomfortable one; I think they could see that.

The man seated next to me looked like a man of means, more so than the man to his right. He was wearing a black raincoat and had a very expensive fedora lying on the counter next to him. He was well groomed and, by his vocabulary, seemed to be better educated than his friend.

After a few minutes of my thumbing through the paper he spoke to me. I was a bit taken aback since he didn't seem to want to have much to do with me earlier.

"I don't recognize you. Are you new to town, or just new to this part of town? Tony and I, you might say, own a good piece of Allentown," he said as he glanced over to his friend.

Tony interjected, "Yeh, we have an interest in whoever comes around here. That is, you don't strike me as a tourist, or a businessman making a sales call. Am I right, or have I got you all wrong?"

I began to squirm as he said this, but not wanting to blow my cover even before I had one, I said, "You guys got me all wrong. I'm just a businessman looking for an opportunity. I just got here from Cleveland and was hoping to get up with a guy that goes by the name of Fitzpatrick; you know, to, uh, see if I could get a little action going here in town. I got people back home that can speak for me. My name is Bob, Bob Graber."

With that I shut up. I learned long ago that the silence between the words can speak volumes. We sat there staring at each other for what seemed an eternity, but in reality was only a matter of a few minutes. Jimmy spoke first.

"I'm Jimmy, and this here is Tony." In a laughing voice he continued, "So you want to do business with a guy named Fitzpatrick?"

Turning to Tony he said, "Hey Tony, do you know anybody by that name?"

Tony replied, "No boss, do you?"

I could sense that they were playing with me, but I did notice him call Jimmy boss. That meant that Jimmy was not just a common street thug. He had some rank in the criminal world that controlled this area, and he might even *be* this Fitzpatrick I was looking for.

Jimmy again looked at me and said, "What kind of business are you looking to get in?"

I knew that this was make-or-break time. If I could convince him I had something to contribute here I might just have found my in with the local crime organization. And a way to find out if this Fitzpatrick guy was really in charge of things in this part of town; more important, if he had anything to do with the string of recent murders.

Trying to play it cool, I replied, "You know, a little with the ponies, a little with the stables, if you get my drift. I'm kind of a marketing manager. I can help build your customer base, bring in more business."

Jimmy looked skeptical, but Tony seemed to buy it.

"Is that a fact? You can increase our business, eh?"

"That's right Tony, and I only require a small percentage."

Jimmy's ears perked up at this, "How small, and percentage of what?"

I could see they were both hooked.

"Well, my usual is 10% of the take, but for you I'd settle for 7%."

"Why do we deserve such a break?" Jimmy said, grinning at Tony.

"The way I see it is, 7% is better than no percent. Look it, I'm new here and I want the fast track in. I can't wait around to break into the business. If you're willing to help me, I'm willing to help you. Seems fair to me."

Jimmy smiled and replied with a laugh, "We'll see how good you are hot shot."

THREE
FRIDAY, APRIL 11

2:00 A.M.

It hadn't been two weeks before things began to happen. There was a scuffle early this morning that everyone would later whisper about, but no one would talk about out loud – at least not to the police.

This time it was a shop owner in the Allentown area. It seems he had a disagreement with some of the local mobsters and was roughed up a bit, to set an example I suspect. It didn't fit in with the string of murders in the area, but there was something strange about this that made me believe there was a connection. The owner was a middle-aged gay man, living above his antique store with his partner and had apparently been trying to push the local criminals out of the Allentown area; they decided to push back.

I was driving by, searching for answers, when I saw them inside the antique shop, working over that poor shop owner. One of the men came out of the shop and saw me, as I sped off.

*   *   *

10 A.M.

"Bob, you look tired today. Were you out late last night or something?" Tony said fishing around to see what I've been up to.

"Naw, I had a girl over to my place and we got into it. You know how women can get sometimes. Kept me up half the night. I wouldn't have minded if we were getting it on instead of her bitching about my other nocturnal activities. You know, they all want to be exclusive. Ha!"

"Yeh, but I thought I saw you driving down Allen Street last night while I was out taking a walk. That wasn't you?" he probed.

"Oh, I know you must be talking about seeing my car. Yeh, I loaned it to my cousin. He came into town from L.A. for a few days on business and didn't want to rent a car so I lent him mine. He's staying at the Lenox Hotel on North Street. Probably couldn't sleep; jet lag I guess."

"Yeh, maybe so, but it looked an awful lot like you. Family resemblance, huh."

"Sure. You know, us farm-boys all look alike. Ha."

"Right. Ha, ha!" he said, laughing it off.

I seemed to dodge the bullet this time, but I'd better be more careful; I don't want to blow my cover. Ha! Here I am thinking I'm some sort of spy or secret agent or something. I'd better just get what I came for and get out fast.

FOUR
FRIDAY, APRIL 18

"Just looking, thanks," I said to the antique storeowner as I was looking for a clue, anything that could help me.

"Well if you need anything my name is Toby," he replied with a friendly smile. Then he went over to the register to check out a paying customer.

After the shop had momentarily cleared, I approached him to inquire about the events I witnessed about a week ago. He seemed a bit nervous when I asked.

"I'm new to the area and was wondering if you could recommend some activities that a stranger might enjoy. I came here from the mid-west a few weeks ago and still haven't adjusted to the time change. I find myself just driving around all hours of the night, ha."

He didn't buy my story, I could tell. He looked at me with even greater suspicion then when I first began the conversation.

Trying to put him more at ease with me, I said, "You have some very interesting pieces here. I'm a bit of a history buff and was looking for something that would have come from this area's past. Do you have anything like that?"

He finally smiled and invited me over to the shop's special collection of period pieces from Allentown's past. I could tell that these were his pride and joy.

Having gained some confidence with him after a short time of discussing the antiques, I tried once again to find out more about what dark secrets he had answers to; especially that curious incident that took place right in this shop a week ago.

I began, "I heard you had a break in here last week. Did you have anything stolen or damaged?"

At that he stiffened up a bit, but responded to my question, "No, thank heavens, we didn't have anything taken; and the damage was minimal. Fortunately, my partner heard the noise in the shop and was able to scare them off. Unfortunately, he got a few bumps and bruises from those awful hoodlums as he so courageously chased them out into the street. He is such a man."

"Isn't that nice. So I take it you live here as well. I'm sure that has advantages, doesn't it," I said trying to get him to open up more.

"It does indeed. For Mitch and myself it affords us, well, a home where people are more readily accepted for who and what they are, if you know what I mean. It also lets us keep an eye on the shop. Besides, this is a wonderful place to live and work."

"Well, that is just great. You and Mitch have a lovely shop here. I hope he is all right after that incident."

"Considering that there were three of them he did just fine. From what I saw I wouldn't have wanted to be one of them. Mitch is quite a powerful man, even at his age."

I was stunned. He was there when Mitch was beaten! He saw the whole thing and did nothing. I'm guessing that Mitch didn't know that he was there watching the whole thing. Why would he stand by and let his partner, his lover, get beaten almost to death? That made no sense. I had to find out more.

"I'm sorry to hear that. I suppose watching that must have traumatized you so."

He seemed more than willing to go on about this or anything else at this point, so I let him.

"You have no idea. I'm just glad he didn't see me cowering in the corner of the stairwell. He would have been so upset. He tries to shelter me from any bad things; so much so that, at times, I get angry

21

that I'm missing out on real life. But I'm rambling on and on; and you must be *bored to tears*. You have been so kind to listen to me. Let me help you find something nice for – your wife? Girlfriend? Or maybe both, ha, ha!" he said in a more jovial tone.

"No, none of the above right now," I replied.

"Oh, you don't strike me as one of us," he said with a sly grin.

This conversation was beginning to make me uncomfortable. Not because of the line of questioning, but because I began to feel like the one being pumped for information.

"Uh, no; I'm currently between wives and girlfriends. But I would like you to help me pick out a nice piece for my own apartment."

"Of course; that's what I'm here for," he said.

As he picked up different artifacts, almost fondling them, I began questioning again.

"So, I've noticed quite a variety of activities right here on Allen Street what with the Brick Bar down the street, the Allendale theater on one side and the Deco restaurant on the other; not to mention that unusual costume shop across the street."

"Oh yes, we do have an eclectic group of people around here. If there's not a fight in front of the bar, there's a hooker getting busted at the corner. Then you have the regulars at the Deco: the old men, the tourists or Fitzpatrick and his mobsters. Oops, I don't believe I said that."

"Oh, don't worry I won't say a word to anyone. If I did, you'd have to kill me – right? Ha, ha!"

At that he laughed, but it was a bit of an uncomfortable one because he knew he had revealed something to me that he shouldn't have. This might just have put his life and mine in danger – especially if one of us told the wrong person.

I tried to lighten things up a bit, knowing I wouldn't have too much longer to play in this role. At some point he would tell Tony or Jimmy, or even Fitzpatrick about my snooping.

The Allentown Murders

"I hear you have quite the art festival here during the summer. I'm sure looking forward to being here for that. Can you tell me about it?"

He then went on about the Allentown Art Festival; it's history, the vendors and artists, and so on. I listened only half attentively. I was more interested in finding out about why these thugs beat his partner, Mitch; and why he stood by and watched. I also wanted to know something about the main reason Kate and I were doing all of this – who was responsible for the string of murders of the prostitutes over the last few years.

As he was wrapping the late 19th century pewter bowl I bought, I asked, "By the way, that costume shop across the street, SIN City, who owns that?"

"Oh, that place is owned by a young man named Si Norom. He has a very interesting collection of costumes for rent or purchase. Mitch and I have rented from him many times over the past few years that he's owned the shop."

"Well, it's always nice to hear about a young person who has that entrepreneurial spirit," I added.

In a bit of a catty tone he said, "I wouldn't go that far. It seems that his father fronts the whole thing. It's strange, however, you never see him; and now they have some young floozy living with them."

That piqued my curiosity. I had to find out more about these people, "Oh? Well the old man might just be an invalid or shy or something of that nature. I'm sure there's a reasonable explanation."

"No, not at all. I have seen him a few times and he seems as spry as you or me. As a matter of fact he doesn't seem to be that old anyway. And the girl; well, she bosses Si around and seems to have an almost father-daughter relationship with Si's dad."

"Well there you are. She's probably Si's sister," I said.

"No. I don't think that it's quite that simple. I remember talking to him when Mitch and I were renting costumes to go to last year's Halloween gala. When I asked him about why he got into the costume business, he said that growing up as an only child taught him to use his imagination. He said that he used to take marionettes and

23

dress them as all kinds of gory creatures. He would make their costumes for them. So I know he didn't have a sibling."

Just as we were finishing our conversation I heard a door slam from the back room area.

Toby turned quickly toward the noise and then back at me with a half-twisted smile and announced, "Oh, that must be Mitch back from a few errands. He's a bit angry with me. You know, one of those lover's spat things. I'd better go see how he is."

Changing the subject I interjected, "Well, I've taken up enough of your time. Thank you so much for your help in finding this piece for my apartment. I'm sure it will look just lovely there."

With that I headed toward the door. As I exited, I turned slightly to see him scurrying to the back room. I wonder if there is any connection between their 'little spat' and Mitch's beating?

I had a few more stops to make before I could put the pieces to this puzzle together. Something wasn't right here.

FIVE
TUESDAY, APRIL 22

"We also sell magic," the young man said as I wandered around the isles of his store.

"Excuse me?" I said, taken aback by this seemingly random statement.

"That is, we sell kits, you know, with magic tricks and card tricks – a little prestidigitation if you will."

"Oh, slight of hand," I responded.

"Yes, exactly. Nothing goes better at a party than being in costume and amazing a small group with a quick magic trick. It tends to really liven things up. Impress the ladies, if you know what I mean," he said with a sly grin.

"Si, Si. Now where the hell did you go?"

Out from the back of the costume shop came a tall, muscular middle-aged man with a shock of red hair, hazel green eyes and ruddy complexion. He seemed to be in a hurry.

When he saw me he stopped dead in his tracks; in fact, he started to spin around as if to hide from me when Si shot back, "Dad, you can come out here. This is Bob Graber, a salesman from the Midwest. He's staying in the area temporarily."

Looking at me he explained, "My father doesn't like to be around too many people. He's a little recluse."

Turning back to his dad, "Mr. Graber here was just asking about our magic kits. Maybe you'd like to fill him in; after all magic is your passion, isn't it," Si said with an expression that told me that there was more to the statement than I knew.

"Why of course. How are you Mr. Graber? My son here has somehow forgotten his manners. People call me RJ; and Si's right; I don't like too many people. I guess, as you get older, you find most people disappointing. But you're not here to listen to the ramblings of an old man. What is your interest in magic?"

I could feel a cold sweat forming around my collar. I had to come up with something, and pretty quickly.

"Well, I, um, you know as a kid, like all kids, I guess. That is…"

At this point RJ began to laugh and said, "I know exactly what you mean. Why I've seen it a thousand times. Most men have had this fascination with magic all of their lives, and when they come here they feel a little foolish in playing out their boyhood fantasies. Isn't that right?"

I felt quite relieved at this and replied, "You've got me. I do feel a bit silly about this, but knowing that I'm not alone. I'm interested in this kit over here, the one with the rope. I always wondered how they would tie knots or cut them and the knots would just slip off, or the rope would be whole again. What kind of rope is it? What is it made of?"

I found I was asking too many questions. As I caught myself I could see a worried look pass from Si to RJ.

At this Si interrupted, "Well, I think my dad can help you better than I can at this point. I'll leave you two alone to talk. If you'll excuse me, I just got a new shipment in that I have to put out."

RJ turned toward him briefly and said, "Sure. You take care of the costumes; I'll take care of our friend here. We'll be fine, won't we *Mr. Griffin*."

At this my heart sank. After catching myself, I replied, "Graber, it's Bob Graber."

He smiled slyly and responded, "Why of course, Graber, Bob Graber."

26

It was getting too dangerous for me at this point. I had to get out.

"Well, I've taken too much of your time already RJ. I'll be staying here a few more weeks; that is, until I complete my business. So why don't I just come back another time. I'd love to chat some more with you. And since you and your son have been nice enough to take the time to show me your magic kits, I'd like to buy one of the rope trick kits."

At this RJ took the kit I was holding and said, "Wait, I have a special one in the back that I know you'll love."

He turned slowly and walked to the back room where I could here him talk with Si in hushed tones. It sounded like they were having an argument over something or someone. A moment later he came out from behind the curtain that separated the two rooms with a large, red box in his hands. I could see his demeanor change from the previously serious one to one now that spoke of pleasure. He had a knowing smile on his face and carried the box as if it contained eggs. As he carefully laid it on the counter and opened it, I could see that it contained the same kind of rope that was in the other kits; only this rope was thicker, much more like the kind used to hang the prostitutes. As he took it out for me to see, he twisted it quickly several times. Before I could tell what he was doing, it was braided into a hangman's noose, the same way the ropes were found around the necks of those poor women.

"This is just one of the many tricks that you'll find in the booklet that accompanies the rope. I hope you find as much pleasure working with this as I have."

There was something very strange about this whole thing. If this were the same rope used to strangle the women, why would he be handing it over to me? And why was it packaged in a blood red box?

Nervously I said, "Thank you very much. I really must be going now, but I will be sure to stop by again before I leave town."

He replied, "Maybe you can show me a few tricks you've learned with the rope. But don't get frustrated if you can't do any at first. *Remember, Rome wasn't built in a day, now was it?"* After a short pause he added, "And maybe when you've mastered a couple I can show you a few more that I know as well."

"Thank you again. I guess I'll need to work on my weaknesses, heh? Anyway, I look forward to another enlightening conversation with you. Please say goodbye to your son, Si, for me. Would you?"

"Of course; it was a pleasure meeting you *Mr. Graber.* And keep in mind; weaknesses are liabilities in a man. *You need to eliminate your liabilities,"* he replied with a grin.

Is RJ the one that I'm looking for? And did he somehow make me? If he did, then I'm a dead man already. I have to make one last call before I can get back to my world. I have to focus on what I came for – who is responsible for the hangings deaths of the prostitutes over the past few years. And does that somehow tie in with the alleged embezzlement of the union funds? I have to talk with Reilly Fitzpatrick. He must be the key to this whole thing.

SIX
WEDNESDAY, APRIL 30

10:00 AM

"We can all meet tonight at, say 11, in Mr. Fitzpatrick's office. It's just above the union hall right around the corner on Elmwood Avenue."

I was a little nervous about being alone with these guys late at night, but that was the only way I was going to be able to meet Reilly Fitzpatrick; and he's the one I had to meet on this undercover adventure of mine.

"That sounds fine, but are you sure he wants to do business with me?" I said, trying to find out what their intentions were.

Tony spoke first, "Sure; ain't that right boss?" He said, turning and smiling at Jimmy, as they sat across from me in the booth at the Deco Restaurant.

As I glanced out the window onto the corner of Allen and Elmwood, something, that is, someone, caught my eye. I was distracted by a most beautiful woman, racing across the street against the light. Part of my distraction was how desperately she seemed to want to get somewhere in a big hurry. As I looked back at the two men seated across from me I could see that they were equally as distracted by this sight.

"I guess some people like to live dangerously, don't they Bob?" Jimmy said, glaring at me.

At this they both looked at each other and then at me and let out a big laugh. Startled at this I let out a nervous laugh myself.

"So Bob, what exactly do you have to offer Mr. Fitzpatrick? You know, he's a very busy man and if it weren't for your contacts back home he wouldn't even entertain seeing you," Jimmy said after a brief silence.

"Well, I'd rather leave it till tonight to get into details; but suffice it to say I have become very well known for my ability to do the laundry, so to speak. I not only can make money disappear, I'm also pretty good at tightening up operations where costs are getting out of control. But I'm sure you already know this, or, as you say, I wouldn't be seeing Mr. Fitzpatrick tonight; right?"

Tony seemed mesmerized by the conversation and blurted out, "That's right!"

Jimmy gave him a look of disapproval at this, turned to me and continued our discussion with, "So you think we need some money laundered, heh? What gives you that idea?"

He then looked over at Tony and said, "Tony, did you steal someone's money? I know I didn't."

I jumped in boldly with, "Look it, I wasn't supposed to say this, but I was invited to come here by someone who has some influence in the neighborhood to do just that. In fact, I was talking with him face to face just last week over at the costume shop."

Little did I know at this time that that would be the last nail in the coffin for me.

Jimmy smiled and just replied, "Is that a fact."

*　　*　　*

The Allentown Murders
11:00 PM

"Mr. Graber is it?"

Shaking his outstretched hand I replied, "That's right. It's an honor to meet so prominent a man as you, Mr. Fitzpatrick. I've been looking forward to our doing business since I was invited to the Allentown area."

"It sounds like you might be useful to our enterprises here. Let's take a look at what you might be able to do for us, shall we?" he said with a knowing smile.

As we talked about millions of dollars, at first in vague terms, then in more specific ones, I got the feeling that we had met before. His voice and mannerisms seemed familiar, while his appearance was totally foreign to me.

This was a middle-aged man of medium height with brown hair and green eyes. He seemed to be fairly muscular in build, but had a big, round belly. He wore wire-rimmed glasses that looked more decorative than functional. The glass looked like window glass and not the kind you'd find on someone who needed corrective lenses. He had a pointed nose with a brushy moustache hanging below, attached to a goatee.

"You see; I have a slight problem. I have been entrusted with several hundred million dollars. It is my job to invest it wisely for my people. Now in the course of moving this money around some of it needs to disappear, and of course, reappear somewhere else – in untraceable currency. You do get my drift, don't you?"

This is what I came for. With a knowing smile I replied, "Yes, I understand completely; and I'm just the one to make that happen."

After a short pause in conversation I continued, "Now as to your profit/loss picture with some of your other ventures, I think I can be of help here as well.'"

With that his ears perked up. He said with interest, "Oh, how can you help with this problem?"

I began, "As I understand it you have several middlemen who control the labor force on the street, is that right?"

"Yes," he said a bit unsure of where I was going with this.

"Well, I also believe you've had some trouble with some of these workers taking advantage of your good nature, shall we say, and leading to their dismissal from the labor force. Am I on track so far?"

Fitzpatrick began to smile and said, "I like the way you put things. Yes, that's right; some of the middlemen and laborers had to be eliminated from service, ha."

"It seems to me that you have a management problem. If management has a tighter control over the labor force the problems just might disappear."

Showing his curiosity, he replied, "And just how do you propose we tighten up?"

"You could kill two birds with one stone, pardon the pun, if you eliminate the middleman. You have men that are close to you, that work for you, that can take over that middle position. By having some of your girls, for a bonus of course, take over the day-to-day petty stuff, your boys can easily control the market. The best part of this is that your profitability will increase!"

Fitzpatrick looked over at Jimmy and Tony, and said, "Now why didn't either of you think of that?"

Turning back to me, and with a grin peaking through his hairy face, he casually remarked, "Well *Mr. Griffin*, I think we just might be in business here. My men will see you out, and I will be in contact with you within the week."

He stood up, smiled and stretched out his hand to shake mine. With that faux pas I was suddenly struck. I had heard that voice before call me by my real name – *but where*? Something about it made my blood run cold. I felt a strange chill come over me. Who was that man that stood there before me? Why did he sound so familiar?

"That's Graber, Bob Graber."

"Why, of course, *Graber, Bob Graber*," he said, with a knowing smile.

SEVEN
THURSDAY, MAY 1

There she is again. I've got to stop her and find out who she is. I don't know if it's just some obsession of mine, or if it's journalistic intuition; but I must talk to her.

As she ran across the street, not minding the traffic light or traffic at all, I followed her. She crossed Elmwood Avenue and then Allen Street headed for the alley between the costume shop and the Greek diner.

As I stood at the front of the alley I shouted, "Excuse me, Miss. Can I talk with you a moment?"

She stopped in her tracks and turned toward me holding her hand above her eyes, shielding them from the glare of the sunlight streaking through the alley.

"What do you want? I'm in a hurry. What is it?" she shot back at me.

"I'm sorry. It will only take a minute. I don't mean to frighten you. I'm..."

But before I could introduce myself she interrupted, "You don't frighten me. And I know who you are. You're that reporter, snooping around Allentown like no one knows what you're really up to. Everyone knows. Now, what is it? What do you want with me?"

I was startled by this revelation. Here I was thinking that my disguise had fooled everyone, but I was apparently the only one who thought that. While it was refreshing to hear someone speak the truth, I at once had a sense of the danger I was in, knowing that these killers knew who I really was.

After I caught my breath I said, "Look it, if we could maybe just go next door to George's for some coffee, I'd like to talk with you about some things that have been happening in the neighborhood."

"I will on one condition."

"Sure. What's that?"

"You leave my father and my brother out of this."

I paused to evaluate the ramifications and replied, "Okay, you have my word on that."

I knew Si had little or nothing to do with things at the top. In fact, he might not be involved in any of this stuff, other than knowing what was going on. I didn't need him.

As for her father, RJ, I could leave him out as well – as long as I had Fitzpatrick to expose!

After settling into a booth and placing our order, I continued, "I'm not interested in your father or brother; who I am interested in is the person responsible for the murders that have taken place in this area over the last several years. I am also investigating the *alleged* missing money from the union pension fund. I think the two are somehow connected. And I suppose you know who I'm really after, don't you?"

"Let's suppose, for the moment, that that is really who and what you're after. If that's true, then what do my father, brother, *or I*, for that matter, have to do with any of this? Why are you snooping around our shop?"

I paused for a moment and wondered if I hadn't already told her too much. Is it wise of me to confide in her, a virtual stranger, what I was about to disclose? This could mean my life!

"I don't know if I can trust you, but I have to find out certain things in order to get the answers I'm after. You seem like the most logical person to me. You're fairly new to this area, you seem to not be involved in much of what is going on around here, and you are in a good place to have access to some of the answers I need. So – I guess

The Allentown Murders

I'm about to put my life in your hands. But please remember I hold a few cards myself. For example, I am aware of what RJ and Si sell at the shop besides costumes. I don't care; that's for someone else to look into, not me. I won't involve you or your family if you play straight with me. No one will ever know what we discuss – in the paper, or in the courtroom if it comes to that."

Her expression changed as I related this to her. I was trying desperately to see what her reaction would be. She was not as innocent as I believed. She could play her hand well.

"All right, what is it that I can help you with? As you yourself have said, 'I'm new to the area and not a part of what has happened or is happening.' So why do you need me?"

"I need to know what the connection is between the recent murders and the missing funds. And, how do these two events involve Fitzpatrick. In order to tie these things together I also need to find out who else is involved and what their roles are."

I watched as she wrung her hands moving them under the table. She didn't want me to see her nervousness at my queries.

After a momentary lull in the conversation she spoke again, "And what makes you think that I know anything about Mr. Fitzpatrick's drug business, or about the hangings of those poor women for that matter?"

As she said this she caught herself. I might have missed it if it weren't for her own reaction to her words.

I couldn't help letting a sly smile slip out for a second. She caught that and, lowering her head for just a moment, I heard a sigh. She slowly raised her eyes to mine and spoke once more, "I can see by your expression that I may have misspoke and given you the wrong impression."

I interrupted, "No, not at all. I believe you gave me the correct impression. You do know more than you're letting on. I don't know if you realize it, but you are in as much danger as I am. These people are serious. Just as I'm a stranger here snooping around, you are a stranger as well. Just because you are related to RJ and Si doesn't make you immune to suspicion. In fact, it makes you more so."

"Oh, how is that?" she responded.

"I believe that Fitzpatrick and his thugs are using your dad and brother – and you through them – as pawns in their game of drugs, death and embezzlement."

I could see I was getting to her, so I continued, "A moment ago you referred to 'Fitzpatrick's drug business' and 'the hangings of the prostitutes'. I never said that that was what I was after. I was referring to the bodies of the two drug dealers that were found at the bottom of the Niagara River. So it seems to me that you have more information than you are letting on. Am I right?"

At this she abruptly stood up, clutching her handbag and said, "*This conversation is over!* If I have anything more to say to you I'll contact you. Until then, stay away from me, my father and my brother or I'll have my own talk with Reilly!"

With that she turned and stormed out the door and out of sight. I was stunned for a moment; I couldn't move. It all seemed to be going the way I had hoped, and then suddenly she's gone.

These and other things kept running through my mind. It was racing a million miles an hour when all of a sudden it occurred to me – "She called him *Reilly!*"

As I said this out loud I banged my fist against the table, startling the other patrons in the diner. George, the owner, who was behind the counter talking and laughing with what appeared to be one of his regular customers, stopped and shot me a look that showed his disapproval at my sudden outburst.

I stood up and, leaving my money on the table, walked over to George who was now reengaged in his conversation, and said, "I'm sorry for my little outburst a moment ago. I just realized something very important. You know how it is when something pops into your head sometimes..."

Before I could finish George stopped my rambling with, "No I don't. We Greeks are a lot more thoughtful about things. We don't just blurt out anything that comes into our heads like you Americans. Have a little respect for your elders next time – *vlakas!*"

The Allentown Murders

They both laughed. I had a feeling that last word he spoke was not a complement. I smiled, said thank you, and left. They laughed some more.

EIGHT
FRIDAY, MAY 2

11:00 PM

"Hi boys, to what do I owe this pleasure? And I thought midnight was the witching hour," I glibly remarked as Jimmy and Tony entered my tiny apartment that sat over the Allen St. Hardware store.

My smile quickly faded as I saw the serious expressions on their faces. This was no social visit.

"Come on with us. Mr. Fitzpatrick would like to have a little talk with you – right now," Jimmy said as Tony stood over me, pulling me up out of my recliner where I was reading.

"Isn't it a bit late for a visit. Maybe we could do this tomorrow; say for brunch?" I said, attempting to lighten the mood and buy some time so I could make my escape.

As Tony helped me up, Jimmy grabbed the papers I was reading which contained some of my own notes. These were statements I had gathered from police reports and some first hand interviews I had just completed from some of the locals who had information on the murders and the drug trade in the neighborhood. I knew I didn't have any more time to make the connection between these things and the embezzlement.

Just then it occurred to me. *What an opportune moment this was.* Who better to find out what the connection was than from the man in charge himself. All I had to figure out was how to get Fitzpatrick to talk and then get away alive. Mm...that could be a problem.

"Jimmy, Tony no need to get excited," I said as I tried to pull the papers out of Jimmy's hands. He pulled back and fortunately for me some of them tore as we struggled.

Trying to throw them off I said, "Come to think of it, what better time to have a talk with 'the man' than right now. Right boys? I mean he needs to know what the buzz is out on the streets."

Looking at the papers now being tucked into a valise I remarked, "And those documents are just the thing that Mr. Fitzpatrick needs to see. I've even been putting some of my own notes on them to help him see who the rats on his ship really are – so to speak."

I could feel a sweat breaking out on my forehead as we made our way to the door and out onto Allen Street, arm-in-arm with Tony.

"So Mr. Griffin, you *have* been busy – haven't you?" Fitzpatrick said with a knowing grin, as he perused my notes.

I knew I had been made and there was no point trying to continue the charade. My only option was to get out of him the missing piece to the puzzle and get the hell out!

"Well Reilly. May I call you that?" I said with a smile.

"Why of course and I'll call you by your first name as well. *Bob*, isn't it?" he replied smiling back.

Ignoring this I began, "There's just one thing that I would like to know..."

He interrupted, "Jimmy, Tony. Why don't the two of you go out and get some coffee for us. I have a feeling we'll be busy discussing things for a while and the coffee will give us that extra jolt I'm sure we'll both need before too long."

"Sure boss," Jimmy responded. Then they left his office just over the union hall on Elmwood Avenue where we sat face to face.

"Now Bob, what is it that I can help you with? I see from these papers that you have already compiled enough information to put me in a very bad light; but I suppose you already knew that, didn't you? Wait, let me guess; you would like to know about the union pension funds, isn't that correct?"

"That and the connection between you and the hangings as well – for starters!" I said.

He laughed and then replied, "Well, well; we are ambitious, aren't we. *Remember Rome wasn't built in a day, now was it?* I will be glad to tell you all about it. That is, all except for the specific details. That would spoil all of the fun, now wouldn't it? That will be for you to figure out for yourself."

His last remark gave me hope that I would get out of here alive, but why? What did he have to gain by letting me live? He could have had me killed at any time and I'm sure no one would have ever found out who did it – or even where my body was, for that matter.

Something else was gnawing at me though. That voice, the gestures, and that expression he used. There was something strangely familiar about them. I heard that phrase and saw those gestures before, not from him – from someone else in Allentown, but who?

He was true to his word; he told me in general terms about the money and how it tied in with the drug trade in the area. He also related how he had ordered the murders and why.

It was becoming clear now to me, why he was telling me all of this. He wanted someone to know how brilliant he was; he *needed* someone to know how he was able to outsmart the police, the FBI, even the courts. I think I was the one he wanted to tell because I've come the closest to finding out about it.

It was as if this was some sort of contest and I was the winner. Now I would win the grand prize – the knowledge of what he did and how he did it, without any way to prove it. So he would let me live; he *had to* in order for there to be someone out there with just enough information to satisfy his ego, but not enough to do anything about it. The added bonus would be that if there were any further digging he would know right away who the one was holding the shovel – me! This was perfect.

"Jimmy, Tony; your timing couldn't have been better. Now that Mr. Griffin and I are finished with all of the sorted details why don't the two of you pack up his things and put them in his car so that he can be on his way after we enjoy the coffee and some light conversation."

As they were leaving he added, "Oh, and by the way, be sure to let his landlord know that he will be leaving – permanently. And pay him for the rest of the term of his lease. That's all."

They left, making me wonder how permanently I would be leaving.

As soon as the door closed he turned to me and asked, "Now is there anything else I can help you with before they return with your things?"

"I do have to ask one last question if you don't mind," I said, not yet satisfied with our discussion.

"Why, of course – shoot," he said.

He could see the strained look on my face at his remark. He laughed and added, "Sorry, poor choice of words. I mean, go ahead."

"I know that what you've related to me is nothing more than a tease. I can't really do anything with it unless I follow it up. But I have the statements of my sources, and even though you'll probably destroy those I can still get them again. Why let me go?"

He put his cup down, and leaning in toward me, he said, "Why Bob, you almost sound disappointed that I'm not going to kill you. You look at me as some kind of monster, killing people at will or whenever they disagree with me. I assure you I'm merely a businessman; I don't enjoy killing people. It's too messy and much too costly. In a business, you don't fire someone that you've spent a great deal of money on in training and grooming for a job just because they may occasionally step out of the bounds you've set. No, you corral them back in and retrain them. I assure you that anyone that I have fired, so to speak, has been because they have become a deficit to the

41

business. Just like any business one must weigh his assets and liabilities. The key is to minimize your liabilities."

I interrupted, "So you just have to eliminate them; is that right?"

He smiled and replied, "Exactly. *You need to eliminate your liabilities.* Now I think you've got it."

Now I knew where I heard that voice before. It was all coming together for me. But before I showed my hand I had to get out of there as quickly as possible – or I might never get out!

Just as he started the conversation, he ended it and, as we finished our coffee, Jimmy and Tony announced their arrival with a soft knock on the door.

"Come," Fitzgerald said as he stood and walked over to where I was sitting.

Taking his cue I stood as well, and, looking first at Jimmy and Tony who stood at the door to my right, I turned back to Reilly who had extended his hand toward mine, shook it and smiled.

As he gestured toward the open door he simply stated, "Now, you may go."

With that I turned and walked toward the door – *exit stage right.*

NINE
SATURDAY, MAY 3

12:30 AM

I would assume that Jimmy and Tony are better hit men than they are packers. The few things I had with me were strewn all over the back seat. I just hope that they didn't supply my trunk with a dead body!

It's time for me to head out to Sunset Beach where I'll find my little summer cottage and hopefully Kate asleep, recovering from her encounter with these guys.

"Damn! That was close," I shouted to myself as I nearly hit a man standing at the foot of the Skyway Bridge hitchhiking. Was it me; am I starting to feel the effects of the late hour, or the stress I've been through lately; or was my steering wheel slow to respond to my jerking it to the left to avoid that man?

I suppose I owe him a ride now that I've almost run him over. Besides he might be good company and also keep me awake for my ride out of town. Hey, he can't be any worse company than I've just experienced.

As the man ran up to the passenger side of my car, I could see he was a drifter headed anywhere. He appeared to be about my age but looked somehow weathered, a bit worse for wear.

"I'm sorry about back there; I wasn't trying to hit you," I said with as friendly a smile as I could muster.

"No harm stranger. Most people would've been grateful to ya if ya did!" he responded with a laugh.

"You're not from around here, are you?" I asked.

"Naw; I'm from Nowhere, Nebraska and I'm headed to Anywhere, South where I can dip my toes into the Gulf or the Atlantic anytime I please. Somewhere I can keep warm and live off the land."

"Well, I can help you out for a little part of the way. I'm headed to Chautauqua County, about 30 or so miles from here. At least I can get you headed in the right direction – and away from the downtown area. A stranger is libel to get into trouble downtown at night."

He grinned and said, "Thank ya mister. That's mighty nice of ya. By the way, I'm Jonah, like the guy in the 'Good Book' that was swallowed by the whale. That's my middle name. My real name is Randolph Scott, like the movie star, ya know."

As he said this he stuck out his hand to shake mine.

"Yeh, right. The movie star; sure," I replied shaking his hand and wondering who the hell was Randolph Scott.

He continued, "I'm sorry about the dirty clothes and all. I gave the maid the week off and, well, you know how it is."

He laughed, an embarrassed laugh. I felt even worse for him.

"Hey listen, look in the back seat. I gave my maid the week off as well and I just can't keep up with folding the laundry as you can see. You look to be about my size. Why don't you pick out some things from the pile and try them on."

I could see a sad, yet thankful, look steal across his face. I didn't mean to embarrass him, but his clothes were not only dirty, but they reeked.

"Thanks friend. That might be a good idea since they might just smell a bit as well," he said.

After he picked out a new shirt, pants, socks and shoes he looked and smelled a whole lot better.

"There. Now isn't that better. When you get to your destination you'll look like some sort of casually dressed executive.

That will get you into more places than what you had on would," I said.

"Y'all got a point there."

For the next 20 miles or so we both sat quiet. It was after one in the morning by now, and he looked just as worn out as I was.

Somewhere a few miles just south of the Town of Derby on Route 5 I felt it again. The steering wheel wasn't responding as it should; a quarter turn and no response, then a half turn.

We stopped to get gas at the Catt-Rez gas station where I filled the tank up, and before getting back into the car, I walked over to Jonah who had gotten out himself to stretch his legs and said, "This looks like the end of the trail for us cowboy."

Michael J Maccalupo

Part II
The Guilty
[RJ & Reilly]

TEN
SATURDAY, MARCH 15, 1986

REILLY

"Jimmy, what do we need to do about this little problem?" I said as I leaned over my desk glaring at the, now sweating, union representative.

As he pulled out a handkerchief that was tucked neatly in his suit pocket he replied, "Well boss, it's like this…"

As he said this I slammed my fist on the desk shutting him up and screamed, "*NO! It's like this –*"

I sat back in my plush black leather chair and, putting my feet up on the desk, began my instructions to this underling.

"I want this job done by you and Tony, do you hear me?"

Wiping his sweaty brow Jimmy replied, "Right Mr. Fitzpatrick; whatever you say. You know we'll get the job done right."

"Good. Now it's come to my attention that one of our procurers has branched out on his own into a business that is in competition with one of our other enterprises. That's not good for business, and it has ruffled the feathers of some of our best agents in the field."

"Got it boss. You want we should eliminate this problem altogether?" Jimmy asked.

"No. That wouldn't make good business sense. RJ is NOT to be touched; is that clear!"

I found myself getting enraged by their suggestion. After calming down I continued, "He is still valuable, but he does need to be taught that he should keep his attention focused on his own house, so to speak. Do you get my meaning?"

"So Tony and I might just pay a visit to his stable and leave him a reminder of what happens to someone who tries to branch out without the union blessing. Am I reading you right?"

I smiled and nodded, "There's a new girl that he is very pleased with at the moment. She's bringing in double of what the others are and trying to literally sleep her way to the top. Her name is Shelly something-or-other. Make it look like a jealousy thing; you know, the other girls didn't appreciate her trying to fast-track it to the front of the line."

"Do you want us to do it the same way as we did the others? You know, the cord around the neck, a little heroine in her pocketbook, maybe a local politician's phone number. That antique shop owner, Taylor, has been stirring things up with the local Allentown Community Board about some of our union activities."

"Exactly what I had in mind. Then we can take care of two problems at once: get Mitch Taylor off of our backs and make sure our 'procurer' stays in line. I like that – this way everybody wins."

*   *   *

"Well? How did it go?" I said as Jimmy and Tony stepped into my office over the union hall on Elmwood Avenue.

"Oh, poor Miss Donlevy met with a terrible accident," Jimmy said with a grin.

"Yeh, she got all tangled up around the neck with a very pretty white cord. Unfortunately, before Jimmy here could help her out she had expired," Tony came back with.

Jimmy continued, "There she was all tangled in this cord; and the harder I tried to help her, the tighter it got around that pretty little neck. I could tell that she wasn't exactly having the time of her life by the expression in her eyes and how hard she tried to get a foot down on the ground."

Tony chimed in, "Yeh, but it took him forever to make that noose to put around her neck. How do you do it so fast? Show us again."

I interrupted, "Okay, enough of the humor. I'd show you, but you two will never get it. So why bother? The job's done. Now let's move on to more important matters. We just got deposits from our union reps for dues and some of the fund-raising activities that have been going on. I want you to count it, deposit it – minus our take – and get with Ivan to cook the books. It all has to look legit you know. Tony, you take our cut and take it through the usual laundering process and wire it to our account in the Cayman's. Got it? By the way, we need to find a new guy to move the money – Ivan is getting sloppy, or maybe just greedy. Anyway, I don't think we can trust him any longer."

"Consider it done. By the way, when do we get to enjoy the fruits of our labor on the warm sandy beaches?" Jimmy asked.

"By the end of this year we'll have taken in enough from the union funds plus our drug, prostitution and other enterprises to live happily ever after. Just a few more months, boys; just a few more months! Now you boys go see what's going on out on the streets. We need to keep our ears close to the ground. If they know we're around, they'll tow the line."

As they were leaving Jimmy turned and said with a smile, "I can hardly wait till Christmas. What a present we're gonna get. Do they have Christmas trees in the Cayman's boss?"

I smiled back and replied, "If they don't, we'll import one!"

"Right boss. We're on our way."

"You're on your way all right; right to the slammer. I didn't need that poor girl, but what a shame to have to sacrifice her; after all, she *was* making a lot of money for me," I said after they closed the door. If my plan works right I'll be rid of these two bozos as well as a few others that I plan to eliminate from the equation, like that Mitch Taylor.

"Sadie, would you come in here for a moment. I've got some things I'd like to go over with you," I spoke through the intercom.

As she came through the door with pen and pad in hand I just leered at those gorgeous legs as they swayed across the room toward me. I drank in her beauty as she reached the chair across from me and sat very business-like for a moment, legs crossed, pen and pad at the ready.

Looking up she asked, "To whom is this to be addressed?"

I smiled as I looked her up and down and replied, "No, I don't need you to take a memo. This is a more person conversation I had in mind."

With that she rose, putting the pen and pad on the corner of my desk; then, turned and headed for the door, which she locked. As she turned back to me she smiled, removed her glasses and came around my desk and sat on my lap.

Unbuttoning the top of her blouse I said, "Now, isn't this more comfortable?"

Sounding annoyed she said, "Is this what you hired me for – sex!"

"Now Sadie, just because you're sexy doesn't mean I picked you for the job for that reason alone. I've always said, 'It's just as easy to hire a beautiful woman as it is an ugly one. Ha, ha!" I added.

She just smiled and ran her hand across my chest as she leaned in and kissed me with a passionate warm kiss. I had no other choice – I kissed her back.

After a few minutes of some very heavy necking and petting I pulled my hand out of her blouse, leaned back in the chair and announced, "Pack your bags, we're leaving for Switzerland in four months! I know you'll need every bit of that time to figure out what you'll want to wear there."

She slapped me across the chest and laughed, saying, "Oh you. Isn't that just like all you men. All you have to pack is socks, underwear and a few tee shirts and jeans. I've got to look good. You know I do it for you."

I was puzzled, "How is that?"

"Well if I don't look good, it makes you look bad. Don't you see?" she responded smugly.

"Right," was all that I could say to that remark.

"But what about the boys. When they came out of your office they were talking about the Cayman Islands. Are they going there?" she asked in a confused tone.

At this point she really didn't need to know everything. In fact, the less she knew about my plans for 'the boys' the better off everyone would be, especially her.

"Well, that is their plan, but they think that I'm going with them. They don't know about our plans; and I'd rather that be kept a secret between the two of us. Besides, they won't need me once they're down there basking in the hot sun, smelling the salt air and lying on the sand. Now will they?"

"I suppose not," she replied.

I think I convinced her. What I don't need is to have to explain to those two idiots why I'm dumping them for my incredibly gorgeous secretary. Actually, come to think of it, I don't think I'd have to explain that one, *even to them*!

ELEVEN
TUESDAY, APRIL 1

RJ

"Si, would you and Connie please come upstairs for a moment. We need to talk," I said in a somewhat irritated state. Things were not going exactly as I had planned.

"I had to close the shop in order for the two of us to come up. Don't forget we don't have any help down there," Si said with a note of distain for my urgent request.

"Oh, did you have many customers?" I said in a sarcastic tone.

He shook his head no.

I said, "I thought not. Now, to business.

"Connie dear, I know this is all new to you and I'm sure running a costume shop is not your life's goal. So I've been giving it some thought. I have some friends down at Canisius College who tell me that the school has a fabulous Creative Writing Program. And I know that you have a very keen interest in becoming a writer. So I took the liberty of getting you enrolled in the graduate program there...well, that's it!"

Before I could tell what her reaction would be she sprang on me like a lioness.

"RJ, you are wonderful! How can I ever thank you?"

That told me all. I may not be the best of dads, but I do want the best for my kids.

"Great. You might start by calling me *dad* or *father*," I said with a smile.

"Sure dad; I think I can manage that," she replied.

"Now, if you don't mind, would you go down to the store and let in all of the customers who have been patiently waiting at the door. I wouldn't want to deny your brother of any sales."

As I said this I shot Si a sneer.

He said, "Yes, *your* father and I have a few things of our own to discuss."

Connie smiled and replied to Si, "Oh, don't be jealous. *Our* dad has helped the both of us; me with school and you with this shop – right?"

Hanging his head he acknowledged, "Right."

Once she was downstairs I began, "Si, it has come to my attention that our neighbor across the street, Mitch Taylor, has been stirring things up again on the Allentown Community Board. He's on a campaign to rid the Allentown district of drugs and prostitution."

"Oh, I'm well aware of what he's been up to. I'm friendly with his partner, Toby, and he loves to gossip. Around here, if you want to know anything about anything just go to the nearest beauty salon or the nearest 'beauty'; and Toby's the nearest 'beauty'!"

I laughed at this and said, "Well, don't get too friendly. I don't want you going over to the other team, if you know what I mean."

Si laughed and replied, "Don't worry, I still like girls."

After a short pause he continued, "But what about Taylor? What do you have in mind to do to him?"

Rubbing my chin I announced, "There is only one thing we can do – kill him!"

"Now wait a minute, I never signed up for murdering anyone. Sure we sell a little dope and run a small stable, but murder is out of my league; out of our league."

I responded, "I know, but what other choice do you see? Unless..."

He could see something was cooking up in my head.

"What; what is it?" he asked.

"We just might be able to get someone else to take care of it for us. After all, if we did it someone might just find out about my past connection with his daughter and that 'do-gooder' son-in-law of his and come looking for me."

Si gave me a puzzled look and asked, "You never told me you knew the guy before. What's that all about?"

"I never told you a lot of things; like why I left your mom back in Denver, or why I left Hari in Cleveland, rest her soul, or a million other things. And frankly, that's my business; you're on a need-to-know basis when it comes to my past – got it? But since this *is* something that you need to know, I'll tell you."

After about 20 minutes of telling him of my experience living around the corner from Hap Pozner and his friends in South Buffalo going back 15 or so years ago, he began to see the importance of my staying anonymous around town. That little bastard and his uncle and friends cost me my job, my home and my marriage.

"So getting rid of this Mitch Taylor pain-in-the-ass will take care of two things at once – stop him from ruining the good thing we have here, and give me a small amount of revenge for past grievances with his family."

"Okay, I get it; but who is it that's going to do our dirty work for us?"

"Why Fitzpatrick, of course. He and his henchmen owe me a few; especially after doing in my best girl, Shelly."

As Si was turning to leave I grabbed him by the shoulder and spun him around and warned, "Connie must never know about any of this. I don't want her involved in any way; got it?"

"Of course, *dad*. I wouldn't think of tarnishing our princess."

With that, he pulled away, turned toward the staircase and hobbled down to the shop, clutching the handrail. I guess he remembered the last time he mouthed off to me, when I shoved him down that very flight of stairs and broke his hip. Since then he's walked a bit funny and always looks over his shoulder when he walks away from me. I can't say as I blame him though. I would too.

I shook my head and said to myself, "I just may have to kill *that* poor bastard someday too."

TWELVE
FRIDAY, APRIL 11

REILLY

2:00 AM

"It's pretty damn cold out here. What's the plan? I want to get back inside before my fingers freeze off," Tony said as he tried to blow his warm breath into the palms of his hands.

He was right; it was a cold April morning; or should I say middle of the night.

"I know it's cold; it's April in Buffalo what did you expect? Besides, people in Buffalo like to suffer – so get used to it," I shot back.

"Mr. Fitz, are you sure about this Taylor guy? Is he the one stirring up all of the trouble in Allentown?" Jimmy asked, trying to change the subject.

"Yeh, I got it from my best source, RJ," I said.

"But can you trust him?" Tony asked.

They had no idea what my connection with RJ was, and as far as I'm concerned they never need to know.

"I trust him more than I do either of you two slugs."

"Thanks boss; that really hurt," Tony replied.

"Just when I thought my luck was going good – it gets better. Boys, grab him!" I said, as one of our local junkies happened by.

Before he could turn and run Tony and Jimmy had him pinned up against the building.

"Tommy; where you running off to? I thought we were friends."

He replied in a shaky voice as he pulled something out of his pocket, "Here, this is all the money I have right now. I'll bring you the rest tomorrow, I swear."

"And to show you I have no hard feelings, Jimmy, give him a little taste – on me! Ha, ha!"

Turning back, I could see movement in the shop, so I told the boys, "Let him go. We've got more important business to attend to now."

I added, "All right, here he comes now. Once we get into the shop we give him the once over; you know, rough him up a bit. Then I'll lay out the terms to him. He'll fold; they all do."

"And what if he doesn't? Then what?" Jimmy asked.

With a stern look I replied, "Then we eliminate him from the picture. Will that be a problem for either of you?"

They both laughed and Tony responded with, "It will be our pleasure."

I could see by his demeanor that Mitch Taylor took my phone call from earlier this evening to heart. His eyes told the story; he knew why I wanted to meet with him and what would most likely be the outcome.

"Thanks for agreeing to meet with us at this late hour, or should I say *early* hour. I didn't want anyone to know about this little discussion so I thought it best to meet now," I said.

He closed the door behind us, then, turning to face me said, "I know what this is about. You think that you can scare me into submission; well, you're wrong. I and a few others want to clean up this neighborhood and only you and a handful of your henchmen stand in the way."

I smiled, "Now don't go getting your blood pressure up. I'm here to let you know that I'm willing to help you out. I understand that your partner has put you and your business into some financial difficulty. I know this, of course, because I just happen to own a piece of the little bank around the corner where you do business."

As I said, this I could see a rage begin to sweep across his face.

"As I was saying, I came here to offer you some help, not to intimidate you. I can make your little problem go away, and all I want in return – all *we* want in return, is your cooperation. And that cooperation can come in the form of your not saying anything. You get off your campaign to hurt my business ventures and I get on one to help yours. Sound fair to you? Sounds fair to me, doesn't it boys?"

As I said this I turned toward Jimmy and Tony who were now standing next to him with their backs to the door. It was then that I saw him, outside on the street, slowly driving past the shop. The car was a God-awful pea green Ford Pinto; just like the one that Bob Graber drives. In fact, it looked like him behind the wheel. The car seemed to stop for just a few seconds, and then slowly move past Taylor's store. The car interior while dark, showed the outline of a man in a trench coat and hat.

"Am I crazy or is that Graber's car?" I asked.

They turned, and Jimmy replied, "It sure looks like it, boss."

We all wanted to see who would be riding the streets at this hour.

Just as I moved out the door to approach the car, it sped off through the red light and off into the distance.

"Did that look like Graber to either of you?" I asked, now in an angered state.

Tony responded, "I couldn't make out the face, but it could have been."

Jimmy added, "Me too Mr. Fitz. With the moonlight coming from the other side of the car it kind of put a dark shadow on his face. I wasn't able to ID him either. But it sure did look like his beat-up old Pinto."

It was very late and I was getting tired; tired from a long day and tired of dealing with these do-gooders.

Turning back and entering the shop again I asked, "Well, what's it going to be? Can we work together or not?"

"I'd rather die than to give Allentown over to you. Is that clear enough?"

I stared at him for a moment and began to smirk. I could see fear come over him; and with good reason.

"Boys, how do you feel about his answer? I don't think we'll have to kill you to get you to change your mind; will we boys? I'll tell you what; why don't I leave Tony and Jimmy here to convince you. I'll be down at the office. I'll give you some time to rethink your answer."

Turning to my boys I said, "Now, not too rough boys; I just want to give him something to think about, not put him in the hospital or anything. After all, we're not murderers; just businessmen, right?"

Looking over at Taylor, I said, "I'm a patient man; you'll see. I can wait for you to come around to our way of thinking. But I won't wait too long."

Almost as an after-thought I said, "Jimmy, there's one other thing I want you to look into this morning. When you're done here come talk to me in my office, okay?"

I needed to find out if that was Graber that drove past – and why.

"Sure boss. This won't take too long, *will it Mitchie?*"

Tony and Jimmy smiled at me as I left. I closed the door to the shop behind me and I could see Mitch Taylor buckle over, with blood beginning to run down his face.

As I was turning toward the street I caught a glimpse of someone lurking in the shadows just at the top of the steps at the back of the shop. It was probably Taylor's partner, Toby, watching in the darkness. That could be a good thing. He can watch the beating and then later convince Taylor to back off for both of their good. This could work to my advantage. As much as I'd like to kill him, it's not necessary – yet!

THIRTEEN
THURSDAY, MAY 1

REILLY

"I think he's on to us. And I think he's gonna run," Jimmy said, as I sipped my coffee sitting in a booth, staring out the window at the Deco on the corner of Allen and Elmwood Streets.

"Yeh, I suppose he will," I said in a slow and distant tone.

It's not that I'm not concerned; it's more about all of the other things I've got to worry about.

"You've taken care of it, haven't you?"

"Oh, Yeh. Has he got a big surprise when he tries to drive out of here. Tony and I did a little mechanical work on his steering. It'll be good for about 40 miles or so, and then, well, I guess we'll read about it in the papers – on the obituary page to be exact!" Jimmy said as he began to laugh.

Coming out of my half-dream state I turned to him and replied, "Good. That's what I wanted to hear. Then we have only one other problem to take care of; but that can wait a little while longer. Now are you sure he's leaving?"

"Oh, Yeh. Tony and I saw him packing last night. He was so busy he didn't even hear us tampering with his car. He looked like a man on a mission. Ha!"

"Good."

"So you're sure it was him and not a cousin from out of town that was driving slowly down Allen Street in his old beat-up Pinto," Jimmy questioned.

"Oh, I'm very sure. You haven't seen that supposed cousin around here anywhere since then have you? No, of course not; cause he doesn't exist – and neither will Griffin after tonight," I replied.

We all laughed at this. It was then that I saw her; Connie was racing across the street against the light, headed toward the alley between the costume shop and the Greek diner. Someone was following her, about to catch up to her as she entered the alley. It was him – Bob Griffin! What was he doing with her? I'll have to let my alter ego find the answer to that one.

"Ah, Jimmy. I want you to do me a favor," I said as an idea hit me.

"Sure. What is it boss?"

"Look out there just inside that alley, that woman and man. If I'm not mistaken that's our man Griffin with the woman that lives above the costume shop."

"Yeh, I think you're right. What are the two of them up to? You want me and Tony to take care of her too? We'll be glad to *do* her; she's quite the looker," he said with a devilish grin.

I must have lost my senses. When I heard this I became so enraged that I grabbed him across the table and pulled his face into mine. Swearing and spitting, I pulled out my knife and pressed its blade against his jugular and laid it out in no uncertain terms for him, "You harm one hair on her head and I take my stiletto and cut off your cogliones so you'll be singing soprano! Got it?"

As I released my grip he slowly sat back down and, straightening his shirt, said, "Sure boss. I didn't know she meant anything to you. You got something for her? Hey, I'm just a fly on the wall, and *that's* between y'all."

"Yeh, you might say I got some interest in her; so lay off!"

*　　*　　*

FRIDAY, MAY 2
10:30 PM

"Jimmy, Tony; it's time for us to pay Mr. Griffin one final visit. Go over to his apartment and inform him that I request the pleasure of his company – *NOW*! I'm sure he will be more than happy to oblige. Ha, ha," I instructed my two stooges.

"Sure boss," Tony responded.

"Oh, and be careful not to break him. I'd hate for him to be in pain when he has his little accident," I added.

Jimmy said, "We'll be right back with the goods – and we'll be sure to say please!"

I could hear the two of them laughing all the way out onto Elmwood Avenue.

"So Mr. Griffin, you have been busy – haven't you?" I said with a knowing grin, as I perused his notes.

He knew he had been made and there was no point trying to continue the charade.

"Well, Reilly. May I call you that?" he said with a smile.

"Why of course and I'll call you by your first name as well. *Bob*, isn't it?" I replied smiling back.

Ignoring this he began, "There's just one thing that I would like to know..."

Our conversation went on for quite some time, so I sent my boys out to get us some coffee. When I was satisfied that he had enough information to make him dangerous, I cut him loose. Victory is never complete until the enemy knows he has lost.

I had my moment's gratification of knowing that I had not only defeated my opponent, but his immanent death would ensure that my secret would be safe with him – forever!

*   *   *

SATURDAY, MAY 3
8:00 AM

"Did you read this morning's paper Mr. Fitz? It says here that a reporter died early this morning in a fatal car crash at the Cattaraugus Creek Bridge just south of Evangola State Park. It says,

Saturday, May 3 Buffalo, NY

A car carrying Robert Griffin, an investigative reporter for the Buffalo News, spun out of control early this morning, crashing through a loose guardrail over the Cattaraugus Creek Bridge on Route 5 in Irving. The car was said to be moving at a dangerously high rate of speed when it struck the guardrail, sending the vehicle into the rock bed below where it burst into flames, killing the driver. His body was burnt beyond recognition, but investigators were able to identify him by a few artifacts that were recovered from the wreck, as well as the vehicle registration information gathered from the DMV".

FOURTEEN
TUESDAY, MAY 27

REILLY

"Hey Mr. Fitz, we're like the Post Office, ain't we?" Tony said with a grin.

"What in the hell are you talking about? It's two in the morning and I'm not in any mood for one of your stupid jokes," I said as I tried to shake off the bitter early morning chill.

"All I meant was that we deliver despite the cold, rain, dead of night, you know just like the Post Office."

Jimmy interrupted, "Yeh, but I suspect Taylor ain't gonna like the package we're delivering."

"All right, here he comes to let us in. I'll be happy if he agrees to our terms and we get a little warm and dry in the shop as a bonus," I commented as I saw the silhouette of Mitch Taylor headed toward the front door of the antique shop.

There was only a single light on the stairs that illuminated the back of the shop. It trailed off as he made his way to the front to let us in. I could see a determined look on his face that told me he would not be easily convinced.

The only other light we saw was that of the waning moon, softly illuminating the streets that surrounded Allentown.

Not a sound could be heard on the street except for the chatter of my two associates and me.

"Well, Reilly I thought we already had this conversation last month. In fact, I still have the bruises to prove it," Taylor said, sounding very agitated.

I smiled, "Can we come in out of the cold, wet weather and talk. We're here this time to negotiate with you. None of us want any trouble. You've got a nice business here. You're a leader in the community. You and your partner enjoy all of the things that Allentown has to offer. We don't want to interfere with that. All we want is for you to let *us* enjoy those same luxuries everyone else does. Is that asking too much?"

I could see him clench his teeth and then he responded, "I'm not trying to stop you or your 'thugs' from enjoying the same liberties we all enjoy here; what I am trying to stop is the underbelly of society that you perpetuate and from which you profit by destroying what the rest of us are trying to rebuild. Allentown has been the second worst area in the city for drugs, prostitution and violence next to Chippewa Street; and I aim to change that."

Looking around at Jimmy and Tony, and then back at Taylor, I smiled and said, "Now there you go, getting the wrong idea about what we're all about. We want to help you clean up the area, but you've got to be realistic about things. You're absolutely right, the drugs, prostitution and violence have gotten way out of hand. And that's where we can help."

Taylor interrupted, "Ha! You're going to stop these problems? Wouldn't that put you out of business?"

I replied, "I didn't say we would stop them; what I was about to say was we would control them. Now, looking at human nature in a more pragmatic way we can all agree that there will always be those who will look for drugs and loose women."

"Oh, I get it. By eliminating your competition you can control the drugs and prostitution in Allentown, thus creating a monopoly for yourself. How generous of you," Taylor said, now with a smug grin on his face.

The Allentown Murders

"Well, I can see you're a man that doesn't like to beat around the bush; and I salute you for that. So I won't either. Yes, I plan to eliminate my competition and control, not only the drug trade and prostitution, but also eliminate much of the violence that has helped to scare away some of the potential business that you and the other merchants could benefit from. Is that so bad? You and your fellow shop owners enjoy a safer neighborhood, won't have to deal with pushers, druggies and hookers hanging around your doorstep, and everybody's hap, hap, happy. In the process, I make a few bucks for all the work I put in to make this all happen. Now what's wrong with that?"

I thought that I had convinced him at this point. I could see that I had convinced my two associates, but they are a bit dim-witted and on my payroll to boot.

"Now, I'll leave you to mull this over. When you have your answer, you know where you can find me. But keep in mind, I won't be coming back again to talk."

As we were turning toward the door to leave, Taylor spoke up, "Wait. You can get your answer right now. There's nothing I have to think over; your argument was clear and very persuasive."

I smiled at the thought of winning this battle without things getting too messy. He was no fool. He knew he had no real choice but to agree to my terms. As I always say, 'Never enter into any agreement where you won't come out ahead of the other guy'.

"Well, I knew you were a smart man, but I guess I didn't give you enough credit for knowing when to grab onto a good deal. Now all we have to do is iron out some of the details. Oh, and by the way, I forgot to mention there's something extra in it for you. I always like to reward those people who are most loyal; right boys."

Jimmy and Tony responded, "That's right Mr. Fitz."

"I don't think you understand. I said I had your answer; I didn't say it would be what you wanted. No, as a matter of fact, you're attempt at bribery now has galvanized my conviction that my response would be the right one."

I turned to my boys who now were flanking Taylor and responded to his statement, "Oh, and what would that be?"

I could see in his face that he was not going to give me the answer I had hoped for – and expected.

"You're answer is NO! No, I won't become one of your lackeys; no, I won't help you build your criminal empire; no, I won't sell my soul to the devil by turning my back on those good people of Allentown who want better for themselves and their families. And NO, I won't stop my campaign to rid the area of you and people like you. That's my answer!"

I could feel the anger welling up in me; but as I tell my boys, 'Never act in anger; revenge is much nicer'.

"I'm afraid you've left us no other choice but to eliminate the obstacle impeding our progress. That would be you," I said.

"Tony, Jimmy; take care of our problem. But make it quick; after all, a brave man deserves a quick death."

As I turned to leave I could see a shadow being cast from the light coming from the top of the stairs. It looked like a slight, curled up form quivering and sobbing. I took this to be Taylor's partner, Toby. I knew that his witnessing this might just be a benefit. He wouldn't have the courage to tell the authorities, and it would probably push him to kibitz with his other 'girlfriends' to help keep them in line as well.

Just before leaving I turned to Taylor, now with a cord twisted around his neck and about to succumb and said, "Oh, I almost forgot I brought a present for you from an old friend. But I guess you won't need it now, so I'll just leave it here for your partner. It's a little present from the old neighborhood; some colored filters that used to go on a black-and-white television to make it look like the shows were in color. The kids loved them, especially your daughter!"

I could see the panic and fear in his eyes. It now changed from that of one dying to one in fear for his loved ones.

"Ha, ha. Yes sir, isn't life strange," I said at the thought of things to come.

FIFTEEN
FRIDAY, MAY 30

REILLY

"Isn't life grand. Brother, you may not have realized this, but we have created the perfect monopoly," I said feigning a conversation with RJ in my office to help perpetuate my persona. Sadie, my secretary, is always listening in on my conversations. Her penchant for gossip helps me out sometimes, since I only let her hear what I want her to hear.

"First of all we're only half brothers; and secondly, as the older 'half' brother and the smarter, I not only know what we've created, but I was the idea man who put it all together," RJ said, a bit irritated with me.

"Yes, of course, dear 'half-assed' brother, but don't forget who puts all of these plans into action to make them a reality," I reminded him.

"I suppose you're right. That's what makes us a good team, brother of mine," he replied with a laugh.

He continued, "Now with Taylor out of the way, and the Allentown Community Board backing off, we not only control the drug and prostitution trade in the area, but we also own the clinics that rehabilitate the drug addicts."

I interrupted, "Not to mention the halfway houses and counseling groups that put the 'girls' on the straight and narrow; and all with government money to help us out."

While we were patting each other on the back RJ added, "Now, if we could only get a piece of the action that the local churches enjoy – and their tax-exempt status we'd be batting 1,000!"

"Now let's not get greedy. I'm happy to be batting 500 at this point. Remember; when you're too greedy people start to pay too much attention to you. I like flying below the radar."

RJ agreed, "I suppose you're right. It took a lot to get this far, let's not blow it."

*   *   *

RJ

"Connie, what's new with you?" Si asked, only half interested as he eyed the Danish sitting in the dish on the counter.

"Since you sound so interested I'd love to tell you all about it," she replied in a sarcastic tone.

I had to interfere in what might turn out to be a brother-sister fight, even though they're only half related, not to mention newly acquainted.

"Wow, you two picked up on this brother-sister thing right out of the box. It makes me glad you didn't grow up together; just imagine what it would be like now!"

Connie was quick to add, "Oh, I don't know that this is the typical brother-sister relationship; it might be more of an instant distain for a narcissistic personality."

"That would be me I suppose," Si commented.

"See what I mean; it's all about him," she shot back.

"Now, if you two are done, I'd like to know how you're doing after only a short time in the area, Connie. Are you making new friends, getting in with the college scene; you know, the typical young adult stuff. I'm not that old to have forgotten what it's like being in my twenties. And I also haven't forgotten what it's like moving to a new town," I said.

Si interjected, "God knows you've moved to new towns every few years for most of your adult life. And speaking of that, why is that RJ?"

"Let's not dwell on the past. I'm home again; we're home and together finally, so let's enjoy the moment. Now, back to Connie. Well?" I asked.

"Well, I have made some new friends at school. I've also met some of the girls in the neighborhood here. I've got to tell you they are not all that different. It seems to me the only difference is that the neighborhood girls are paid professionals and the ones at college are still working toward their credentials. Ha!"

"Very funny. Keep in mind the ones in college will one day command a much higher price for their services, assuming they meet a rich guy," Si responded.

I interrupted their joking, "I don't find this all that amusing. Connie, I don't want you hanging around the locals. People will start to get the wrong impression of you. You know, 'we're known by the company we keep' and all that."

"That goes for you to RJ. I see what company you keep," Connie shot back.

"Fair enough, but I just want what's best for you; and, by the way, do either of you think to call me *dad*?"

As if choreographed they both said, "*No,*" in unison.

A little hurt, but with full knowledge of why anyone in his or her right mind would not call me dad I said, "Fair enough."

Just as we three were about to fall into an abyss of silence, Connie had a thought and blurted out, "Oh, I almost forgot. I'm going to be a graduate assistant to a young man from North Carolina who will be a guest professor for the summer and fall semesters. He's a writer; he writes murder mysteries and I'll also be in one of his graduate writing classes. I'm excited about it."

71

"See, now that's what I want to hear. Don't end up like me or your brother; get your masters' degree and get a good job."

Si looked up from the Danish he was devouring and said, "What am I chopped liver? I'm right here. Don't talk about me in the third person; and, by the way, I've managed to build a very nice business here in Allentown. My costume shop is the envy of Western New York and beyond."

"Beyond is right. Mars I suspect is very jealous of you," I added.

"Oh, there's one other thing," Connie said ignoring our little tit-for-tat remarks.

"Well, what more do you have?" I asked, smiling at her enthusiastic demeanor.

"I also found out that he is originally from South Buffalo, right near where you used to live, *dad*."

"How about dad without the sarcasm," I replied.

I added, "And did you get his name? I might have run into him when Hari and I lived there. How old did you say he is?"

She thought for a moment and then responded, "I believe Dr. Crenshaw said he's somewhere around 34. He also told me his name is Hap something; but I think that that's a nickname, not his real first name."

I felt an uncontrollable grin cross my face, and I could see that they both recognized it.

Si was the first to respond, "What is it? Do you know this guy?"

I pulled myself together as quickly as possible and, looking very casual, replied, "No, I don't believe so. You know there were a ton of little rug-rats running around South Buffalo then; I imagine there still are. The poor immigrants had lots of kids in those days, and they all had nicknames. Find out his last name, maybe that will ring a bell."

Connie and Si just looked at each other, a little suspicious of my sudden nonchalance, I suppose.

The Allentown Murders

Before I could say another word Connie added, "Oh, I almost forgot; he's got a wife. Dr. Crenshaw mentioned her because her father was just murdered, right here on Allen Street; the guy that owned the antique shop across the street, Mitch Taylor. That was her dad. How tragic. Anyway, her last name was Taylor."

Another piece to my plan was now in place. I knew I wouldn't be able to hide it any longer so I said, "Oh, I think I do know who they are. He's probably Hap Pozner and she was Joanie Taylor, or JT as they called her as a kid. Sure I knew them. Great kids. They lived around the corner from Hari and me. They, and a few of their friends, used to come over to watch my color TV."

Connie laughed and said, "How long ago was this anyway? Didn't everyone have a color TV?"

Si spoke up, "Sorry little sister; not everyone had a TV at all. In fact, there were no color TV's back then; at least not in the working poor neighborhoods like South Buffalo and where I grew up."

I explained, "No, there weren't color TV's; in fact, we had one of the few televisions in the neighborhood. I say color because they used to sell these colored acetate sheets that would fit over the TV screen to give the picture the appearance of being in color."

Connie, looking confused, asked, "But wouldn't that make the picture just one color, the color of the acetate?"

Si, in a sarcastic tone, cut in with, "Blonde, beautiful and brilliant – my sister has it all. That's right it was in one color, unless you changed the sheet to a different color. Then it was only that color. And before there were computers there were typewriters and before that there were..."

Connie interrupted, "I get the idea. It just sounds so silly to me."

I explained, "It may sound silly now, but don't forget that that was the late 1950s and it was just the dawn of the age of technology. Televisions had been around for a while, but there weren't many programs to watch and not too many people could afford them anyway. So, when someone in the neighborhood could buy a television set the neighbors came out of the woodwork to be your 'best buddy'."

"If that was television when Si was young, I shudder to think what you grew up with RJ. I guess I'm just glad I didn't grow up in the dark ages."

I had to laugh, "Okay, let's not dwell on the past. But I do want you to find out more about Hap and his wife for me. Maybe you could be a little nice to Hap, you know, see what they're doing back in town; maybe find out what she's doing. Let's say I could put you on the payroll of Bossco Enterprises if you do a little research for me."

Connie said, "Now would that move me up from one of those girls who are just studying for the profession to a paid professional?"

Being a bit embarrassed by this I replied, "Do you think I would ask my own daughter to prostitute herself for a little information? I don't believe my ears."

Not convinced Connie shot back, "Oh, from what I've seen of the way you work, I believe you'd sell your own mother to the highest bidder!"

I hung my head and feigned hurt, "That hurt. I loved my mother."

At this Si burst out in laughter; I followed. Connie left the room.

SIXTEEN
THURSDAY, JUNE 19

RJ

"Now I want you to tell me every word of what transpired between you and Hap Pozner. Leave nothing out," I said to Connie after she returned from her graduate assistant job at the college.

"All right. It went something like this. First Professor Crenshaw brought me to the office in the tower where I will be working. Then he introduced me to Hap. I said something like, 'Professor Pozner, I am looking forward to working with you this term. I just hope that I will be able to give you all the assistance that you will need'; and it went on from there. We made small talk, you know, call me Hap, call me Connie, etc."

"And?" I said impatiently waiting for more.

"As I said we did the usual small talk, getting to know a little about one another for a few more minutes. He asked about me and I found it to be an opportune time to learn about him and his wife's work. Mostly about him, I have to admit."

"After a few moments he interjected, 'Well Connie, you seem to know something about me; now how about you telling me something about yourself. Where you are from, what your goals are, whatever you'd like to share.'"

"I said, 'I don't mind. I don't have anything to hide, do you?'"

"That took him aback a little, but he just coyly smiled and said, 'I suppose we all do, but I'm sure mine would bore you, so please go on.' We talked a while longer, giving us a chance to get to know each other and to get a little closer to him. I could see him begin to squirm a little. I could tell, while he felt uncomfortable with me almost on his lap, he was hoping I would be there soon."

Once again I interrupted, "Did you find out anything about Joanie's research project?"

"I'm getting to that part; but I thought you said you wanted to hear everything. You'll just have to be patient. Besides, you sent me to seduce him, so now you have to hear how I did it. You men all want to be seduced, but you don't give a damn how much work it is for us women!"

"All right, I'm listening. Amaze me!"

She smiled at her victory and then continued, "Sitting on the corner of his desk and leaning in for him to get a good look inside my partially-unbuttoned blouse I almost began to laugh at the typical male reaction I saw. Men are all pigs – thank God! As he began to get that 'deer in the headlights' stare I had to say, 'See anything you like?'"

I began to snicker at this.

"See what I mean. You're all pigs," she added.

"Where was I? Oh, Yeh. That snapped him back to reality. He began to blush; I to laugh. I smiled and said, 'Oh, don't be embarrassed. If you didn't stare I would worry about you. Besides, we're both adults, right. I'm sure you've seen women's breasts before, or, at least, I hope you have.'"

I almost felt like I was pimping my own daughter. But what the heck, the ends do justify the means sometimes.

Connie continued, "He became noticeably flustered at the conversation. He replied, 'Oh sure, I've seen thousands. I mean two at a time of course...I'm sorry, what was I saying. I mean I've seen a few, maybe a thousand times...uh, uh, what I mean is...'"

I began to laugh at the poor slob, almost feeling sorry for him.

The Allentown Murders

"At this point he pulled out a handkerchief from his back pocket and was swabbing his forehead. I just laughed all the more. Putting my hand to my mouth I tried to control my laughter. I replied, 'How about we change the subject. We'll be working pretty close and sometimes very late together in this tight space so I don't want you to think that my only purpose here is to seduce you.'"

"He replied with something like, 'Good. I didn't think that for a moment. I mean, sure. We're both adulterers... I mean big people. Well, not big in the sense that you think I mean...' I couldn't help but laugh at his continued bumbling around for the right words. I stood up, took his hand and pulled him up out of his chair. As I moved to within an inch of where he now stood I put my hand over his mouth and said, 'Now let's talk about your wife. What does she do?'"

When she said this I felt a cold chill, "You didn't do that to the poor slob. I'm beginning to feel sorry for this guy."

"I knew that all you had to do was bring up *the wife* and any man would snap back into reality – his own reality, good or bad. Just the thought of the wife has the same effect as a cold shower on a married man. And it worked."

I interrupted, "Is there a handbook for women somewhere?"

Connie looked cross and said, "Don't interrupt if you want to hear the story. *Ahem*. Walking toward the window, with his back to me for a moment I could hear him take a deep breath and then, turning facing me once more, said, 'Yes, my wife, Joanie. Right. Well, she does research for a pharmaceutical company called Vericon. She's working for the remainder of this year at their Grand Island home office. She's in charge of a big project there; something to do with drug addiction and helping addicts break the habit. I don't know much else, and, if I did, I wouldn't be able to tell you anyway.'"

I was chomping at the bit, "Was that it? Is that all he said?"

Ignoring my latest outburst Connie continued, "Feeling in charge I brashly stated, 'Oh, I think that if you knew more I would be able to get it out of you.' And when I said this I could see his face begin to get red once more, telling me that I was right. He tried to worm his way out of this one by saying, 'Well, I never was one who could keep a secret. When I was young my mother could always tell when I was lying – and then she'd get the truth out of me. I guess I was born to tell the truth.'"

"I'm not his mother, but I sensed that he was lying. He did know more than he was telling me," she added.

At this point Si, who had been doing some paperwork for his business looked up and asked, "Didn't you find out any more about what she is researching and why it's such a secret?"

She began to get annoyed at, now, our constant interruptions.

She went on, "I could tell he was had, and knew it. But what was it that was so top secret that he would try to lie about it? I need to do some more investigating."

After a short pause she looked at me and added, "And what is it that makes this so important to you two?"

I replied, "Connie dear, I don't want you to become too involved in the family business. There are things about me...about us, that you'd be better off not knowing. Suffice it to say that we have business interests that you will certainly profit from in the near future, and you won't have to get your hands dirty in the process. Just do what I ask and don't ask too many questions."

Si added, "Yeh, princess, *our dad* doesn't want to pull you down into the muck with him and me, and *Uncle Reilly*."

When Si said this I backhanded him across the table, knocking him off his chair and onto the floor. As he picked himself, and then his chair, up off of the floor I glared at him; he glared back at me, turned to Connie and smirked. He then went to his room and slammed the door locking it behind him.

All the while Connie sat in her chair – frozen.

After I had a few minutes to cool down, I smiled at her and reached across the table to touch her face. I guess after what she just witnessed, she didn't know what I was going to do next.

Seeing her reaction, I pulled my hand back and said, "Honey, you're my princess. I would never hurt you. I was just going to touch your beautiful face. There are things that you don't know about your brother that maybe you need to be aware of. He often speaks when he should listen. He has a bad temper, which, I admit, he gets from me; or at least in my younger days. Since I've grown older I've mellowed out a bit. But worst of all he doesn't know when to keep things to himself. That will cost him dearly someday. That little love tap I gave him was just a reminder of a much stronger sting he may feel if he says the wrong thing to the wrong person. I'm just trying to protect the two of you. You see that, don't you?"

Connie squirmed in her seat as I talked, and then, after a short pause, responded, "Sure, I understand; but what did he mean calling Mr. Fitzpatrick – 'Uncle Reilly?'"

I laughed and replied, "Oh, that's sort of an inside joke. Mr. Fitzpatrick and I have done business together for several years now and own some properties and businesses together. So your brother refers to him as Uncle Reilly to kind of throw a dig at me, I guess. No big deal."

"So the two of you are not related?"

"No, of course not. His last name is Fitzpatrick and mine is Sweeney."

She was not convinced and added, "Well mine is Dilworth and Si's is Norom and we're related; unfortunately. In fact, we're both related to you and none of us have the same last name!"

"What can I say; welcome to the '80s!" I said trying to get us off of that subject.

SEVENTEEN
MONDAY, JUNE 30

RJ

"I'm sorry, Mr. Fitzpatrick isn't in yet," Sadie announced as I attempted to make my way into his office.

"Oh, I'm sure he's there. He probably just snuck in before you got here or came in the back way. He just called me not 10 minutes ago and said he had something urgent to tell me," I said as I opened his office door making my entry.

I could tell his secretary looked a bit miffed at my lumbering in, but I had a peace offering, knowing I might meet some resistance from her.

"And I almost forgot, this coffee and Danish are for you. I know how hard he drives you. I figured you probably could use something to give you some extra energy."

She smiled and said, "Oh, how did you know that I like cheese Danish and cinnamon in my coffee?"

She then told me I could wait in his office if he wasn't there. As soon as she closed the door behind me Reilly greeted me, "Well, hello RJ. Thanks for coming so quickly. Please have a seat."

I looked back and could see the doorknob release as I suspected it would at hearing her boss's voice. We talked and laughed for about an hour, mostly about the past – our past.

"RJ if it weren't for different mothers we could be twins!" Reilly said as he sipped his morning coffee.

"I wouldn't say that too loud; your secretary has big ears, you know. And big tits, I might add. Ha!" I laughed.

Reilly just smiled and replied, "As I always say, 'It's just as easy to hire a good looking woman as it is an ugly one'."

"And I wouldn't want it to get around that we were related," I shot back.

"Well, do I detect that you are ashamed of your little brother? Or are you waxing on how history has a way of repeating itself? You know, your own family," Reilly added with a slight chuckle.

"There's a lot at stake here, so let's stick to business. Besides, your checkered past is nothing to be proud of either. You and your penchant for young girls," I said in a strike back at him.

"Now I believe you're confusing me with yourself. I seem to remember one of us being run out of town – several times, I might add," he said in an angered tone.

"The past is the past, damn it! Can we get down to the business at hand?" I shouted.

I put my hand over my own mouth at the thought of his secretary, taking note of everything she heard.

I began again, "That Bob Griffin business last month was a bit messy, and we were lucky it hasn't come back to haunt us – yet. Now we have that pain-in-the-ass Pozner resurfacing, along with his nosey friends."

Reilly interrupted, "Not to mention his wife and her research project on drug addiction. If she comes up with a cheap and simple way to get addicts off the stuff our whole system will be ruined."

"The question is, 'Do we *off* her, him or maybe someone close to them as a warning. You would have thought that her old man's murder might have sent a message," I conjectured.

"Yeh; that was one of those unintended, but fortunate, consequences of trying to maintain continuity in the neighborhood. Mitch Taylor's death, to her, might look like it was related to her research. Maybe we can capitalize on that...Mm," Reilly added.

With his suggestion, it came to me, "We can send Hap a message through Connie; she's his assistant at Canisius College," I suggested.

Just then Reilly chimed in with nothing less than brilliance, "Yeh; she can seduce him and threaten to tell his wife if he doesn't get her to kill that project of hers."

"You amaze me brother; sometimes when you speak so lucidly it almost sounds like me talking!" I said with a laugh.

"You mean it isn't?" he chortled.

I added, "I'll have a talk with Si. He can give Connie the marching orders, so to speak. They've seemed to bond, and she trusts him. Besides, how would it look if a girl's own father asks her to sleep with some guy just for his own benefit? That would make her look like a hooker, and me a pimp."

Reilly came back with, "You are a pimp; did you forget about your stable?"

We both laughed and toasted our genius and the plan to destroy Hap and Joanie – and save our business ventures in the process.

*　　*　　*

REILLY

"Sadie, would you come in here for a moment; I'd like you to take a message," I announced over the intercom.

"Sure Mr. Fitzpatrick. I'll be there in just a moment. Will I need anything besides a pen and paper?"

"No; nothing besides your sexy self," I said feeling like I'd already won the battle.

As she opened the door to my office and entered I could see a puzzled expression cross her face as she looked at every corner of the room. I knew what she was searching for, so I addressed RJ's absence in order to satisfy her curiosity.

"I suspect you're looking for RJ, aren't you? Well, he left just moments ago, out the back door. He didn't want to disturb you on his way out. He's funny like that, you know," I said.

"Oh, well, he sure wasn't worried about disturbing me when he came in," she was quick to add.

I managed to get out a slightly uncomfortable laugh; but I could see by her look that she was satisfied, if not annoyed.

After I gave her the message I was ready to make my exit to check on Jimmy and Tony, who were supposed to have already reported back on what they've learned about this little project of Joanie Pozner's. One of the perks of being a union boss is that I have my own spies in factories and plants all over Western New York.

I say I was ready, but it seemed Sadie was far from ready to let me leave. She can be a big help most of the time, but every once in a while she tries to poke her nose too deep into my business. But, I've learned to live with it; her nosiness has worked to help me on many occasions. So I'll do as I always do – tell her nothing in a way that makes her feel like she has walked away with a treasure trove of information.

"I get the feeling our conversation is not over. Is there anything else I missed Sadie?" I asked.

"Well Mr. Fitz, there is one thing that I am curious about," she said in her sheepish voice.

"Okay, I know there's no avoiding it. What is it?" I said with a fatherly smile.

"Well, it's actually two things. First, why is it I've never seen you and RJ together? He comes in the front; you come in the back. He goes out the back, you go out the front."

"And?"

"And...well, I couldn't help overhearing him say something to the effect that you two were twin brothers. Is that right?"

I let out a big laugh; as I did, I could see her face begin to turn red.

"Oh, I'm sorry. I'm not laughing at you; I'm merely laughing near you – so to speak. No, he didn't say that, I did. And I meant it metaphorically, not actually."

"I don't get it," she said, looking very puzzled now at my reply.

"Well, you see, he and I have done business with each other for many years now, as you know; and we are even on boards together. So it almost feels like we're twins. Get it?" I said trying to explain my way out of that one.

"Sure, I get it now; of course. But what about my first question?"

"Oh Yeh, I almost forgot; the one about the disappearing man, right? Well, that's an easy one to explain – it's like Batman and Bruce Wayne or Superman and Clark Kent."

She looked even more confused than before.

As I attempted to escape on this note she stuck out her arm and pressed it to my chest stopping me in my tracks as I about made my way to the door and freedom.

"Hold it right there mister! You're not getting away that easy. What exactly does that mean? That you and RJ are the same person with two different identities?"

I grabbed her hand and pulled it away from my chest, looking her in her eyes and said, "Why yes, of course. But now I'm going to have to kill you."

She gasped at my remark and dropped her pad and pen to the floor. I could see she was about to wet herself so I let out a laugh and hugged her. I gave her a big smooch on the top of her head and said, "Come on Ms. Myers, lighten up. I was only kidding. I couldn't kill you. If I did, who could I get to work as hard as you, and at the same time ease-drop on all of my conversations?"

At this she stooped down, picked up her pad and pen, shot back up and out the door exclaiming, "*Men!*"

* * *

RJ

"You want me to do what!" Si shouted after I explained what I wanted him to tell Connie to do.

"Look it, you're just her newly discovered half-brother; I'm her father. For God's sake, how would it look if I asked her to prostitute herself?" I said, trying to reason with him.

"Just when we were beginning to like you enough to call you dad, you turn back into the weasel you really are," he shot back.

"Hey, it's not like I'm asking you to do it. Besides, I'd much rather you'd try to seduce Joanie – you know, go right to the source of the problem; but you're too ugly," I added.

"Thanks a lot, *dad*."

"And even if you weren't, women are harder to get into bed than men. It's a statistical fact. And we don't have a lot of time to work with here," I said, pretty impressed with myself.

"Okay, leave it to me. She gets him in bed, blackmails him and he does our work for us, right?"

"That's right. The alternative is we kill the both of them. Oh, and you might want to mention that to Connie if she baulks at the first solution. I think that might just change her mind, if she is disinclined to honor our request. I'm sure she'd rather have him around. But only use that as a last resort. I wouldn't want my daughter thinking that I'm a murderer or anything," I said with a snicker.

"Right RJ. I would hate for her to learn the truth about you," Si said in a sarcastic tone.

"Oh, and by the way, you need to convince her that the research project Joanie's working on is flawed; that it has the potential to kill many more than it could possibly save – like that DDT thing. You remember; it caused a big stir when that woman, Rachel Carson, wrote the book saying that DDT was harmful and all. Anyway, the results since then have been hundreds of thousands of people dying because of its ban, all to save a few birds. Go figure."

As he left the kitchen to go back downstairs to the costume shop I couldn't help but get a bad feeling about this. While it's been good for the two of them to become close this quickly, I worry that they may betray me. It might not be a bad idea if I kept an ear to their conversation just to make sure no one was going off script.

EIGHTEEN
WEDNESDAY, JULY 9

RJ

"Well?"

"Well, what?" Si responded.

"Well, it's been over a week and I don't see any results. Did you have the conversation with your sister yet or not?" I asked.

"I was waiting for the right time," he said.

"*WHAT!* The right time was when I told you to do it. Now, go upstairs and have that conversation before she leaves for school. Don't forget, you have as much to lose in this as any of us. Now take her into the kitchen, sit her down at the table and have that talk."

He nodded and slowly shuffled his way up the stairs. I barked those orders at him knowing that the table in the kitchen sat right next to the heat vent; and that vent led directly to the vent in the back of the shop. I knew neither Connie nor Si would even suspect that I would be listening in on their conversation at the other end of the duct. But I did.

"Connie, we need to talk about something. I know that we have just met recently and discovered we're brother and sister; and I also know that we're really beginning to bond, and I like that very

87

much. So I don't want you to take what I'm about to say in the wrong way."

"Oh? You've got my attention. What is it that you have to tell me that's so urgent? You know I've got to get to school in about 20 minutes."

I could hear him clear his throat and hem and haw. Finally, he began, "Well, our dad is involved in some business ventures that involve drug rehabilitation, along with Reilly Fitzpatrick. And those businesses employ quite a few people in the area."

"Yes; so what does that have to do with me, or you for that matter?"

"It seems that your boss's wife, as you've told us, is involved in some research concerning cures for drug addiction."

"That's right. So…"

"Well, RJ and Reilly are on the board of Vericon, the pharmaceutical company that she works for, and, because of their positions on the board, have found out that the research is flawed and is potentially dangerous if it is released. The company has put a halt to the project, but this Joanie person has intimated that she might find a competitor who would produce it if Vericon doesn't let her finish it."

"Again I have to ask, what does this have to do with me?" I could hear the stress in her voice.

Si went on to lay out the details to Connie and I could hear her questioning begin to fade as he made his argument. Just as I thought he had convinced her she interrupted him. This time when she spoke it was in a hushed voice, as if she didn't want anyone to hear – or as if she suspected that someone was already listening. But I was able to catch snippets of the conversation; enough to alarm me.

"Si, I know what's going on here. I think I can trust you. I know you have a stronger loyalty to RJ than I do; after all he…"

"Sorry to interrupt you sis, but I probably have less of an allegiance to that old pervert than you think. You've seen how he slaps me around like I'm his servant. This limp I have; well, I didn't have it until he knocked me down those stairs. So save your concerns for someone who gives a damn about him."

"Well, it just so happens that I went to Mr. Fitzpatrick's office a week ago this past Monday, and did I get an earful. I always thought that it was just in the movies how the secretary listened through the door to hear the conversations going on in their boss's office; but Sadie proved me wrong. Apparently, it goes on in most offices. We listened to Reilly and RJ talking and found out all about this little plan of theirs. It was a very odd conversation though."

"Odd in what way, sis?"

"Well, we could hear them both clearly, but they never seemed to speak at the same time."

"Maybe they were just being polite."

"Yeh, but they never even seemed to laugh at the same time, or anything. Very odd."

"Well Connie; do you trust me?"

"I think you're my only hope. I have to. What do you have in mind?"

"I might be stabbing myself in the back as well, but it will be sweet revenge to beat him at his own game. Besides, I'm far enough removed from the underhanded dealings of those two that I might just be able to cut a deal with the D.A. once they're arrested. Here's what we'll do…"

Damn it! They know too much. I'll have to deal with the two of them myself; and just when I was beginning to feel like a father to them. Oh well, c'est la vie – and their *death*!

Michael J Maccalupo

Part III
The Murder
[Hap Pozner]

NINETEEN
SATURDAY, MARCH 15, 1986

"AAAAAAHH!"

"Hap, wake up, wake up! It's just a bad dream."

I found myself sitting up in our bed, a cold sweat drenching my PJs and Joanie holding onto my arm shaking me, shouting to get my attention.

"It was her; that strange little girl. She couldn't be more than four or five years old, the one that has been haunting my dreams these past six months or more. It's the same dream played over and over. She doesn't say anything; she just stands there looking down at something on the ground – a sign, a marker, possibly a gravestone. She's standing on the sidewalk in front of a shop on Allen Street; it's during the Art Festival in early June. She's there with all of the people walking around, but yet she's not with them; she seems somehow apart from the masses. There's a man, a puppeteer holding two marionettes behind her – one on either side.

There's a haze or mist surrounding her, as the passersby look in the shop windows and at the booths lining the street. They don't seem to see her; only I do. She stands there silent, looking at the ground. Then a single tear slowly falls from one of her beautiful green eyes and rolls down her cheek. Her expression is one of sadness, but just as that single tear falls from her face, her eyes roll up to catch mine and a sneer steals across her pale white lips."

The Allentown Murders

As I relate this, my hands begin to tremble and I feel a cold chill run down my spine. I have to pause to regain my composure. Joanie sees this and tries to lighten thing up a bit.

"You're fine Hap; everything's okay. You've probably been working too hard on your new book. I think writing murder mysteries for a living has got you thinking that they're more than the fiction you write."

As she took my hand and smiled I felt some sense of comfort and safety. After all, it was only a dream.

She could see that I was coming back to my senses and she added, "I know you and your mother think that you have some sort of sixth sense, but this was nothing more than your overactive imagination at work. Now, how about some breakfast?"

She always did know how to get me in a better mood.

"Who's buying?" I said kiddingly.

"Why you, of course. But I'll tell you what; since I'm in such a good mood I'll help. Let's see…okay I got it. Make some bacon and poached eggs with rye toast."

"That's it? That's how you're gonna help?"

"Yeh, what did you expect? As I've heard you say many times, 'Planning takes more time and energy than doing the actual task."

"Thanks for reminding me. Remind me to keep my philosophy to myself in the future."

As we both got out of bed and prepared for the day the conversation turned serious again.

"Hap I'd like you to go to see Dr. Milborne. It might help to have a professional listen to this nightmare. He might be able to help you."

"Yeh. That's all I need right now, a shrink! I have a best friend who slips and slides in his own shit; his girlfriend, who I suspect is a bit psychotic; a wife who thinks I'm losing my mind; then add to that mix a shrink to tell me that I'm all screwed up because my parents didn't love me or my brother tortured our pet rabbit or some other stupid reason! No thanks; end of story."

"So what are you trying to say? Spit it out, don't be shy."

With her last remark I held my breath in anticipation of getting reamed out, but her scowl turned to a grin and we both broke out in a fit of laughter.

"Now what was that? Pork sausage and sunny-side up eggs?" I said after we caught our breath.

"*Bacon and poached eggs! Bacon and poached eggs!* And coffee. *DON'T FORGET THE COFFEE!* Do you *ever* listen?"

"All right, all right. Such drama, sheesh."

There was a long pause in our conversation as I prepared to make breakfast. Somehow I knew that this would not be good.

"So. Have you thought about what I said?" Joanie asked, standing right next to me at the stove. I knew she was serious because she stood there with one leg out in front, her knee bent and her toes tapping the ground, her arms folded and her lips drawn tightly together.

"Thought about what?" I said hoping to change the subject or at least lighten the conversation.

"*Don't be a smart-ass!* You know very well what I'm talking about. Dr. Milborne," she said in a firm voice.

"Oh, that. I thought that maybe you were reconsidering the breakfast thing. You know, actually getting your hands into the cooking process."

She just stood there without saying a word. I knew that that was a bad sign. There would be no way out of this one.

"All right, I'll go see him."

This, of course, was only the beginning. She had won this round; she saw me flinch, so she was going in for the kill.

"Well?"

"Well, what?"

"When are you going?"

"I have to call and see when he can take me."

"Well?"

"*WELL, WHAT NOW?*"

"Well, when are you going to call?"

The Allentown Murders

"Oh geez. I'll call right after I make our breakfast and have a chance to eat it, so I have the strength to dial his number and have a conversation with his secretary, and write the appointment date and time in my calendar. All of that takes energy you know."

"AAAAAAHH!"

"What? What did I say?"

TWENTY
THURSDAY, MARCH 27

"It starts very happy and calm; Joanie and I are just walking around the Allentown Art Festival. We're on Allen Street looking at the booths filled with paintings, jewelry, small sculptures and whatnots. We're holding hands, you know, taking it all in – the sounds of people talking and laughing, the smell of Italian sausage, peppers and onions being grilled and popcorn being popped, and the money changing hands as the happy customers walk away with their prize."

I could see Dr. Milborne nodding as I spoke. I don't know if that was a nod of approval or just to confirm that he was listening. There was no other reaction. I couldn't tell, as I told him my dream, if he really understood how this dream had taken me over night after night for the past six months.

I continued, "As we passed Mulligan's Brick Bar and then the Allen Street Hardware Store, which was right next to the Allendale Theater, I looked across the street and there, next to George's Restaurant there she was, standing on the sidewalk right in front of a costume shop. Behind her I could see a marionette dressed as a Wizard with another dressed like a Court Jester; both being held by a puppeteer; they were staring into my eyes, with one hand each extended toward me with a finger pointed directly at me. Their mouths had an unnatural grin on them, not at all like the expression you would find on a puppet. Somehow they looked human, or maybe demonic."

"Go on. What happened then?" he interrupted, as he did every few minutes. I suppose to make me feel like he was paying attention.

"It was then that I focused on her, the little girl."

At this, he stopped writing, looked up at me, and with a sobering expression painted across his face said, "Please describe her in as much detail as you can. This could be very important."

After a short pause he said, "Continue."

His interruptions, while encouraging me on with my tale, kept me too much in his world. I needed to dig deep down and relive the dream if it were to make any sense to anyone else.

As I began again I could feel myself back on that street and in the dream once more, retelling what I saw and felt.

"She was very young – about four or five years of age, maybe three and a half feet tall, piercing green eyes, strawberry blonde shoulder length wavy hair. She was wearing a white dress that had lace or tulle on it; it almost looked like a First Communion dress. She wore silver shoes with white socks. On her head, surrounding her beautiful hair was a pink band of some sort that had pink ribbons falling gently down the front of her shoulders."

I could see from how he was looking at me from over the top of his glasses that I had piqued his curiosity. I continued.

"At first she was just standing there, much like the marionettes dangling behind her – except, of course, she wasn't pointing or looking at me. Instead, her gaze was directed at something on the ground, on the sidewalk. It appeared to be rectangle in shape and was raised several inches above the ground. It was red; blood red, in fact. There appeared to be a white rope or cord of some sort around it, and it was tied like a hangman's noose!"

I paused to look around, not at the room, but at the scene that I was now envisioning.

"There was a mist or light fog that surrounded her where she stood. The street was crowded, but no one seemed to notice her."

Once again he interrupted, "Did she say or utter anything?" But at this point I was too mesmerized by this vision to be distracted.

"She was singing a children's nursery rhyme; 'Hush Little Baby' I believe; she sang only a few lines, then, just as suddenly as she began, she stopped. I could see a single tear slowly fall from one of her eyes, down her cheek, off her lip and onto that marker she stood staring at. It was at this time that she slowly looked up and stared right at me, as if I were the only person there. I felt her glare reaching deep into my eyes and into my soul. It was then that a twisted smile stole across her lips, but only for a second. She turned her back to me and, with one step, she was gone."

I could see that he was intrigued by this story. He wanted to know more, but more I didn't have...or at least didn't think I had.

"Can you tell me what, if anything, was written on that marker? That may be a critical piece in understanding what this is all about. We need to get to the root cause of these dreams, and this may be the key."

"I'm not sure I want to know. What if it's my gravestone or of someone I love. I don't want to know."

"You must confront your fears in order to defeat them," Dr. Milborne added after a long pause.

"What do you think it means, doc?" I said, feeling a cold sweat break out on my neck and forehead.

Looking up from his notes and over the top of his glasses he added, "And what do you think it means, Hap?"

I was surprised by his remark and asked, "That's it? That's the best you got? Look doc, between you, me and God I'm only here because my wife made me come."

"How refreshing. Usually, my patients blame it on the Devil," he responded with a snigger.

I could see that this would go nowhere, so I relented with, "Okay. You're saying that if I go to the Allentown Art Festival in June and stand in the street in front of the costume shop where I see her, with the crowd milling all around, I won't see her and all will be over? Is that right?"

I could see that he was getting annoyed with me, or maybe it was frustration I saw. I figured he was smart enough to see that I was being sarcastic.

"Well, Hap; it's really all up to you. Take what I've said and embrace it or continue on this path of self-destruction. It's your choice."

"And it's my money too! And speaking of money I see that our time is up. Thank you for this delightful chat we've had." I said, as I got up to leave.

At this he grabbed my arm and reminded me, "I get paid either way. I try to listen carefully to people's problems and to help them. This is *your* problem and you need to solve it, or it will only get worse."

I sat back down with a feeling of hopeless resignation. I knew deep down that he was right – I had to confront these fears.

"All right, maybe you are right; but what do I do after I go there and the dreams don't go away? Then what?"

"Don't get ahead of yourself. Half of what happens in life is predicated on our will to make it happen. The other half is just dumb luck."

"Well, I needed to go to Buffalo to do research for my book and to visit family anyway, so I guess I could go for the Festival and take care of several things at once; right?"

I could see him smile for the first time during our talk. But was it a smile to cheer me on like a coach might give a player going onto the field, or was it a smile to say, 'I won and you don't even know it'. Regardless, I knew I had to do this.

As I got up to leave once more, Dr. Milborne spoke up; but this time with some force, "Hap, I'd like you to sit down again...please. There's something else that we need to talk about."

Sensing the topic, I said, "But there's nothing else that I want to talk about; and besides, our time is up isn't it? Don't you have some person who needs your help more than me waiting out there gnawing on the carpet or your secretary's leg?"

"Hap, I purposely put your appointment at the end of the day so that, regardless of whether or not you were ready, we could at least broach the subject. You know what I'm referring to – the one you avoid. I believe it has a lot to do with your dreams and the troubles in your marriage."

"What troubles? Have you been listening to Joanie again? I love her, but she can sometimes make something out of nothing. We've just been going through a rough patch, as all couples do now and again. We'll work it out. I've been in a writing slump lately, that's all."

He sat there shaking his head at me and said, "Hap, I'm not talking about your writing slump. What I'm talking about is Joanie's miscarriage. I've known you two, both personally and professionally, for a while now. Why I sometimes I think that I'm your father and not your therapist."

I sat there silent as he talked, feeling alone and detached from the world around me. Finally, I spoke up, "Look doc, I know you mean well and, as a therapist you have the best interest of your patients at heart; but this is too personal for me to have a 'Kumbayah' session with you."

"Hap, you're missing my point here. I believe that little girl that's in your dreams might just be your projection of what your daughter might have looked like at that age. Her features as you described her – hair color, eye color, stature, etc. – would almost certainly match that of Joanie and you. Why she sounds to me like she's the image of Joanie as a little girl. Am I right?"

I slumped in my chair, putting my head into my hands for a moment. After I was able to control the shaking that had overtaken me, I looked up at him and said, "Yes."

After, what seemed like an eternity of silence, he said, "I have a feeling there's more to this than I'm being told. I can't reveal what another patient has said to me, even if it is your wife, but I somehow get the impression from the both of you that there is some undercurrent to this whole thing."

The Allentown Murders

"All right, I'll talk to you about it. Maybe I'm doing this for me, maybe for Joanie; but for whatever reason you can't ever even give her an inkling of what I am about to tell you."

"Of course not, Hap. You have my word."

"Somehow, throughout our entire friendship – and that goes all the way back to kindergarten – our friend, Susie, has been somehow at the root of most of the bad things that have happened to everyone around her. Now, I'll be the first...well, okay, the second...to admit that I do have a bit too much paranoia about some things, but I can't help feeling that Susie somehow, in some way, had something to do with Joanie's miscarriage. That's why, ever since they moved to Charleston shortly after that, I've avoided seeing them whenever possible. It kills me to think that she might have caused it. But Joanie has never given any indication that Susie was at fault, or had anything to do with it for that matter. It's just a gut feeling I have."

"There must be more to it than that, isn't there?" he asked after hearing my conjecture.

"There is. It was probably the week before that Susie and Joanie were out shopping for some baby things at a store when a clumsy sales clerk tripped over a baby toy that had fallen on the floor. As she was going down she said she felt something hit her back sending her directly into Joanie who was leaning over a crib with her back to the woman. When she fell on Joanie the force of her weight slammed Joanie into the rail of the crib and then onto the floor with the baby hitting the floor first. We went directly to the doctor and had tests done. Her doctor said that she would be all right, but needed to stay in bed for a week or so. All that week she was in pain; and then it happened – she began to hemorrhage. By the time we got to the emergency room it was too late to save the baby."

"I'm so sorry Hap, but you can't live your life and have a good relationship with Joanie until you let this go. Whatever happened – happened. I don't know your friend Susie, but you have to come to terms with your relationship with her as well. This is too many years to carry that much weight, don't you think?"

TWENTY-ONE
FRIDAY, APRIL 4

"I just hope Slick and Susie appreciate our coming to Charleston to help them move – *again*."

Joanie shot back, "Oh stop your bitching! These are our friends. So what if they aren't quite settled yet. They're finding themselves."

"Yeh, they're finding themselves getting kicked out of every decent rental house and apartment in Charleston. My greatest fear is that they'll decide to move back to Wilmington and want to move in with us."

I could tell Joanie was in no mood for my sarcasm. I'm just glad that I was driving; she might have driven the car off a bridge or into a ditch to get me to shut up.

"Well, it would be nice to have our two closest friends back in town with us; don't you agree?"

"Sure, in town would be nice, but you remember how it was before we were married and we all lived at each others apartments, don't you?"

"Don't be so dramatic. And you call Susie a drama queen! They won't live with us because I wouldn't let them. I love them and all, but I do draw the line somewhere, and moving in with us is over the line," she added.

"All right, I got it. Now let's see what they think about your plan for them. I'm not getting a good feeling about this whole thing, but I know that once you've got your mind made up there's no changing it. So I'll just go along for the ride. But do me one favor, would you?"

"Maybe, what is it?"

"Try to keep yourself from telling me how to drive. I've been doing it for 17 years!"

At this last remark she backhanded me across the chest.

Then she added, "Shut up and just drive. And don't miss the exit; we're almost there."

I knew better than to say anything at this point, but I couldn't help letting one of Slick's 'shit-eating grins' escape and find its way to my lips. Joanie caught it and smacked me again and said, "*Drive!*"

"What was the exit number or name?"

"I don't know how you find your way around our house sometimes without a map. It's exit 220 off Interstate 26, then down Sans Souchi Street to Clemson. Now I'd like to shut my eyes for a while. Do you think you could at least keep us in South Carolina while I get some beauty rest?"

"Take as much as you need, please."

With that she backhanded me a third time; this time with her eyes closed.

"Good shot!"

*   *   *

"Hap, Joanie come on in. It's good to see you both. Why, since Slick and I've moved here we don't see you but about every three months," Susie said as she greeted us at the door.

"Yeh, you seem to only come when we have to move. Ha, ha," Slick added.

That's Slick for you. He could find humor in hemorrhoids.

"Hey, buddy. What you been up to? Wait, let me guess – you've been busy studying the mating habits of giant squids, which by the way don't live in waters less than about 700 feet."

"No, I did that for a few months, but it didn't work out. As you pointed out they don't live in the waters where I do my research, which, by the way, I wished you had mentioned to me before I wasted three months!"

Joanie jumped in with, "When you two boys are done I'd like to have an intelligent conversation about something more important than some big fish. All right?"

"Well, actually squid are not fish; they are..."

At this point Joanie, Susie and I had had enough of Slick, so we all turned to him and shouted, "*SHUT UP!*"

A little annoyed at our response, but not enough to actually shut him up Slick went on with, "Look it guys, Susie and I asked you to come help us move, but this time it's a little different."

Before he could fill in the blanks Susie chimed in, "Not now Slick. Can't you see they're tired from their trip; and Lord knows tired of our problems? We can talk about this later."

Slick hung his head and said, "I guess you're right."

Susie was quick to add, "Of course I'm right. Aren't I always?"

As a smug grin found its home on her face, Joanie changed the subject.

"This might be a good time to unload and clean up a bit; okay?"

After we all had a chance to take care of things, unloading the car, cleaning up after the three and a half hour drive, and just relaxing a bit, Susie brought us back to Joanie's earlier request for an intelligent conversation.

The Allentown Murders

"Well, what are these big plans that you mentioned? You know that if you and Hap need help, Slick and I would be more than happy to help you in any way we could. Isn't that right Slick?"

I could see from his strained look that he wasn't quite in with Susie on this one. Oh, I know he would do anything for Joanie and me if we really needed help, but lately he seems to be in his own world. I guess he's feeling the strain of having to move often and the lack of support for his projects. I've told him many times that there's work for marine biologists all along the coastal area, but he would rather dream up research projects and try to find funding on his own. Hey, who knows, he might just be kooky enough to get it right with one of his hair-brained ideas. Who am I to judge anyway?

"Well, sit down everyone and let me explain our situation. As a matter of fact, we do need your help, and I have a feeling you're going to love my idea," Joanie said.

Oh boy, that's not a good way to start out. I just hope they actually do love her idea or she'll be crushed.

"Okay, here me out before you say anything."

Susie and Slick looked at each other, then at me, and finally at Joanie; then with a nod they both said, "Okay."

As Joanie related to the two of them how I needed to do some research for my new book in Buffalo, and how during the upcoming Allentown Art Festival was the perfect time to do this research, they sat quietly listening; in fact, they appeared somewhat mesmerized as she began talking about the little girl in my dreams.

"...I know it sounds crazy, but Hap does seem to have what some refer to as 'the shine', just like his mother. In fact, I sometimes call him Nostra-dumb-ass, 'cause he knows when he's going to say something stupid!"

Not wanting to miss an opportunity, Slick jumped in at this point with, "Yeh, I once heard about this old lady who had this fortune-telling business; it must have been down in Lily Dale. Anyway..."

"Slick, if you're going to waste our time with one of your stupid stories – please *DON'T!*" Susie interrupted.

With an annoyed glace at Susie, and then turning back to us, Slick got quiet.

At that Joanie went on with her story.

"Hap has been having that dream again, almost every night, where that little girl all dressed in white appears on the sidewalk in Allentown, during the festival, right in front of a costume store. She seems to be looking at a marker or sign or something on the sidewalk. Then, after shedding a single tear, she turns and takes one step away from Hap. Then, just as suddenly as she appeared, she vanishes."

With that, Joanie fell silent, as did we all. After a few moments, Slick spoke up.

"Let me use some of my powers to see the future here. Mm...I'm thinking that you two want us to go with you to the festival and grab this girl before she can get away, and, with my superior power of interrogation, shake her down for answers. Should I use the usual; you know, the spotlight in the eyes, the dripping water on the forehead; or are we going to play good cop – bad cop?" At this, we could all see that Slick was full of himself, because he had his 'shit-eating grin' on.

"I was thinking more in the line of going there, standing where I do in the dream, and, when I don't see the girl or the marker, breath a sigh of relief and enjoy the festival."

"Oh, that confronting your fears thing; I see," Slick was quick to add.

Looking first at Joanie and then to Slick and Susie, I said, "Now to the favor. We would like the two of you to move back to Wilmington so we can all be together again. I know that it may take a while for you to find jobs and all, but we hope you can come back and find an apartment and make it your permanent home."

After a few minutes of chitchat, drinking coffee and eating some of Susie's delicious cinnamon coffee cake, Joanie brought us back to Slick's earlier comment.

"Now that we have that out of the way, what was it that you wanted to talk about Slick?"

The Allentown Murders

At this, Slick's demeanor took on a more serious expression. He looked at Susie, I suppose for approval, and, after a nod from her, he began.

"Well guys, as you know Susie has been holding down the fort here for the both of us while I've been trying hard to make one of my research schemes work. I guess there comes a time when you have to just wake up and say 'this isn't working' and try something different."

I tried to lighten up the tone of the conversation with, "Let me guess. So you've decided on a career in nuclear physics and are about to complete the home study course and become certified from Guatemala U., right?"

Seeing his expression remain serious, I backed off.

"I wish it were that easy. No, we're flat broke – again, and are being evicted – again. This time it is time for the whole truth."

Susie stepped in, "I'm very proud of you Slick. I am seeing a big change in you; you're finally starting to grow up and become a man."

Joanie jumped in here, "Yeh Slick, we're all proud of you, but what does this mean? Do you have a plan?"

I added, "Listen, if you guys need some money to help you get through this, we have a little saved that we could give you."

They both smiled at this and Susie said, "Thanks Hap, and you too Joanie. We love you two, but we don't need any money. We have a plan; tell them about what we've decided to do Slick."

"First of all, we need to move our stuff out of this house; then..." he paused and a smile ran across his lips as he said, "...we're moving back to Wilmington. Susie got her old job back at New Hanover Regional Medical Center, and I got a grant to do research through the Marine Biology department at UNC-W. How great is that!"

Joanie and I burst into shouts of joy and laughter. We all were jumping around the room when Slick dropped the bombshell.

"And we're going to move in with you guys...for a while. How about that for great? Now we'll be able to see each other every day!"

Joanie and I stopped our laughter and jumps for joy. We just stood there looking at each other in horror. Joanie was quicker to come up with something to say to this surprising news than I was.

"For...for...how...l-l-long?"

Susie broke in, "Don't worry; it'll only be a few months, six or eight maybe – at the most. I hope its okay. We didn't mean to spring it on you like this, but we couldn't find any other way to survive."

As she said this a few silent tears began to run out of her eyes and down her cheeks. Slick lowered his head, embarrassed by the situation.

A bit ashamed of our reaction to this, Joanie and I began to feel what they were going through. Joanie moved over to Susie and put her arms around her saying, "That's okay dear, after all we're all family here. We were hoping that you guys would move back to town anyway. It'll be great to have you both back where we can have fun like we used to. I know you will be back on your feet in no time; and this time it'll work. Besides, it will be fun, just like when we had our apartment together. Right?"

Susie wiped her tears away with the back of her sleeve and responded, "Sure. It'll be great."

Seeing she wasn't quite convinced, I added, "Come on, it'll be like camping out. You know, Chestnut Ridge, Chautauqua Lake..."

Just as I was about to name every place we all camped together Slick jumped into the conversation with, "If you say Zoar Valley I will drop you on the spot!"

At this we all laughed and sat back down at their kitchen table to plan the move.

Joanie and Susie began to busily make plans while Slick and I traded lies about things we never did and which cartoon character was the best and why. Slick and Susie would come to our house to stay for a while as we made our plans for the trip.

TWENTY-TWO
TUESDAY, APRIL 15

"Do you realize that this July will be our 10th wedding anniversary?" I said, pleased with myself that I not only remembered the year, but also the month. I didn't want to push it and guess at the day, so I left it there.

"Why Hap you never cease to amaze me. You remember our anniversary. I missed what day you said it was." She knew she had me. *SHIT!*

"I didn't say," I said with a big smile. That is, until a smirk stole its way across her face. Then I knew I was in trouble.

"Okay. So when is it?"

In desperation I blurted out, "*Ah ha! You don't remember.*"

"Well, of course I do. You're the one who doesn't remember. This is your last chance. When is it?"

Just then Slick burst in and without missing a beat said, "When is what?"

I quickly snapped back, "Our wedding anniversary."

"July 31st; don't either of you remember your own anniversary? Sheesh." Slick paused, and shaking his head, added, "And they call me stupid!"

Feeling good about himself Slick slapped his hands together and said, "So, what's for dinner?"

Disgusted, Joanie remarked, "Somehow Slick I think you've earned it. Isn't that right Hap?"

All of this was lost on Slick so he moved on with, "Well, I'm here and Susie's on her way. She's coming right from work. What's the urgency for a meeting?"

As we moved into the kitchen and sat around the table, I began, "Well, you both know how I've been troubled lately with Devon's death. I'm feeling more and more like he's reaching out from his grave to tell me something. I'm beginning to see him in my dream, you know, the one with that strange little girl in white. You remember the puppets in the picture where the girl is standing in front; one of them is Devon dressed like a Court Jester. He's one of the puppets, and he's looking at me and pointing toward me. It's as if he's trying to tell me something. I know we found the guy who actually killed him, but it's like Devon's trying to tell me that someone else was behind it. It just might be the person whose face I see on the other puppet in my dream."

I paused to draw a deep breath, and then continued, "And that other puppet, the one that I thought looked like a Wizard, is also looking at me and pointing. I see it more clearly now in my dream. There's a puppet-master pulling the strings of the two puppets dangling behind, and on either side of the girl. The face on the Wizard is someone that I've seen before or possibly have known in the past; but I can't quite tell who it is. When I look at him I just see his evil grin and his hands. There's something in his one hand, a book possibly; the other hand is pointing at me. Somehow Devon's death and that little girl are connected; but I don't know how. But I know we have to go back to the beginning."

Joanie interjects, "What does that mean, go back to the beginning?"

Before I could comment Slick spoke up, "Exactly; the beginning of what? When? Whose beginning or what beginning?"

Trying to slow things down to make better sense of it, I add, "Well, if my dreams have any meaning to them there's certainly something important about a beginning. If Devon is trying to warn me of some danger, then maybe his death is related to it. In any case we would need to go back to a beginning that was before his encounter with Jake the Snake back in Buffalo. Does that make any sense to you two?"

They both nod in agreement. Just then Susie came bounding in the back door to the house and into the kitchen where we three had stopped and turned at the ruckus coming from the garage.

"Hey Susie. How was work?" Joanie said, as her eyes shifted from Susie to Slick. She didn't see any humor, or irony for that matter, with Susie working so hard and Slick being a part-time researcher.

"An accidental self-inflicted gunshot wound, one accidental concussion caused by a Louisville Slugger across the back of the head, three not-so-accidental stabbings, and two DOAs." She paused for a moment, "Oh, I almost forgot, two botched finger reattachments; the usual stuff."

Slick was intrigued by all of this, even though this was the daily report ever since Susie transferred to the ER. He commanded, "Well, give us the details!"

"Must I – really?" Susie asked. We could tell she was exhausted; and her day wasn't over yet. "All right. Now let's see...mm...the three stabbings; one was a domestic – the wife caught her husband cheating on her and stabbed him and the girlfriend. The third stabbing was unrelated. That was where two drunks got into an argument at Brusky's Bar on Carolina Beach Road. The girlfriend and the one drunk didn't make it."

"So far, so good. Keep going," Slick said as he leaned in so as to not miss a word.

Susie looked over at Joanie and me and begged, "Must I?"

Joanie just rolled her eyes and walked out of the room.

I thought for a moment and responded, "Of course. You've gone this far. That would be like putting a bowl of ice cream in front of Slick and saying don't eat it."

Slick turned to me and asked, "Rocky Road?"

Thankfully Susie went on, ignoring his comment. "The self-inflicted gunshot wound was accidental. Some idiot was trying to clean a loaded gun. Too bad he only shot himself in the hand. And the concussion; that was two grown men playing with one of their kids baseball bats, trying to show who had the fastest swing."

Slick was really into it now, "Well, who did?"

"The guy that didn't get hit I imagine," Susie stated.

I was beginning to find this interesting as well, "What about the two reattached fingers?"

"I almost forgot. Remember the guy cleaning the loaded gun? We tried to reattach what was left of the two fingers he blew off. I don't think they'll work. And even if they do, they're going to look very strange."

Susie saw that our attention was waning and that Joanie had drifted back into the kitchen, so she changed the subject, "So what is this big meeting all about?"

I proceeded to get her up to speed on our conversation from earlier.

"So what do we do now?" I asked.

"Well, it seems to me that we need to find out what exactly Devon was trying to tell you; if, in fact, he was trying to tell you anything." Joanie added.

"If that's true, then how do we find out?" Slick questioned.

Joanie had a look on her face that she was cooking something up in that pretty little head of hers.

"Hap, tell us again what you think Devon was saying to you in the dreams you've been having," Joanie said as she took out some paper and a pencil.

"Okay; if I remember correctly he said a few things over and over. He kept repeating these three things, 'You must go back to the beginning.' Then he would say, 'We remember – I fear him the most.' and then only, 'SIN'. It's the strangest thing. It's like he can't talk or ..."

"Or maybe that's all he wants you to know. Like these are the things that will lead you to his killer," Susie interrupted.

Just then Joanie stood up and announced, "Then let's start at the beginning!"

The Allentown Murders

Slick cocked his head to one side and said, "The beginning of what?"

Seeing the humor in all of this I added, "I think we're back there again."

Joanie snapped back, "No, I mean his beginning with us – Devon's."

"You may have a point there. He might be trying to tell me to go back to when we all first met and became friends. But what happened that could have led to his death?" I wondered.

"That's what we need to find out," Susie spoke up.

Just as the three of us were settling into our own little trances Slick jumped up out of his chair and onto the back of it without ever touching the ground and startled us.

"I've got it!"

Susie looked skeptical, "You've got what?"

"Well, I'm glad you asked. 'Going back to the beginning' can mean many different things. It can mean whose, which in this case would probably be Devon's. It could mean what, as in his beginning friendship with us. It could also mean where, like when he came back to Wilmington from Buffalo after his experience with that biker gang – that led to his murder! And that's what I'd put my money on."

I couldn't help myself at this point, "Slick; you're forgetting one thing."

"Oh, what's that?" he said in a smug tone.

"You don't have any money," I shot back.

Joanie interrupted, "If you two are quite through Susie and I would like to move on with this."

"All right then Slick, what do you propose?" Susie asked.

"I think we can kill two, or even three, birds with one stone when we go back to Buffalo."

"A poor choice of words, but what birds are you talking about?" I added.

"You can do the research for your new book you need to do, we can confront the mystery girl of your dreams, and we can possibly find out why Devon is reaching out from the grave to you, if, in fact, he is.

I jumped in here with, "Okay, I get the first two. We go to the Allentown Art Festival, I stand in front of the costume shop and don't see the girl, and I look for the marionettes and see that they aren't there. Now you're going to have to fill me in on how we will figure out what Devon's trying to tell us."

We could all see Slick's mind going; he was doing his finger-tapping, eye-squinting, teeth-grinding thing that he always does when he's deep in thought.

"Back to the bar and the biker friends of ours," Slick blurted out with a smile.

I remarked, "I hate to bring this up but didn't we put their leader in prison for murder not that long ago? And didn't we infiltrate their gang to do it?"

"You bring up some good points, but I think that you forget that we also bailed a few of the guys out when they got in trouble with the law. Besides, didn't you go to high school with that guy Tripp? The one that took over as the leader once Jake was taken off to prison?"

"Ironically, he was our class president. Okay, you made your point. But I hope that they will be as happy to see us *now*, as they were when we put down the cash for their bail. And, by the way, Tripp was the guy that I stuffed into the locker our sophomore year and later went up against and beat at student court when I was a senior. He wasn't too fond of me then, and didn't seem too fond of me at our last meeting. So I can't imagine that he would be thrilled to see me again, especially asking for his help. But, hey, you seem to know more about people than I do, so what the heck. Let's do it."

"Hap, you worry too much. It's like I always say..."

"*SHUT UP!*" was all you could hear from the three of us.

TWENTY-THREE
THURSDAY, MAY 15

"Hap, when are you going to open that letter? It's been sitting here for over a week," Joanie asked with her usual lack of patience with my dutiful adherence to my new found sense of procrastination.

"Never? Well, maybe not 'never'; but it might be a bit premature for me to open it. After all, it doesn't have a return address and it's postmarked from Buffalo. I don't know anyone in Buffalo that would send me a letter, let alone one that has no return address. Why don't you open it if it's bugging you so much?"

"No. You're not going to sucker me into opening it. I know why you're not opening it. It's because you're afraid it will blow up or have some sort of poison on it. Right?" Joanie said with a sarcastic tone.

"Hey, just because I'm paranoid doesn't mean everyone's not out to get me! Besides, it could be a letter bomb or have ricin on it. If I opened it and I was right, then what would you do? Huh?"

"Mm, what would I do? Let me think. I don't know; maybe replace you with a newer model," Joanie said as she handed me the letter.

"Now open it for God's sake!"

"All right; but I'm not liking this one bit."

After a short pause to figure out what it was I was holding in my hands I blurted out, "Ah ha! Just as I suspected."

That piqued Joanie's curiosity. She asked, "Okay, what does it say?"

"There's a short note here, hand written by some guy named Bob Griffin, addressed to me. And there seems to be newspaper clippings and the beginning of an article or news story he must have been working on, with some notes at the end with names, dates and, and...murder victims!"

"What?"

"Wait. Let me read the note to you."

As I sat down on the sofa next to Joanie I put the envelope and other papers on the coffee table, focusing solely on the letter addressed to me:

"Dear Hap,

I address this note in a very informal fashion, not because we know each other personally or even in a business way; no, I do so because I have been following you (figuratively) for a while, looking for someone that I can trust to carry through with what I've started if something were to happen to me. The fact that you received this means that I am no longer alive and must rely on the person that I believe you are to finish the work I've begun.

I must, here, warn you that, as I have met an untimely demise, there will not be the same threat to you unless you let the wrong people know what I am asking you to finish for me. I believe your character, intelligence, unswerving desire for truth, and your honesty and integrity are the backbone of what led me to you. But most importantly it was your inquisitive nature that led me to believe that my story, here enclosed, will find its way to fruition in your hands.

If, for some reason, you don't find it in your soul to right this wrong then simply destroy the contents of this message and put me out of your mind. No one, with the exception of myself, knows anything about this information being in your hands. There are, however others whose lives are, or will be, in danger

116

as you finish the task I have begun; that is, exposing the murderous greed and other crimes in the city that you and I both love – Buffalo."

Your brother-in-arms,
Bob Griffin

At that both Joanie and I slumped back onto the sofa and just stared into space. After a few moments of collecting our thoughts she said, "Hap, what are you going to do?"

"I don't know," was all that I could utter.

As if struck by lightning, Joanie jumped up and said, "Come with me. I think I have a clue here."

Dumbstruck I followed her to the garage where she started rummaging through the box of old newspapers. Paper was flying everywhere.

"Well, don't just stand there, help me!" she shouted out to me.

"I would if I knew what you were looking for," I replied.

"The article; the one with a picture of a burning car that was on the section that has stuff from around the country."

"Oh, I remember you telling me about that," I said.

"You remember me telling you about the reporter dying in a terrible car crash that was thought to be suspicious, but you didn't actually read the article, did you?"

"Well, I...um...not exactly the whole thing."

She shot back, "'Not exactly the whole thing?' Not exactly any part of it to be more precise, right?"

"Well, now that you put it that way; I didn't have a chance to get to it – you know that procrastination thing I've got going for me – but I had every intention of reading it. But somehow, poof, it disappeared. Now here it is so I can read it."

"You're impossible!" was all that she could muster.

"So what was so special that it made the wire?"

"Here read it for yourself."

"Saturday, May 3 Buffalo, NY

A car carrying Robert Griffin, an investigative reporter for the Buffalo News, spun out of control early this morning, crashing through a loose guardrail over the Cattaraugus Creek Bridge on Route 5 in Irving. The car was said to be moving at a dangerously high rate of speed when it struck the guardrail, sending the vehicle into the rock bed below where it burst into flames, killing the driver..."

"It says here that his body was so badly burned that they were not be able to make a positive ID. They were able to use DMV records to identify the car and used the few remaining artifacts belonging to the victim to identify him. It goes on to note that investigators suspect that there might have been foul play involved, but are quick to add that no suspect has been named. Wow, why didn't you tell me about this?"

At this she threw down the remaining papers that were still in her hands and, looking at me with daggers, said, "You idiot! I did tell you about it. And I did tell you to read it for yourself."

"Oh, that article. Yeh, now I remember."

After a brief pause in our conversation I said, in a serious tone, "Why don't we go inside and take a look at what his story and notes have to say."

"Good idea."

As we sat on the sofa once again, we picked up the articles and other papers he had enclosed with his hand scribbled notes, and remained silent with Joanie holding one side of the papers as I held the other. We read in amazement of what he had uncovered about the goings-on that occurred at the teamster's union headquarters located right in the middle of...Yeh, that's right...Allentown!

"Six people were murdered over the course of three years in the Allentown area, all either gay males or female prostitutes," Joanie said out loud.

"I don't get it. His notes are incomplete. What does union corruption have to do with murders of gays and prostitutes, or the murder of the reporter himself? It doesn't make sense to me; does it to you?"

I could see that she was mulling this all over. After a few minutes silence she responded, "I don't see the connection, but the more important question is, 'What does this have to do with us?'"

I got her point and asked, "So what you're really asking is, 'Are we going to get involved in this mess?' Right?"

"Right. Just because he asked you to do it doesn't mean you're obligated to follow through with his wishes. No one else knows that we even have this information, and besides, aren't our plates full enough already with your nightmares about the girl and the puppets, your writer's block, not to mention our semi-permanent house guests. Isn't that enough to chew on for a while?"

"I guess you're right...but, on the other hand..."

Joanie could see that it was already too late – I was deep in thought, trying to figure out how I could manage all of this.

"But, and let me just posit this, what if there were some relationship among all of these things? What would you say then?"

Joanie shook her head in disbelief and said, "Have you lost your mind? What could any of these things possibly have in common?"

"You mean outside of our house guests, right?" I asked.

"Of course," she responded.

"I don't know, but I just have this feeling about the whole thing. Let's follow up on his notes and see where they lead us. We're going to Buffalo anyway, and maybe it'll make more sense once we're there. And besides, if we don't like the way things look, we can get out of it at any time. Don't forget, no one else knows that we know anything. As far as anyone else is concerned we're just doing research for my book. And I mean even Slick and Susie are on a need-to-know basis; and they don't need to know anything right now. Okay?"

"Okay, but you have to promise me that if anyone should become suspicious of our inquiries, we bail," she cautioned.

"Agreed."

TWENTY-FOUR
TUESDAY, MAY 27

"Joanie, I've got some great news!"

Not showing any enthusiasm, Joanie responded, "This better be good. I'm exhausted from three solid days of meetings on the new project."

"That's great!"

"What? Do you like to see me suffer?" she questioned.

"No, of course not. But my great news ties in with your constant trips to Vericon's home office on Grand Island. Do you remember last fall when I sent the paperwork in to become a resident writing instructor for a semester at Canisius College?"

"Yeh, so what about it?"

"Well, I just opened their response today and was floored when I read that they actually want me to teach there! A Mr. R.S. Fitzpatrick, the chairman of the board of directors of the College, signed it. They have invited me to be a guest lecturer for the second summer session and through the end of the fall semester in their Creative Writing Department. I'll be teaching undergraduate and graduate courses in writing. Isn't that good news?"

Once she heard this she became as excited for me as I was.

"Congrats! That *is* wonderful. Now we can be there together. In fact, I can ask for a temporary transfer to that facility since I'm there most of the time anyway; and I can take care of things here that I need to by phone or fax. When do you start?"

I scanned down the cover letter to see the date they expected me and responded, "They would like me to start in two weeks. Pack your bags!"

"What! They sure didn't give you much notice, did they?" she asked.

After a short pause, she continued, "You did just get the letter in today's mail, didn't you?"

I squirmed a little and then replied, "Well, not exactly; but I did open it today."

Folding her arms and tapping her foot, she demanded, "When did you receive the letter? Better yet, what is the postmark date?"

"April 10?" I said in a sheepish voice; but came back strong with, "Okay, so I didn't open it right away. I thought that it was a rejection letter; the envelope was too thin. So I let it sit for a while."

"*A while!* Five days is a while; hell, even two weeks is a while; but six weeks is *forever!* What were you thinking...no, better yet; *were* you thinking?" she said in a very agitated state.

"Well, the first two weeks were my usual procrastination thing; but after that I just forgot about it," I replied matter-of-factly.

"All right. Now that you've put us in the 'hurry-up offense', so to speak, what plan do you have for getting everything ready to move so quickly?" she asked.

"Not to worry. I've got it all planned out, right up here in my head. I'll take care of everything. All you have to do is pack *your* things. Okay?" I said with an air of confidence.

Joanie stopped in her tracks and reminded me, "Oops! I'll bet you forgot one important thing; well, really two – Slick and Susie. They weren't planning on us staying in Buffalo for the next six months. What can we do?"

I thought a minute and then said, "Not to worry. Do you think that they will be terribly upset to finally have jobs and a place to live where they probably won't get thrown out of?"

"Do you mean that you would leave them in our house in Wilmington while we live in Buffalo? Have you lost your mind?"

I pulled up a chair next to hers in the kitchen and sat, staring at her for a moment. Then it hit me.

"Look it, they will be home within the next 10 minutes, so we have to have some answers ready or, knowing them, they will figure out answers of their own; and I guarantee you that we won't like it."

She responded with, "You got that right. Let's think."

"Ah ha! I think I've got the answer!" I said as I jumped out of my chair. Just then we heard the garage door open. They were home.

Joanie looked over at me and said, "We'll have to wing it I guess."

"Susie, Slick, so good to see you. How was work today? Here, sit down – get comfortable."

Looking very suspiciously at me, Susie said, "Okay, what's up? Are you two throwing us out? We only moved in last month. We thought things were going well. What did we do wrong?"

At that Joanie and I both started laughing. Slick and Susie looked even more puzzled.

"We're sorry; we didn't mean to alarm you. I guess Hap did sound a bit strange. It's just that we have some great news that we just got – in fact, only moments ago. So we're a bit stunned ourselves," Joanie explained.

Slick grinned and asked, "Well, what is it, or do we have to wait all night?"

I spoke up, "Sorry. Well, as you know Joanie has been traveling to Buffalo quite a bit with her research lately and has to go back again later this week. Several months before you became *permanent* houseguests I had applied for a semester residency program at Canisius College. Well, it came through! I've been invited to work there beginning this upcoming summer session and working there through the end of the fall semester. This will be about the time Joanie will need to complete her new project at Vericon. That will bring us back here for Christmas. How does that sound?"

I thought that the news would make our friends happy for us, but instead they just looked at each other and acted dejected.

"Okay, I know that I'm not the most sensitive guy around, but even *this* is obvious to me. What's wrong?" I asked.

Susie spoke first, "Well Hap, Joanie, we were honestly just getting settled in to our new jobs and our new home – yours; but it looks like we'll have to move once again. We're tired of moving so much, but we understand."

Joanie and I just looked at each other in disbelief. She spoke up, "What are you talking about? You don't have to move. We want you to stay here to take care of the house while we're gone. We'll only be gone about six months anyway."

We could see the relief on both of their faces. After a few hugs and a bit of laughter over the misunderstanding, Joanie and I began our narrative of what we hoped to accomplish in terms of my research and dreams while there. Slick and Susie again thanked us for letting them stay here.

Just as we were reliving some fun moments of our youth, the phone rang. As they all stopped to focus on who will answer it, I sprang to my feet and announced, "I've got it; don't all get up…"

I stopped mid-sentence as Joanie answered the phone and I could see her demeanor change from one of playful laughter to dead serious.

"What is it?" I asked as the three of us moved closer to her.

Just then the phone slipped out of her hands and onto the floor, followed by Joanie.

I raced to catch her before she hit the ground and the three of us moved her to the sofa. I went back to the phone, now dangling off the end table and onto the hardwood floor. Picking it up I could hear a familiar voice. It was Katherine, Joanie's mom.

I grabbed the phone and asked, "Katherine, is that you? What's going on? Joanie has passed out. What was it that you said to her?"

I could hear sobbing at the other end, and as she was about to speak I could see Joanie coming around. Susie was there, doing her nurse thing, with Slick spinning in circles talking to himself – as he usually does in a crisis.

"Hap, I'm sorry to bring this awful news, but Mitch, Joanie's dad is dead. He's been murdered!"

"Are you all right? How's Toby? Oh, sorry. I guess that's insensitive of me."

"No, that's all right. I'm doing okay. You know that I still cared about Mitch, even after he left us for his 'friend'. But that's who he was, I now understand. And Toby? He's completely unraveled over this. He did love Mitch; they had a good relationship even after the hell I put them through at the beginning. He does talk to me now; he's quite a forgiving guy. After all these years, I guess if he had to leave me, at least it was for someone who cared about him. Sorry, I'm rambling."

"No, that's quite all right. But tell me, how did it happen? Did someone try to rob his store?"

"It's too early to tell. The police think that it may have been a botched robbery attempt, or possible a part of something that has been going on in the Allentown area for several years. There have been six or so murders of gay men and female prostitutes in the area in the last three years that bear a striking resemblance to the way that Mitch was killed. I don't know if you are aware, but people in Allentown are talking about a serial killer being on the loose. Mitch may have been the latest victim," Katherine said between sobs.

She questioned, "How's Joanie doing now?"

Coming back to reality, I responded, "Speaking of Joanie, I'd better go; she's coming around now and I'd better be with her. We'll call you back soon. Take care."

"What happened?" Joanie said as she was regaining consciousness.

"You passed out," I responded thinking that that was what she was inquiring about.

"No, I know that; what happened to my dad?"

"Sit down, I'll tell you as much as I know."

The Allentown Murders

After I went through what her mother had told me on the phone Joanie said point blank, "Well, you know this means we are going to Buffalo tomorrow morning. Let's get packed; we're going to be there a while."

At this Susie jumped into the conversation, "And Slick and I will be coming with you, and staying as long as it takes to find out who killed your dad."

We could see a warm smile cross Joanie's lips as she responded, "You guys are wonderful; but what about your jobs? We were going there already for our work; how will you take an indefinite leave and still have a job to come back to?"

Slick, with his usual air of confidence, said, "Don't you worry about that. Ever since Susie moved to the ER she's been working anytime they were shorthanded, besides doing her own shift. They owe her a favor. And me, I have enough data to last me six months for my current research project. I can spend my down time in Buffalo doing all of that nasty number crunching and compiling. Besides, if I need more information, I can have my assistant get on the research vessel and collect whatever data I need."

"Then I guess that's it; we're all going to Buffalo in the morning. But, there is one thing."

Slick gave me a look of 'What is it now?' and quipped, "Okay, I'll bite. What's the problem?"

"Well, if we're all going to ride together, then we're going in my car. You can borrow Sarge's car when we get there; he never uses it."

"Oh, is there something wrong with my car?" Slick was quick to add.

"Not if you don't mind surprises. Your car has so many things wrong with it that there is no telling what will fall off."

Joanie interrupted, "That's about enough boys. We need to make our arrangements now and also call ahead to Buffalo and let them in on our plans. They weren't expecting us this soon."

Slick jumped in with, "Well, what are we waiting for, let's get moving!"

TWENTY-FIVE
WEDNESDAY, MAY 28

"This kind of reminds me of when Lucy, Ricky, Fred and Ethel moved from New York to California. I remember when..."

Susie stopped Slick with, "That's about enough. We've heard all about this and your other 'fond reminiscences of days gone by' for the last hundred and fifty miles! Enough already."

Slick slumped down in the back seat and, turning toward his window, just stared quietly; looking a bit dejected.

I couldn't stand to see him that way; odd as that may seem. Finally, he's quiet and I can't stand it; oh well.

"Slick, how about you drive for a while; my eyes are getting tired," I said, trying to cheer him up.

"Sure. I didn't want to say anything, but I also noticed your hands and feet were also getting tired too."

He couldn't just be grateful. So I asked, "What does that mean?"

With a smug look on his face, probably because I bit, he came back with, "Well, unless there were cones in the road that you were swerving around, I'd say you have a warped sense of a straight line. And, maybe the music was just in your head, but I sensed a strong rhythm being tapped out with your gas pedal foot as well."

The Allentown Murders

At that I jerked the wheel to the right and slammed on the brakes sending everyone flying to their left, and announced, "Maybe you're right. Here, you drive."

They could all tell that I was very annoyed – even Slick; so no one said a word for the next couple of hours. Then Joanie spoke up at last.

"I want to talk about my dad and what happened. All we know now is that he was murdered, hanged; much in the same way several others had been killed in the Allentown area over the last several years. The obvious answer would be that someone had it in for gays and prostitutes; maybe some religious fanatic."

Slick jumped in here, "Or maybe all of those that were killed knew something that someone didn't want anyone to know about. You know, they might have witnessed something, or they might have all owed this person money or something."

Susie posed, "Whatever the connection, they might have had something in common; or possibly these were random killings and the killer just found them to be at the opportune place at the right time for him…"

"…Or her," I interrupted.

Susie continued, "…or her, to do the job and be able to get away undetected."

I could see that Joanie was taking this all in. Suddenly, she blurted out, "What did you just say Susie?"

Looking a bit confused she responded, "What? Well, let me see, I think I just said that the killer might have been looking for the opportune time to do their job so that they wouldn't be caught."

"Yeh, that. You may have just found a clue," Joanie said.

"What did I say? I was just speculating," Susie replied in a somewhat dazed tone.

"It might have been any one of those things, or even reasons we haven't even looked at yet; but it might have been someone who was hired to kill these people. If that were the case, we would have to look beyond the obvious to see how all of these people are connected, possibly to someone not from the area, not going after them for who or what they are now, but maybe for who or what they were sometime in their past!"

"Joanie, sometimes you amaze me. I do believe helping me with my murder mysteries has given you some insight into how the criminal mind works," I said with a smile.

"Yeh, and don't forget that. She can off you anytime and you'd never know it," Slick added with a sly grin.

"That doesn't make any sense at all, not even for you," I responded.

His only response was, "Exactly."

Changing the focus Susie said, "And what about that rope or cord that was used to kill Mr. Taylor and the others? Your mom said the police detective told her that they were made of unusual fibers. What do you make of that?"

I jumped in here, "Look it, we've got another three hundred miles to go; that's enough time to totally confuse the issue. What I mean is, we can speculate on the few facts we have and come up with all kinds of scenarios, but that might only tend to cloud our judgment once we have more information. So, what I'm saying is, let's not make ourselves crazy here trying to figure this out without more things to work with. Okay?"

Joanie spoke up at this, "I guess you're right, but I want to know, *NO, I have* to know who killed my dad and why."

Seeing her angst I said, "I understand what you're going through; we all do. We've all, in our own way, gone through this with people we love. I was just trying to keep the rest of our trip from being a tense one."

Seeing my concern for her, Joanie responded, "Thanks, but I want to go over what we know and hear what you all say about these few facts that we have. Maybe we'll get lucky and find some possibilities that the police won't even think to pursue."

"That's the spirit JT. You're dad, despite his going over to the other team, was a hell of a good guy. I've known him all my life, as we all have, and he was always straight with us...so to speak," Slick said, wishing he had stopped with '...a hell of a good guy'.

As he caught this latest faux pas he stopped, what might have been, one of his longest filibusters in recent history.

"Slick, I think you've covered enough ground here. Why don't you give it a rest for a while," I said, trying to bail him out, as usual.

Susie spoke up, "Slick, you called Joanie, JT. I haven't heard anyone call her that since high school. What brought that back up?"

I jumped into the conversation, "Yeh, I noticed it too. Why did you call her that?"

Looking confused by his own remark, he said, "You know; I'm not quite sure myself."

After a moment's pause to think about it he began again, "I guess I called her that because this whole situation reminded me of when we were younger and used to get into all kinds of messes. She was JT then, so, I guess I thought of her as she was then...as we were then."

Joanie had something to say about this and added, "Slick, I'm right here you know. You don't have to talk about me in the third person."

"What are we, back in Ms. Nicholson's sixth grade English class? I don't need a grammar lesson, thank you," he said, a bit indignant.

"Can we *please* stick to the matters at hand? We'll never be any help to anyone if we bicker all the time," Susie said in frustration.

The car went silent, but only for a few more miles; then I broke the silence with, "So Susie, you, of course, know Sarge, but you've never stayed at his house for any period of time have you?"

Joanie could sense this one coming and cut me off at the pass, "Hap, I don't think fifty miles outside of Buffalo is the time to be bringing this up, do you?"

I just grinned and said, "Why not? Susie should know what she's getting herself into, shouldn't she?"

Slick got into the conversation with, "What does that mean, exactly? Okay, I admit, he is a bit quirky; but Susie will be fine."

"A bit quirky? Are you kidding?" Joanie couldn't help herself.

Susie, looking puzzled, inquired, "What are you all talking about? I've known him since I was little, just like all of you. Oh, maybe not as well, but he seems all right to me. I don't see that we'll have any problems whatsoever. In fact, you are aware, that I'll one day be his daughter-in-law; that is, if Slick ever finds the cajones to ask me."

"Yeh, what she said...wait a minute!" Slick said before he could digest her rant.

"All right, we're just trying to give you a heads-up on the situation; but hey, as Sarge always says, 'Children should be obscene and not heard!' So I'll just mumble to myself," I said sarcastically.

By this time we were almost to South Buffalo and the old neighborhood. Joanie and I had previously arranged to rent an upper flat on Indian Church Road, off Seneca Street near Cazenovia Park; but because of our early arrival we would have to stay at my mom's or my brother Jeffrey's for a week – and there was no way I was staying at Jeffrey's. His flat was so filthy that even the rats refused to live there!

We would, of course, stay with her mom for a few days, but neither of us could take her for more than that.

Besides, my mom was the best cook in the neighborhood and she didn't butt into our business; we'd be free to come and go as we pleased. How perfect is that?

Slick and Susie would be staying with Sarge, right down the street from my mom's house. It may be a bit sadistic of me, but I couldn't wait to see the three of them in action, especially after a few days.

Once we were settled I planned on making an obligatory stop at my old high school, St. Stephen's, to see my old friend and teacher, Fr. Christopher; partly to see how he was doing, but also to get his advice on this situation with Joanie's dad.

Fr. Christopher has helped me, and the others for that matter, on several occasions. He had Slick's and my back when we hunted down our friend Devon's murderer. Without him, neither of us would probably be here today.

The Allentown Murders

"Well, we're here; beautiful downtown South Buffalo!" I said with a grin.

Slick jumped in, "See, that wasn't a bad ride, now was it?"

TWENTY-SIX
THURSDAY, MAY 29

"It's just strange seeing the two of them sitting there together. I don't know."

"Keep it to yourself; someone might overhear you," Joanie responded to my comment.

"Okay, but what do you think of it, Slick?" I asked.

I, for some reason, couldn't let it go. It wasn't that I was trying to be funny (that's funny ha, ha) or anything, but seeing Toby sitting there right alongside Mrs. Taylor, sharing Kleenex and all, just doesn't seem natural to me.

"Hap, we live in a modern world; this being the eighties and all. You have to start thinking like an eighties kind of guy. What I mean to say is..." Slick was on a roll.

I interrupted him, "I guess you're right."

He stopped mid-rant and said in a surprised voice, "I'm what? I wasn't even done yet."

I stopped him before he could begin again, "I get it. I get what you're saying, but I don't think either of you get what I'm saying. I'm not talking about Toby being gay. I'm not contrasting Mr. Taylor's old, straight life with his new, gay one. What I'm referring to is seeing two spouses, so to speak, sitting together like that. Imagine if it were two women, or, for that matter, two men, sitting next to each other. Do you think that they would be so chummy as to share tissues to dry their eyes? No, they'd be scratching each other's out!"

Joanie was about fed up with my observations. After all, it was her father's funeral.

Realizing the situation I decided to give it up. I just said, "Sorry, bad timing."

At that Joanie swung toward me and shot daggers with her eyes. I didn't move – I didn't even breathe for a moment.

Just as I thought that I was off the hook Slick turned to me from my other side and said, "So which one do I refer to as the misses?"

Before I could say or do anything Susie gave him a shot to the gut with her elbow, then quickly turned away from him and smiled at the old ladies who had seen the whole thing. Meanwhile, Slick was still trying to catch his breath, as he sat there, doubled over between Susie and me.

I got up and walked over to where Katherine and Toby were seated. I could tell that Joanie was ready to tackle me, but instead shot me a look that said, 'You'd better not stir anything up'; and I returned a look that said, 'Don't worry, I value my life'! I think she understood, since she let me go.

"Katherine, Toby. I'm so sorry for your loss. Mr. Taylor was always good to me as a child and even as a father-in-law. I was hoping our trip here would have given me the chance to get to know him better."

Katherine spoke first, "Thanks Hap. I know that he thought the world of you, even after he and I split. He often remarked how you were always there to help me in his absence."

She paused for a moment, collecting her thoughts; then continued, "Looking back now, I guess he felt guilty about the circumstances and how he was almost forced to abandon us. But that was partly my fault; I was angry for a long time – and drunk, I might add." She laughed and then cried a bit at her own remark; then she continued, "I guess it was just a bad time in life for us, just as it is now. I know that Joanie would hate for me to say this, especially right now;

but I want to know who did this to him. You know, 'Hell hath no fury like a woman scorned'; well, the greatest peace a woman can have is revenge! I want the person or people who did this found and punished."

At this she glanced over at Toby who seemed to be squirming in his seat, and then back at me and said, "Please find out who did this terrible thing. Let the law handle him or her, but don't let his death go un-avenged. I don't trust the police to find his killer. To them this is just one more case, one more gay guy in Allentown dead." Before she could continue, she began to cry. Toby looked very nervous to me, in fact, too nervous for someone who knew nothing.

I'm not sure it was the appropriate time, but as I held Mrs. Taylor I looked over her shoulder at Toby and asked, "It was very unfortunate that you're such a sound sleeper and didn't hear any ruckus going on in the shop as Mr. Taylor was fighting for his life. I suppose even the items that were knocked to the floor and shattered as they hit the hardwood weren't loud enough to wake you. Because I'm sure, if you heard anything, you would have gone down to help your partner because he meant so much to you. Wouldn't you? Of course you would."

At this Katherine lifted her head, wiped her eyes and turned toward Toby who was visibly shaken by my statement.

She glared at him and said, "Yes, how is it that you didn't hear anything? Mitch was a strong man; he must have put up quite a fight as he was being hanged."

Almost in a panic Toby said, "I wear earplugs while I sleep. You know, Mitch snored so loud sometimes, that I was afraid he'd wake up the neighbors!"

Feeling the need to calm things down I interjected, "Why of course; that would explain it. It's just unfortunate for Mr. Taylor that you had to wear them. But I guess that wasn't *your* fault."

Before letting it go, I was curious to find the answer to one question that was puzzling me. It was something Katherine had told Joanie and me when we first got to town and she was going over what the police had told her.

I got up to excuse myself. I hugged Katherine and kissed her on the cheek and said, "We'll be close by if you need us. And don't forget we're taking you over to my mom's for a late dinner tonight. She'd be here now, but she's home getting everything ready."

I leaned over to Toby and took his hand to shake it and said, "I'm truly sorry Toby. Mr. Taylor was a wonderful man and, I'm sure, a good partner to you. He would have done anything to protect anyone he loved, as I'm sure you would too."

I said this hoping to get a reaction, but didn't see anything that would tell me if he was hiding anything. So my next move was to ask the *big* question.

I turned away from him to go back to sit with Joanie and the others seated across the room. As I took a step toward them I turned back to Toby and Katherine and, looking into Toby's eyes, said, "Oh, I just remembered something Katherine told Joanie and I when she related the details of the murder as the police reported them to her. I found it a bit curious, but maybe it's nothing. Naw, I won't bother you with it. Sorry. It was good seeing you again, even under these unfortunate circumstances."

I turned once again to walk away, but knew I had piqued his curiosity; and I knew Toby well enough to know that he wasn't going to let me go without finding out what I had to say, even if it put him in the hot seat.

He spoke up and grabbed my arm as I was about to leave, "Hap, what was it that you wanted to ask me? I loved Mitch as much as you all did. I would do anything to help find his killers."

I paused and said, "Well, it's probably nothing."

He took the bait and, with a cocky grin asked, "No, really; what is it?"

Acting puzzled, I said, "Well, the police told Katherine that after you called in the morning, you know, after you found Mr. Taylor's body lying on the floor of the shop, they were there within five minutes."

He smiled at me and replied, "Yes, that's right. In fact, it might have been less than that."

"And they told her that when they arrived and knocked on the door you were slumped over his body crying and holding him."

"Well, of course. Wouldn't you, if you just found the one you loved lying on the floor, dead?"

"Naturally, anyone would. When they saw you and tried to open the door it was locked; so you got up and unlocked the door to let them in."

Toby began to look skeptical of where I was going with this and said, "Yes, that's right. What about it?"

"I don't know; I'm no detective. You know sometimes Joanie has to snap me back into reality. She says I sometimes think I'm one because I write murder mysteries. But what I don't understand here is, if you didn't kill Mr. Taylor, then he had to open the door in order for someone to get in to kill him. Right?"

At this Toby puffed up in a defensive posture and, with a stern voice, said, "Are you accusing me of killing Mitch? Because if your are, you'd better have proof!"

I patted him on the shoulder trying to calm him down and replied, "No, of course I'm not accusing you. As you say, 'You loved him' and, you're not nearly strong enough to hang him, no offense."

"None taken."

I continued, "No, what I'm curious about is, if you had to unlock the door for the police to get in, then who locked it after the killers left? Mr. Taylor was in no condition to lock it, and, I assume the killers didn't have a key. So how did the door get locked? I'm just curious."

I could see him panicking, looking for an answer that didn't exist. Not wanting to let this explode right here at the funeral parlor, where I know Joanie would immediately blame me, I concluded with, "I was just wondering. But I suppose there is a logical answer, isn't there? Well, anyway, I can't figure it out, but if you do, let me know. And once again, I'm sorry for your loss – both of you."

TWENTY-SEVEN
MONDAY, JUNE 2

"Mr. and Mrs. Pozner, we're sorry for your loss. Your dad was, by all accounts, a good and generous man who helped build the Allentown area into what it is today. You can be very proud of him for that," Detective Holmes stated.

"Just out of curiosity, do you get a lot of inquiries about your name? You know, the old, 'No shit Sherlock' or 'Hey Holmes, what's hap'nin' or possibly, 'Brilliant deduction Holmes'. Just curious," Slick said out of nowhere.

Turning to Slick, and with a deadpan look he responded, "No, not really."

At that Slick and I stiffened up thinking that he might be taking offense to that remark. When all of a sudden his partner gives him an elbow and they both burst into laughter. That seemed even weirder to us than the deadpan look they had on a minute ago.

"I've heard it a million times or more. By the way, before you even ask, my first name is Sherwood; Yeh, that's right. I guess my parents had a sick sense of humor."

Seeing Joanie's serious demeanor he moved on with, "And my partner here is Joni Dobson. She and I are the lead investigators in your father's murder."

"What have you learned about his death? Was it really part of these serial killings? Do you have any suspects yet? What can you tell us?"

Just then Dobson jumped in with, "Well, Mrs. Pozner, we can tell you that the person who did this was a strong man who your father probably knew. We believe it to be at least two men; at least one over six foot tall and quite strong. They would be men who knew your father's habits well. You know, when he opened the shop, when he closed it, etc. We don't suspect robbery, although the killers would like us to believe that to be the motive – you know, to throw us off."

Susie questioned, "How do you know this?"

I interjected, "Elementary my dear Watson. If I may: they mess the place up a bit, open the register and take what cash there is, and maybe even take a few items from the shop. This would make it look like a botched robbery. But, in reality, the only goal was to kill your father. The rest was for show; a little prestidigitation, or slight of hand."

As I said this I flashed to that scene in my dreams with the little girl and the puppets pointing at me and was startled. I jumped as I snapped out of it.

"Hap, are you all right?" Joanie asked.

"Yeh, sure. I just saw that girl again."

Holmes, looking around the room at this remark, asked, "What girl, where?"

I responded, "No one. It's a dream I have with two puppets being dangled behind a little girl in a white dress. It's nothing. Never mind."

Dobson continued with their analysis, "We say two men because it would take at least that many to overpower and then hang a man of your father's size and strength. We are looking at this and the other six hangings in recent years in this area as being done by serial killers. You know, sometimes these killers work in pairs."

The detectives told us that all of the victims in these cases were hanged with a cord that was not found in stores around here;

you would only find it in boating stores. The cord appeared to be the same kind that is used on anchors of boats.

We had been here only a few days, but our meeting with detectives Holmes and Dobson of the Buffalo Police Department was helpful. Slick and I were a little disappointed that the sidekick's name wasn't Watson, but, apart from this, they seemed reasonably intelligent and appeared to take their work seriously.

Our meeting lasted more than two hours during which they meticulously went over every aspect of the case with us – that is, every aspect that they were allowed to let us in on; after which we said our goodbyes for the time being, knowing that we would be talking with them as the case unfolded.

Joanie and I were satisfied with what they had gathered in the short time after her father's death; so we made plans for our move to an upper flat on Indian Church Road off of Seneca Street, and to begin our own work – the work we had originally planned to be there for; Joanie to work on her research project dealing with a new drug that could be used to alter the brain's addiction patterns; hopefully, to be used to help get people off of drugs – and to stay off.

My three-fold goal was to rid myself of that mysterious little girl in my dreams, teach writing classes and research cold murder cases for my new book.

In fact, I was hoping that being a guest lecturer at Canisius College might give me better access to police records on cold cases, and possibly even provide me with several bright, eager grad students who would be willing to do some of the leg work looking into these cases.

While Slick spent most of his days with Sarge, or at least at the house doing his reports, and Joanie was spending her days between the Vericon headquarters on Grand Island and at the Provistar Lab Research Center on Sheridan in North Buffalo, Susie was right next door to me at Sister's of Charity Hospital on Main Street, only a block or so away from the Canisius College campus where I worked.

She had somehow managed to get a position in the ER there on a temporary basis; that is, during our stay in the Buffalo area. It had been quietly arranged with her boss at New Hanover Regional. I don't know for a fact, but I suspect her mother had something to do with it – up to her old tricks, just like in the old days. I just hope she doesn't push Susie over the edge like she did our senior year of high school.

All of this would be all right if it weren't for the fact that it put Susie and I a bit closer than I liked. We would ride to and from work together, she planned on coming over to the campus everyday to have lunch with me, and even stop by during any down time that she had while on call.

I'll have to admit, it would be nice seeing a familiar face during the workday, but I was worried that her old obsession with me might be rearing its ugly head again.

When we arrived back at my mom's house in South Buffalo she was already cooking up one of her favorite recipes, and one of mine as well – pot roast.

After a wonderful dinner with some pleasant conversation with my brother, Jeffrey, my mom and my Uncle Sallie, Slick and I left to go down the street to spend some time with old Sarge. He was invited to dinner, but declined saying that his rheumatism was acting up. We went down to help him with his medicine – that's right, a case of Genny Cream Ale. That always seemed to help him.

The girls stayed with my mom to help clean up and to give them time to complain about Slick and me.

Uncle Sallie was off to meet some of his old buddies at Greene's Tavern, one of the local 'gin mills' around the corner from his house; and Jeffrey found an excuse for getting out of helping clean up. He claimed he had date and was already late. He probably was just meeting the guys down on Seneca Street to listen to a band at the old movie theater.

*　　*　　*

"Sarge how's the neuritis and neuralgia today?" Slick asked mockingly.

Not to be outdone Sarge replied, "Not bad *junior*, but its my rheumatism that's giving me a fit."

I jumped in to head off what would quickly turn into a brawl.

"Hey Sarge, how about a cold one."

"Help yourself; and get one for this 'sorry son-of-a-sea-cook' son of mine while you're at it."

"Will do," I shot back with a grin on my face. Slick was already irritated with Sarge, but a few beers would mellow things out for both of them. Sarge already had a head start on us though.

"Well, what are you back in town for this time; besides the funeral, that is?" Sarge said to us; then turning to Slick he added, "And I suspect you're here because you got evicted again and lost your job. What do I mean *job*? You don't really have one yet, do you? No, what I meant to say was, 'Are you broke because you can't get a job that actually pays you money and need to move in with old Sarge.' Is that about right there – *junior*?"

I could see it coming; Slick was fuming. Before I could get in between the two of them, they were at it. Slick pounced on Sarge who was sitting reclined in his Lazy Boy.

Fortunately, it only took a few minutes, with a few blows, before they both were tired. Slick got up, grabbed his beer, mumbled a few obscenities and was out the back door.

Sarge, on the other hand, got up off of the floor where they both had rolled onto and, taking a swig from his bottle, announced, "Well, I can still kick his ass; and don't *you* forget it either!"

All I could muster was, "Right Sarge. I'd better go check on Slick."

I grabbed my beer and headed out the back door to see if I could calm Slick down.

Five or six beers later Slick was ready to go back in and have the conversation with Sarge that we intended to have in the first place.

Seeing that the two of them were not about to concede, I spoke first, "Sarge; Slick and I – and the girls for that matter – are here for a number of reasons. As you know Joanie has been flying into Buffalo fairly regularly for the past six months to work at her company's home office on a new drug that she is developing for them, and I just got a position at Canisius College as a guest lecturer in the Creative Writing Department. So we both made arrangements to come here to live for the next six months, until her project was completed and my term at the college was done. We weren't planning on coming here, however, until two weeks or so from now, but with the sudden death of her father we had to come sooner."

Slick's anger had subsided and he added, "And Susie and I had just moved back to Wilmington where she got a position at the hospital in the ER, and I, believe it or not, just took a position at UNC-W in the Marine Biology Department as a marine biologist. Yes, I actually finished college and got a job."

Sarge couldn't let it go, "So you weren't thrown out of your apartment in Charleston?"

Relenting, Slick responded, "Yes we were, and we're now homeless – that is, except for the kindness of our friends Hap and Joanie who are letting us stay with them until we get our own place there."

Sarge grinned and smugly said, "I figured as much."

Seeing that they were about to go at it again I spoke up, "Well, anyway, we asked them to come along with us because we all think that there's something suspicious about Mr. Taylor's death, beyond the fact that he was murdered. Yeh, the police are investigating it as a murder, since he was hanged, but we're not convinced it's just a part of the string of murders that have taken place in the Allentown area over the last few years."

I could see Sarge's curiosity had piqued, "How so?"

I continued, "Well, the others that were murdered, while hanged with the same type of cord, don't seem to have as many similarities to Mr. Taylor as they do to each other."

Slick jumped in here, "Yeh, they were all either prostitutes or gays – all were junkies; pretty much the dregs of society."

Sarge interrupted, "But wasn't Mitch Taylor a fag too?"

"How eloquently put. Well, he was gay, but he wasn't selling or using any drugs, he wasn't homeless and, in fact, was a leader in the community. It seemed no one around there had a bad word to say about him," I added.

Looking pensive Sarge said, "Well, I guess someone didn't like him, did they."

After a brief moment, where Slick and I were able to regain our wits after Sarge's brilliant remark, the conversation led to our proposal.

Sarge spoke first, "So boys, what are you going to do? And what is it that you want me to do? I know you didn't come here to just drink my beer; although you do seem to put them away all right."

I Looked at Slick as if to say, 'you handle this; he wears me out'.

Slick began, "There's more."

"No shit Sherlock!" Sarge interjected.

Ignoring his comment, Slick continued, "Hap's been having a reoccurring nightmare where..." He explained about the strange little girl and the puppets and how I needed to confront my fears, etc.

When he had finished Sarge just sat there.

After what seemed like hours of him just sitting in his chair shaking his head, I asked, "Well, what do you think?"

Sarge just leaned back in his Lazy Boy and, with his hands folded behind his head responded, "I recline to answer that question."

Confused I asked, "What? You don't want to tell me why you're shaking your head at me?"

He just laughed and said, "No. I said I *recline*, not *decline*. That is, this is going to be a long answer so I'd better get comfortable; and I suggest you two do the same. But before you do, get me another beer from the frig, would you?"

After we were all 'comfortable' and Sarge had a cold one in his hand he began, "The way I see it is you two don't know what fear is really like. Why when I was there during the Big One, you know WWII, that was fear!"

Sarge went on, as promised, for the next hour and a half about the war and how he saved the world from Hitler and the Nazis.

After he had exhausted himself, and us as well, he looked up at me and said, "Hap, if you didn't hear a word I just said about the war, I hope you caught the part about how we used to set false traps to lure the enemy to the real ones. Well, that's what I think you have here."

Now that he had us totally confused Slick asked, "What in the hell are you talking about? What does Mr. Taylor's murder have to do with the war, or traps, or anything for that matter?"

"You never were a good listener; I used to always tell your mother that. Oh, she used to stick up for you and tell me that you listened, but were just a bit slow. I think we were both right. What do you say Hap?"

Trying to change the subject and avoid another fistfight I said, "I'm not exactly sure what you mean by that? Would you mind clarifying it a bit more?"

"Now see; that's what I'm talking about. Instead of saying something stupid, be more like Hap and ask nicely. As the Good Book says, 'Ask and you shall perceive'."

I just rolled my eyes and tried to move Sarge along with his explanation, "So Sarge, you were about to say."

"Right. Where was I? Oh, Yeh. You see boys, we would put together some elaborate plans, only to fool the enemy into thinking they figured us out and then they would fall into the real trap. Get it?"

I was beginning to see his logic, "So how does that apply here?"

"The way I see it is you boys are going to have to go back to the Eastside and hook up with that motorcycle gang for some help.

The Allentown Murders

Let me give you some details here. They are going to have the connections to help you find out about the drug trafficking business in the Allentown area; and they can find out what connection Mitch Taylor had to that business or his murderer. And I think that your nightmare even has something to do with this whole thing."

Slick, seeming impressed by his dad's insight said, "Sometimes dad you amaze me; but only sometimes. Don't you think I've already suggested that?"

Not moved by Slick's half-hearted accolade Sarge went on, "There you go again, stealing my ideas."

Without skipping a beat he continued, "And there's something else that might lead you to his killer. I was reading about this reporter fellow that was killed in a car crash a month or so ago. His car crashed and burst into flames. His body was so burnt that they couldn't even identify it, so they used the car information, and the basic size of the remains to make the ID."

I was stunned, "What would that have to do with Mr. Taylor's murder?"

"The way I see it is that this reporter was supposedly working on a big story. He was going to bust the drug trafficking business in the Allentown area wide open. They say he had names, dates, and all kinds of information that would implicate a lot of people, including some local bigwigs. But since his death, no one has been able to find out where he put all of that information. Maybe Mitch was involved in that somehow...just a thought."

I was amazed, "Sarge, it's incredible how you come across so crass most of the time, and then you have these bursts of genius every once in a great while. How do you do it?"

Before he could answer Slick added, "The real trick is being here when it happens. I doubt if *he's* even around then!"

TWENTY-EIGHT
FRIDAY, JUNE 13

"Do you really think this is the best day to confront my fears, being Friday the 13th and all?" I asked.

"Now Hap, don't go getting superstitious on me," Joanie said with a bit of disgust in her voice.

"I just mean that the festival will be going on all day tomorrow and Sunday as well. Do we really need to be here at night on this day? That's all I mean."

I still couldn't convince her, but, as usual, there was no talking her out of it once she had her mind made up.

"Okay, I surrender. We'll do it your way, but remember I'm not the one who voted for this," I remarked.

"Fine. But let me remind you that this might just be the perfect time; you know, the planets are lined up just right and so on," she said with a sarcastic grin.

As we found a spot to park on Summer Street and walked the short distance to the corner of Allen and Elmwood the four of us were hoping that with this carnival atmosphere, dusk just beginning to creep upon us, not to mention it being Friday the 13th, that we would find the spot on Allen Street where I stood in my dream, look out across the narrow street to the costume store and see only normal looking puppets in the windows dressed with period costumes from Buffalo's younger days, and, more importantly, no ghostly little girl

146

dressed all in white standing there in front of the windows looking down at anyone's bloody gravestone, and no marionettes standing behind her – pointing at me.

"Hap, can you lend me fifty bucks?" Slick said to me out of nowhere, as we walked down Elmwood Avenue.

I stopped, turned to him and said, "What? What do you need fifty dollars for? I don't have that kind of money on me."

"Oh. Well, I can wait until tomorrow. You see we got this pool going on and I needed to cover my bets, that's all," he said matter-of-factly.

"Okay, I'll bite. What pool is it now? You know you've never paid me back for the last three pools you lost money in," I said in response.

"Yeh, well I told you that I would give you double back if I won, but I didn't win. So what are you complaining about?" he said, as if that gave me any sense of consolation.

A bit irritated I asked, "What pool?"

"Well, some of our old friends from the neighborhood have this pool about whether you're going to see this little girl or not, that's all," he said very nonchalantly.

"*YOU WHAT!* I suppose you are betting that I don't see her and the other idiots are betting that I do, right?" I said, mad as hell by this time.

"No, of course not. I wouldn't bet against my best friend. I bet you'd see her," he responded with a smirk on his face.

This exchange had caught the girls' attention and Susie jumped in with, "There are winners and there are losers...and then there's Slick. If he's not my meal ticket, at least he's going to be my ticket to heaven. *(Folding her hands and looking up)* Thank you Lord!"

Slick and I turned around at this. Seeing the two girls laughing, Slick said, "I suppose you think that's funny?"

"We're here," I announced, stopping the group at the corner of Allen and Elmwood.

Looking across and down the street a few shops I could see the costume shop. In Gothic letters across the top of the entrance way was written 'SIN City Costume Shoppe'. On either side of the sign, above the middle of the two display windows were gargoyles carved in the edifice surrounded by snakes.

I tried to see what was in the display windows, but there were too many people moving around, putting up tents, setting up for this weekend's event, not to mention that we were still too far to get a good enough look.

By now the others were leading the way; I was lagging behind, a bit apprehensive as to what I might see. Slick began to pull me along.

"Come on Hap. At this rate it'll be tomorrow when we get there," he said.

Just as I was about to argue back, I turned to realize we were there. As I stood on the very spot as in my dream they all backed away and became silent. I felt the world around me spin and become very still, as light from the costume store began to beam out toward where I stood, frozen in place.

Quickly I closed my eyes and rubbed them as if in disbelief, or maybe due to the light now radiating from the store. The people on the street began to move once again as the light dimmed. There in front of me was a blood-red wall; in front of it were two marionettes: one dressed as a Wizard holding a book in one hand, and the other as a Court Jester. The Wizard had an expression of sinister pleasure on his face. It looked very familiar, as did the face of the Jester.

As I was trying to determine whose faces these were, I began to hear a tune being hummed, at first; then slowly and a little louder I could hear words to the tune. As the words became clearer I could see a faint image begin to appear in front of the puppets. It was...that girl! She stood there singing the nursery rhyme that she always did in my dream - 'Hush, Little Baby'. She was looking down at the sidewalk at something sticking up. As I strained to see what it was I could see that it wasn't a marker or a gravestone, but a blood-red box with a white cord wrapped around it. Suddenly, the singing stopped, the lights went out and I found myself lying on the street with Slick, Joanie and Susie crouched down around me, shaking me and all talking at once.

"Put his head between his legs. Get the blood flowing back to his head," I could hear Susie say to the others.

By now several of the people who were putting up their displays and tents had stopped to see what was going on and came over, leaning over me with expressions of curiosity on their faces.

"Is he dead?" one of them finally asked.

"No he's fine. Now get back to whatever you were doing. Give him some air, all right?" Slick said in a stern voice.

The crowd dissipated as quickly as it had gathered. I sat up to look at the store across the street. The girl was gone; so was the box. In the windows were two marionettes dressed as festival-goers – one a Wizard dressed in black and holding a book of magic; the other a Court Jester dressed in tights with a costume of colorful patches and a pointy hat and shoes with bells on the point of each. I just laughed seeing normal puppet faces on them, but my laughter slowly turned to panic when I remembered whose faces I had seen on these puppets in my dreams.

"I feel sick. I think I'm about to throw up. Let's get out of here – *NOW!*" I shouted as I turned and started to run back toward Elmwood Avenue.

"Let's go – stay with him. He's acting very weird," Slick said as he was right on my heels.

*   *   *

"All right Hap, what was that all about back there? You had us all scared to death. What did you see?" Joanie said in a concerned voice.

"It was her," was all I could get out.

Susie said, "Who? Did you see the little girl back there?"

Slick started laughing and hooting, "That's great! I won. What did I tell you? Hap you should be happy. I've made enough on this pool to pay you back for all the other bets."

Joanie and Susie shot looks at Slick at this point.

"What? Did I say something," he remarked.

Ignoring his remarks I said, "It was her. That strange little girl dressed in white appeared. She was singing and looking down at the sidewalk; but it wasn't a marker or gravestone or any such thing. It was a box, like one that a dress or shirt might come in."

Joanie interrupted, "Or costume?"

I paused for a moment to consider her thought and responded, "Yes, of course! That's what it was; a red costume box, and it had a white cord tied around it."

Susie broke in, "Do you mean a ribbon or decorative string?"

I shook my head, "No. I mean a cord; like the one that was used to hang all of those people here in Allentown. And it wasn't wrapped like a ribbon would be around a gift. It was tied like a *noose*."

There was silence for a few moments.

I spoke at last, "And just before that girl turned and disappeared, the puppets pointed, not at me, but across the street. As soon as that happened a single tear fell silently from her eye, rolled down her cheek and off of her lip, landing on the cord that held the box shut. As it hit the cord it burned it so that the cord fell away from the box and the box opened."

They all sat there stunned by this revelation.

"What was in the box?" Susie asked, finally getting up the courage.

I paused as I looked through my mind's eye to get a clear look at what appeared to be sheets of colored cellophane or acetate; one blue, another green, still another yellow, and finally, one that was blood red!

TWENTY-NINE
TUESDAY, JUNE 17

Something else was eating at me; I couldn't quite get past it. What if someone did know about the letter that I received, and what if Mitch Taylor's death was just a copycat murder making it look like it was one of the murders committed by the serial killer? There has to be some connection; I just hope I can find it before it's too late...for all of us.

"Hap, are you all right? You've been staring off into space for almost an hour now. What's going on in that pretty *big* head of yours?" Joanie said with a smirk on her face.

"Pretty *big* head? Heh! I'll have you know that despite it's size my head serves to hold a massive brain that would otherwise be crammed for space, thank you very much."

"Oh, don't get bent out of shape; it's just an expression," she came back with.

"No. 'Pretty *little* head' is an expression; 'Pretty *big* head' is an insult!"

"Okay, I'm just trying to lighten things up a bit. You seem so sullen."

"Well, I have been..."

Just as I was about to open up Slick burst into the kitchen where Joanie and I were preparing some vegetables to cook in our Wok.

"That's it? Zucchini, mushrooms, broccoli and whatever that is. That's all we're having for dinner?" Slick said without skipping a beat as he strolled past us on his way to the bathroom.

Spinning around I said, "No there's meat; and those are water chestnuts. Please tell me you've at least heard of them!"

"Of course I have; I've never actually seen one though," he said in a matter-of-fact tone.

Joanie chimed in, "Where's Susie? You rode together today; did you forget her?"

We could hear him, now in the bathroom with the door half open saying, "Of course not. Do you think I could leave her at work and live? She's out in the car still. She made me stop at the store to pick up some groceries. I told her that you had plenty of food and didn't expect us to feed you, but she nagged me until I stopped. Anyway, she's carrying them in."

"Hap, go help her, and Slick you can shut the door. *We don't need to hear you going to the bathroom!*"

As I was about to go help Susie, Joanie grabbed my arm, stopping me.

"Now Hap, before you go, remember what we talked about," Joanie said sternly.

"Do you really think that it's a good idea for me to be in the car alone with Susie to and from work every day?" I said trying to get out of it.

"Hap, now that you're starting at the college it will save Slick from driving all over town to bring Susie to the hospital and then get to his office. Besides, I trust you; and as for Susie, she knows I can still kick her ass if she tries any of her old tricks and you tell me about it – and *you will* tell me about it! Right?" she said with even more conviction than before.

"Of course. I know that you can still kick my ass as well," I replied in a sarcastic voice.

"That's right – *and I will too.* Now go out there and help her carry the groceries in before she has a chance to bitch about Slick," she added.

"That was a lovely dinner. Thanks again for all you're doing for us. I told Slick we needed to contribute more, since we come here to eat almost every day. Living with Sarge is bad enough, but having to listen to him while you try to eat is too much! Slick sometimes has no sense of the right thing to do," Susie said, almost apologetically.

"Sometimes?" I shot back looking at Slick.

"All right. I get it. I'm not dumb; and I'm right here, so stop talking about me as if I weren't!" Slick remarked in a feigned hurt tone.

With this the direction of the conversation changed to a more serious one when Joanie brought up her father's murder.

"Let's put our heads together and see what we come up with. What things have we each observed so far? I have a strong feeling that things are much closer to us than they appear to be," Joanie said.

Slick spoke up, "How so? Do you think that your dad's murderer is someone we know?"

"I'm not sure. I feel like there's more to this than meets the eye. You know, that premonition of things to come that you and your mother say you have, Hap. Well, we all have that sometime or other; and I am having it now," Joanie remarked.

Susie jumped in, "Well, I for one, know that there's more to the story than those two detectives are telling us. I think we should go back to your dad's shop and look around some more."

Her comment made me curious, "Was there something you noticed there that seemed odd to you?"

Slick, at this point, chimed in, "Yeh, there was something that I think we all noticed, but didn't really pay any attention to. But let's go back and see if we all are seeing the same thing."

"What are we waiting for; let's go," Joanie said as she got up from the table, grabbed the car keys and raced out the door.

*   *   *

"Just be careful not to disturb anything or anyone. This is still a crime scene. The police would just love it if we messed it up. We'd be the ones going to jail!" Susie said.

"There!" Slick said pointing to a shelf right next to where the murder took place.

"Where?" I responded.

"Right there, on that shelf. Don't you all see it? It's as plain as the nose on my face," he shot back.

"Oh, no. That figurine – it's the little girl! The one I see in my dreams and the one I saw the other day standing across the street. She's pointing at something just like I saw the puppets do every time in my dream; she's pointing toward the shelf behind the counter – pointing at a box on the shelf. And that box looks exactly like the one in my nightmares," I said in a stunned voice.

They all came closer to see the figurine of the little girl all dressed in white pointing. After a few moments in silence Joanie cautiously walked over to the shelf and paused in front of the box. She looked back at the three of us waiting, frozen to our spots, with some degree of trepidation at what that box might contain.

Slowly she reached up and, pulling the box off of the shelf and onto the counter that lay between us, she set it down. We all just stared at it and, in his typical, impulsive manner Slick grabbed the top to the box and jerked it off to reveal its contents.

In shock at what we saw, we all stood there silent - until I spoke up.

"It's the colored acetate sheets from my dream. Blue, green, yellow...and blood red!"

My head began to spin. I didn't know whether I was passing out or just lapsing back into some sort of flashback of those horrible dreams.

"Hap, Hap. Are you all right?" Joanie asked, seeing the state I was in.

I collected myself and replied, "Yeh, sure. I'm fine. But this is what was in the box in my dream. What does it mean?"

"Hap, this may be what was in your dream, but now we have a better clue to what it is," Slick said in a knowing voice.

I responded, "What are you talking about?" somewhat confused.

"Look it. When you described these sheets from your dream you only said that they were colored acetate sheets. You didn't say how large they were," Slick added.

"I know. And that's because in my dream I was across the street and they appeared to be smaller than these. So what?" I was totally confused now.

"So what? So now we know that they are large and not the size of a sheet of paper, nor the shape. So they must be used, or should I say, must have been used for something specific," Slick said with a 'shit-eating grin' on his face.

"Okay," Joanie added, "what does that tell us?"

All of a sudden that knowing look left Slick's face as he replied, "I don't know. Geez, do I have to figure everything out for you guys?"

Susie, after a long and unusual silence, added, "All right, we have something more than we did before. Let's keep looking. Maybe something that will tell us more will jump out at us."

After hours of carefully looking in the shop we decided to call it a night, when it hit me. I ran outside to look at the costume shop across the street where the girl in my dream had appeared. I imagined her there again, with the puppets pointing past me and toward Mr. Taylor's shop. This time looking for the exact location of where they pointed. It was to the right front corner of the shop, just where the store window begins; which is visible from inside the shop. I ran back in and over to the counter – there it was, as plain as day!

"I've got it!" I ejaculated.

Slick came back with, "You've got what? And whatever it is I don't want it."

"Oh, be quiet," Susie said.

She continued with, "What is it Hap?"

"All of you come here." They all raced to where I stood behind the counter.

"Here; from this perspective what do you see?" I questioned.

"Hap, I don't feel like playing games now," Joanie responded.

"Just go along for a moment, please. Now what can you see from here?" I asked again.

Slick said, "Well, I have a clear view of that area just outside the shop window, on the sidewalk – and all the way over to the alley next to SIN City Costume Shoppe."

"Exactly!" I shot back.

I could see Slick and the girls were miffed by my observation.

"Okay; let's suppose your dad was behind the counter late one night doing something, and, with the shop being closed he didn't bother to turn on any lights," I began.

"So?" Slick interjected.

"He's here behind the counter getting something and hears a noise outside his shop – right over there by the window. So he goes a little closer and sees something he's not supposed to see going on. He recognizes the people. They see him. He unlocks the door and lets them in. They exchange words and the men rough him up as a warning; then they leave.

Susie stops me with, "Where are you going with this? It all sounds like conjecture; but from what evidence?"

"Wait, let me finish. Now Toby, hearing the ruckus, comes downstairs and sees the person or persons leaving the shop, and making their way down the alley next to the costume shop. There; that's it," I said, feeling good about my hypothesis.

"That's it? That's it? And where did this all come from? Where is the proof?" Slick asked.

"Well, as our old friend Billy Shakespeare once put it, '...there are more things in heaven and earth that are dreamt of in your philosophy...' That is, based on what the detectives told us, that he was doing something at the counter in the back of the shop, but was beaten near the front, close to the door. This occurred only a few weeks before he was murdered. Also, the letter I received back home, before we came here..."

As I started to tell them about the letter from the journalist Joanie interrupted.

"Do you really think that this is a good time to bring this up, Hap?" Joanie questioned.

"I do. In fact, I think that this is the perfect time. It seems to me that finding your father's killer is much more important than this reporter's accident; no matter how tragic."

Joanie added, "I guess you're right. Go ahead; lay it out for them. Maybe with this information we can solve my father's murder."

Turning to Slick and Susie she said, "But you two must never breath a word of this to anyone. I mean it. It could mean the difference between life and death for Hap if this gets out. You have to SWEAR!"

They could see the seriousness of the situation and both responded with, "*I swear.*"

So we left the shop and headed back to our apartment.

"Okay Hap, finish it," she said.

I could see Susie and Slick's eyes light up as I explained about the letter from the journalist and about the newspaper article concerning his death in the burning car.

"Also in his letter he talked about witnessing something in front of the antique shop on Allen Street; while there are several antique shops on Allen Street, he was talking about this antique shop, Mr. Taylor's."

I pulled out the letter and notes and skipped over to the part where he observed what went on that night.

May 2 –
As I drove slowly down Allen Street, heading away from Symphony Circle, I finally saw what I was looking for night after night while driving this same route. It was in front of an antique shop near the corner of Elmwood that I saw them. There were

three men, one slightly taller and at least twenty years older than the others. I couldn't see their faces, but I believe them to be the same three I've been investigating since my arrival in Allentown – Tony, Jimmy and Reilly. They were all dressed in long black raincoats with black fedoras on their heads. The oldest one was smoking a cigar while the others had a fourth man 'jacked up' against the outside wall of the shop, near the front window.

They seemed to be exchanging money and a small package, drugs I would imagine, given the lateness of the hour (sometime past midnight). Just as I was about to pass them something caught my eye. It was from the only angle that I would be able to see this. It was a man, standing behind the counter in the darkened antique shop. I wouldn't have even seen him if it weren't for the fact that he started moving toward the door. It was then that the men let go of the other man, who now raced away into the night. They walked over to the door and the man inside opened it and let them in. They exchanged words and then two of the men began to beat the shop owner. The one smoking the cigar turned toward me and stopped briefly. Seeing that I had come to a stop across the street from them, he exited the shop and began to come toward my car. It was then that I hit the gas pedal and raced off.

"Well? Now do you think that it's all my imagination?" I added.

"Hap, if what you just read is fact, then there's much more to this whole thing than we know about," Slick replied.

THIRTY
THURSDAY, JUNE 19

"Hap, I really think it's sweet of you to drive me to and from work. I know our hours aren't always exactly the same, but I'll make it up to you, I promise," Susie said in her most seductive voice.

"Not a problem. It was a...really...a Joanie's idea," I replied. I could tell she could see me start to get nervous.

"That is, we talked it over and thought that it was foolish for Slick to have to drive you to work and then go halfway across the county for his work, when he wasn't working at home. Canisius is only a block away from Sister's Hospital and it seemed logical that we ride together. A...a...save gas and all," I finished.

"Not to mention have time to be alone together to, you know, talk and stuff," she added.

I thought that this was a good time to change the subject so I made the mistake of saying, "Hey, if you have time maybe we could get together for lunch once in a while."

Big mistake!

"How thoughtful Hap. I was just thinking the same thing. In fact, my lunchtime is flexible so I can schedule it around your free time. I can even walk over to your office to eat with you. After all, you're driving me to and from work every day, and I can use the exercise as well," Susie said with a devilish smile that I caught out of the corner of my eye. I was trying to not look at her, not just because I was driving, but mostly because she was making me feel very uncomfortable. I almost believe Joanie was doing this to me on purpose to make me suffer – or maybe to appreciate her more. Well, it was working already; and this was just the first day.

*   *   *

"Now, Mr. Pozner this is Miss Connie Dilworth she will be your graduate assistant for the semester. I thought it best that she start right away working with you. This summer session will give you both a chance to get acquainted and better equip you when the fall semester begins," Professor Crenshaw said, just before making his exit.

We had just completed a tour of the campus, and now, after bringing me to my office in the tower, Miss Dilworth arrived almost on cue.

"Professor Pozner, I am looking forward to working with you this term. I just hope that I will be able to give you all the assistance that you will need," she said with a charming smile.

"Thank you, but first, please call me Hap, and I'll call you Connie. If that's all right with you, of course," I replied.

"Yes, of course. In class I'll call you Mr. Pozner. I wouldn't want the other students thinking that I was too familiar with our professor," she added.

A bit surprised I said, "Oh, I didn't know that I would have the pleasure of your being a student in one of my classes as well as being my assistant."

"Yes, I'll be in your Mystery Writing class during the fall semester. I'm hoping to complete the MFA program so I can work fulltime as a writer – like you. I have been following your career for several years now and just love your work. I'm sorry, I'm beginning to sound like a writing groupie," she said with a laugh.

I laughed as well, thinking I actually had a fan and responded, "Well I have one fan. That hardly makes up a fan club, but it's a start." And then we both laughed together.

After a few moments I interjected, "Well Connie, you seem to know something about me; now how about you telling me something about yourself. Where you are from, what your goals are, whatever you'd like to share."

"I don't mind. I don't have anything to hide, do you?" she remarked.

That took me aback a little, but I just smiled and said, "I suppose we all do, but I'm sure mine would bore you, so please go on."

"I lived with my mom in Indianapolis until about eight months ago, then I went on a search to find my father. After a few months I found him; in fact, right here in Buffalo, and I've been here with him since then.

It seems that my mom and he had an affair and I was the product of it. He was married at the time, to some other woman. Well, after his wife found out about me, they left town and moved east; to Ohio, I think, and then finally to Buffalo. My mom is a wonderful person and all, but a girl needs her dad; and I was a bit pig-headed about things and was hell-bent on finding him. My plan was to get back at him for abandoning my mom and me, but as it turned out, he found me, his wife had just died and he welcomed me like a long-lost friend. After we had a chance to talk I saw that he wasn't such a bad guy. I wrote my mom about it and she suggested I spend some time with him. And here I am."

We talked a while longer, giving me a chance to get to know her and help her to feel more comfortable with me. I figured we would be working closely together and it would help if she had her hand on the pulse of my work, so to speak.

This semester was not only going to be a teaching semester; it was, more importantly, going to be a research time. It may be a bit devious on my part, but she seemed bright enough and knew the area well enough that she could be a big asset in helping me find out the background story of the Allentown area; who really ran things there, what the history was, and maybe even find the killer or killers of Joanie's dad.

*　　*　　*

"Well?"

"Well, what?"

"Well, how did riding together work out; and don't try to hide anything from me. You know I can always tell when you're lying," Joanie said with a stern look on her face.

"No. *My mother* can always tell when I'm lying; you can kick my ass if you find out," I said with a grin.

"So let's have it. Did she behave?"

I squirmed for a moment, trying not to get caught in the half-truth I was about to tell, "It went fine. We talked about Buffalo, Slick, you...did I mention, the weather?"

Just then she nailed me in the stomach, and, with a devious smile said, "Now the truth!"

"Okay; *OW*, that hurt! It went fine until she mentioned about coming over to my office to have lunch with me – every day. But don't forget that this was your idea, not mine."

She smiled and said, "That's okay. She can keep an eye on you and that young, and I'm sure beautiful, graduate assistant you have working with you."

"Who, Connie? No, she's ugly; fat and ugly," I said without thinking that at some point Joanie would meet her and really be pissed to find out that Connie was, well, young and beautiful.

"Oh, so you're on a first name basis already? I suppose she calls you Hap; or is it honey, or sweetie maybe?"

I could see that she was writing her own story here, even before it happened. I had to stop it.

"Okay, so she is young and she is fairly good looking; and as a matter of fact I told her she should call me Hap – but only when she's working as my assistant and definitely not in class," I replied.

As soon as I said this I regretted it, but it was too late. It was out there.

"Oh, I see. She's not only your assistant, but she is also in one of your classes as well. Is that right? Or is she in all of your classes?" she said now fuming.

"No, of course not. I only have one graduate class that I teach. She wouldn't be in any of the undergraduate classes."

Once again, as I heard the words I couldn't believe I could be so stupid; but I was. Fortunately, or maybe unfortunately for me, she stormed off. But I knew I'd pay later.

It only took a few hours before Joanie came out of our bedroom; in a much better mood, I might add.

"So you've had a chance to think it over and found that you were just being a bit overly jealous. I can certainly understand..." I said. But before I could finish she interrupted.

"Stop while you're ahead. No, I came out because I felt like I might have been a touch too 'concerned' about you and your newly found fame. But after thinking about it, I figured that any woman, after seeing that you're no different than anyone else, will get over that 'I love my professor' school-girl crush. Hey, after she gets to know you better, she may even grow to hate you!"

"Thanks a lot," I responded.

Joanie got serious now, "I came out because I was going over some of my notes from the lab and I'm a little concerned about the potential fallout from the project that I'm working on at Vericon. You know that with the recent breakthroughs my team has had here we could potentially eliminate drug pushers and cartels, not only here in the States, but around the world. It could have *that* big of an impact!"

I wanted to know more. Up until now she has been very secretive about her research on this particular project.

"Since you opened the door, what exactly are you working on? I didn't pry because you usually tell me all about projects that you're working on; but this one, you've been very closed-lipped about."

"Yes, and I'm sorry; but this is something that needs to be a secret and, with you being a writer, I didn't want you to spin a tale about it and have it show up in your next book – and get someone killed – especially me!"

"I understand," I said.

"But now I think I'm going to need your help. It seems last week, before we got here and I had a chance to bring some new findings to the Buffalo lab, there was a break in at Vericon. Fortunately, nothing was taken. But it looked like whomever it was that broke in was looking for something specific. We don't know if it was company spies from one of our competitors, an inside job – you know someone looking to steal the research and sell it to the highest bidder, or possibly even someone who has reason to see our project stopped, like a drug lord."

This concerned me to the point of saying, "Look it. Maybe you should bow out of this project and let one of your lead researchers take over. We can go back to Wilmington and you can work on something a little less risky."

She was quick to state, "No! This is my project. I'm not going to abandon over a year of research because of a little scare. I just wanted to let you know. Besides, the management at Vericon has beefed up security. My team and I are escorted from the locked parking ramp to the building and back to our cars each day. And while we're inside it's like a fortress. Every room has finger print access only. I'm safe – there."

"So what can you tell me about your research then?" I asked.

"I can only tell you that we're working on a drug, how ironic to call it that, that will alter the part of the brain that creates the addiction to drugs. In effect, it blocks the habit-forming pattern that one acquires from taking drugs such as heroine, crack, etc. It's safe and because of the nature of how it acts on the brain it is not habit forming and there are few side effects. So there's really little downside."

I was quick to add, "Except for drug pushers losing business!"

"Right. And that's why this must remain top secret until we're ready to unveil it to the public; and that comes after the FDA approves it," she said.

I was quick to add, "But what about the testing? Surely you'll be conducting blind tests using volunteer junkies."

"We've already started that process. That's why I'm so concerned about leaks. While they aren't told anything about the drug, or, in fact, if they are even receiving it or a placebo, we want as little known about what we're doing as possible. But, just because someone is addicted to a hard drug doesn't mean they're stupid. In fact, many of our volunteers are quite intelligent; and that worries us a great deal."

"So you think that someone in your test group might be wise to what you're doing and leaking it to someone on the outside, possibly a competitor or dealer?" I questioned.

"That is exactly what we're worried about. While these junkies are told that what they are taking might be a placebo, they are also told it might be a drug that will help them kick their habit without having to go through the usual painful withdrawal they would normally experience, and without harmful side effects. But that's all they're told."

"How long have you been in the testing phase; because you have been incredibly good at keeping all of this from me up to this point," I added.

"Strangely enough I can remember exactly when we started because it was only one week before my dad was murdered. I remember thinking that maybe there was a connection, but I laughed it off as you rubbing off on me."

I was a bit offended by that and had to ask, "Oh, and what exactly do you mean by that snide remark?"

She saw that I had taken it badly and replied, "Now don't get your bowels in an uproar. I didn't mean anything by it except that, as you always say, 'Just because I'm paranoid doesn't mean that everyone's not out to get me'. Come on, you brought it upon yourself."

Licking my wounds I said, "Okay, but that is true you know. I think I've proven it more than once."

"Well, I don't know why, but for a moment then it struck me that there was some connection. I had this eerie feeling that's all. But it passed. I mean, what possible connection could there be between my research and my father's murder? I guess I was feeling guilty for not being there to help him, or maybe for not having much to do with him since he and my mom split up. I don't know. Maybe I'm the one who needs to see Dr. Milborne.

"I know you blame yourself for a lot of things that have nothing to do with you – the Catholic guilt thing. Hey, look on the bright side; I've got that and the Italian guilt thing too. It looks like you got off easy!"

"Thanks, but that's no consolation because here we are, back in Buffalo with my dad murdered, my research possibly compromised, not to mention you and your women troubles."

At this we both began to laugh, but her laughter slowly turned into tears. I held her silently for a moment and then whispered, "It'll be all right. I promise. I love you."

She smiled and all was again right with the world – at least for now.

THIRTY-ONE
MONDAY, JUNE 23

"Good morning students. My name is Mr. Hap Pozner and I'll be your instructor for this brief, but hopefully eventful summer session; and this is my graduate assistant Ms. Connie Dilworth. Her job is to make sure that I don't forget anything and that I don't get bogged down with paperwork. I am very happy to be here at Canisius College, and want you to feel free to visit me at my office in the Tower during my office hours."

This went on for a while, as in any first day of class in almost any classroom. They all looked like eager young college students ready to take on the rigorous challenges that a college course has to offer.

All except for one man, that is. There was one man who stood out. He seemed a bit older than the rest, in his early thirties perhaps; much like myself. He also seemed to have a special interest in my assistant as he kept looking over at her, occasionally nodding. She seemed unaffected by this so I simply put it off as a man who appreciated beauty and maybe looking for a Saturday night date. I guess I couldn't blame him.

"Now that you know a bit about me I'd like to hear from you."

There was a noticeable moan from the small group of students that made up this second summer session class.

"Just a little please. It can be as little as your name and what you enjoy doing outside of class; and possibly even why in God's name you chose to spend what's left of your summer in a classroom?"

That seemed to break the tension and they all, in turn, revealed something about his or herself. Each ones story all seemed to blend together, that is, all except for the man that seemed fixated on Connie.

"My name is Sigmund Ignatius Norom, everyone calls me Si and I run a costume shop in Allentown called SIN City..."

I commented on how his was a very unusual name.

He volunteered, "It is very unusual, and ironic as well. My first name, Sigmund, is, of course, from Sigmund Freud, the father of psychoanalysis. My middle name, Ignatius, is from St. Ignatius of Loyola, the founder of the Jesuit order – who, by the way founded *this* college."

He added, "The irony is, with both of these brilliant men I'm named after, my last name spelled backwards is MORON!"

We all got a good laugh from this – all except Si. He just sat, looking stoic; his demeanor quickly turning the laughter into an uncomfortable silence throughout the class.

He then continued, "My shop's name is sort of a double entendre – my initials and the *sinfully* wonderful costumes I rent and sell."

He went on to tell why he was taking this course, but my ears began to ring, my head to spin and I didn't hear another word after he said the name of the store. I knew I had to find out more about this man, hoping he might know something – anything – about my dreams or Mitch Taylor's murder.

*   *   *

Just as promised, or threatened, depending on how you look at it, Susie showed up just as my last morning class ended and I had

168

made my way back to the fifth floor of the Tower to sit and relax and eat my lunch.

"Hap, it looks like I got here just in time. I thought that you would at least wait for me," Susie said as she burst into my office without even knocking. She at first ignored Connie, who was at the filing cabinet putting away some notes for me, but seeing her turn and glare at her, Susie turned toward her, flashed Connie her sinister smile and said, "Oh, I didn't realize you had 'the help' here working during your well-deserved break from all of them."

Trying to keep this from becoming a catfight, I stood up, got between them and quickly responded, "Oh, I'm sorry, Susie, this is Connie. I'm fortunate enough to have her as my graduate assistant this term. She was kind enough to work through her only break to get some of my papers filed."

Turning to Connie, I said, "Listen, Connie; it might be better if we do this after lunch. You've been working non-stop all morning and I'd hate to burn you out in the first day."

"I suppose I could go and relax a little; I can see what happens to a woman when she doesn't take care of herself as she gets older."

As she was leaving I could see smoke coming out of Susie's ears, so I quickly led Connie out the door, closing it behind her, and escorted Susie to a chair.

She snapped at me, "You don't need to hold my arm and sit me in the chair. I'm not that old, or as she might have you believe, too haggard to sit myself down. Where do they find these nasty children anyway?"

Not knowing when to keep my mouth shut, I replied, "Well, she' hardly a child...I mean, a...a...nothing."

"That's right nothing!" she scolded.

After a few moments of silence, enough to let the temperature in the room go down a few degrees, I said, "So how about lunch then? You know, you didn't have to come all the way over here just for me."

Seeing that this seemed to make matters worse, I quickly added, " I mean, I'm glad to see a familiar face and it's really nice of you to come over to eat with me."

I could hear a sigh and then saw a glimmer of a smile cross her face. Then she said, "Oh Hap, I'm sorry. But women know things that men just can't see. The minute I walked into your office I could tell by the way she was holding herself that she had a huge crush on you. You had better watch out for that one. Just remember *me* – and Joanie, of course. That is, remember that I'm here protecting Joanie's interests. After all, we're best friends and I wouldn't want any tramp like that coming between us."

Feeling a bit uncomfortable about this whole conversation, I said, "Don't worry, I love Joanie and you and Slick, of course. And I wouldn't let anyone break up our team, all right?"

With a nod, all was well again. Somehow, strangely, that nod gave me a flashback to the man in my class, Si, as he gave a nod to Connie. Again it seemed very strange.

"Hap, are you all right?" Susie said, seeing me drift off into another world.

"Yeh, sure. Just going off into one of my trances; you know, where I find my stories."

"I'll never get used to that. But if that's what makes your books so good, then I guess it's a quirk that we'll all have to live with."

"Quirk!" I said, offended at her remark.

*   *   *

Allentown wasn't always what it is today. In fact, Allentown wasn't even Allentown! Back in the early to mid-1800s Allentown was the name of Lewis Allen's farmland at the southern end of Grand Island. But, while history can be fascinating, it can also be nothing more than that – history. The real history of Allentown is a rich one; one filled with sterling moments as well as moments of despair. The truly memorable ones for those living in modern times has to be those of the Art Festival and the richness it brings to the area, accenting the strong eclectic and artistic side of this part of town juxtaposed with the darker side, with the string of drug-related murders that left law enforcement baffled for years.

Even now you can find every kind of human wandering the streets in Allentown, by day or by night. Prostitutes hanging out in front of the Allendale where one could watch porn, or members of the gay community as they pranced along the streets trying to 'out-gouache' each other, or even junkies, pimps and pushers. There are daily brawls bursting out into the street from Mulligan's Brick Bar, and even the occasional gun shot from almost anywhere in the neighborhood. Alongside this though you will see artists painting, sculptors sculpting and musicians playing their own arrangement of some popular song – or even a song of their own. It is a wonderful place to see, and I suppose, to be (some of the time).

But it started out as a place between Buffalo and Black Rock back in the days before this nation became one. Over the years the Allentown area emerged, touched by people like Frederick Law Olmstead, Grover Cleveland and William McKinley – who unfortunately for him, met his demise not too far from this area during the 1901 Pan-American Exposition.

So it is to be expected that this place would be one of intrigue, mystery, mirth and sometimes mayhem.

*   *   *

Shortly before my next class started Connie came back into my office. I guess she must have seen Susie leave.

"Well, isn't she a pleasant one," she remarked, followed by, "Oh, I'm sorry; that wasn't your wife I hope."

I smiled and replied, "No, just an old friend."

"I would watch out for that one if I were you. She's got her eye on you for more than just friendship," she snapped back.

She doesn't know how right she is about Susie, or at least how she was in the past.

"No, don't be silly. That's just Susie; she flirts like some of us chew gum. It doesn't mean anything." I tried to laugh it off, but I do wonder about Susie sometimes. I just hope she's not slipping back into old habits. Sometimes I don't even think that it's me that she's really interested in; she just seems compelled to act that way out of habit or a flirting addiction, if there is such a thing.

Trying to change the subject, I asked, "Well. What did you think of the class?"

"Oh, it was wonderful. You are such a good professor. I could see the whole class was mesmerized."

I laughed, "No, not me. I meant the students. What did you think of them?"

She paused for a moment and then said, "They definitely have a lot to learn; but I guess that's why they're here. Isn't it?"

"What about that man named Si? How did he strike you? Did he seem to act a little strange to you?" I asked, fishing to see if she had any connection to him.

She closed the filing cabinet where she was working and walked over to my desk where I was seated, sat on the corner of my desk right next to where I sat and, leaning in to me, said, "No, not really. Did you think he acted strange?"

As she leaned in to me her low-cut top revealed a breath-taking view of what lie beneath. I caught myself, pushed my chair out, stood up as if to get my briefcase lying on the floor across the room, and responded, "Well, he did seem out of place with the rest of the class, being a bit older and a businessman and all. But I suppose that's what makes summer sessions and night classes interesting – 'viva la difference'; right?"

"Yes, I'm sure that's true. If you don't mind I'd like to go do a few errands before your next class. Would you mind terribly if I were a bit late?"

I found this comment a bit odd, but chalked it up to it being the first day. It's hard to establish a routine that quickly, and I'm sure it would be good for our relationship if I weren't too strict about procedure at this point. Besides, she will be with me as my assistant throughout my stay here, so I might as well take things a bit slow now.

With a friendly smile I replied, "Why of course. I'll be fine until you get back."

THIRTY-TWO
SUNDAY, JULY 6

"Slick, do you really think it's such a good idea snooping around this place at midnight? Someone might see us and think that we were burglars or peeping Toms or something."

"Hap, you worry too much. You *do* want to find out about this guy, especially since he's in one of your classes, don't you?"

"Yeh, but it would, at the very least, be embarrassing for one of my students to find me looking in his windows late at night; and at the worst it might get me a few nights in prison for who knows what!"

"Hap, you're always so dramatic. First of all, we're not going to get caught. Any decent person is fast asleep in their bed at this time of night..." Slick began.

"Right – except us!" I interrupted.

"If you would let me finish. Where was I? Oh, Yeh. As I was saying, they'd be asleep in bed, secondly...I forgot. Don't interrupt me when I'm..."

I interrupted again, "Shh! The lights are on in the kitchen – and look! It's Si and – *Connie*!"

Slick whispered to me as we both held onto the window ledge that we had climbed up to, "Who's Connie?"

"Shh! She's my assistant at the College. But how does she know Si? And what is she doing here at this time of night?"

Slick gave me one of his 'shit-eating grins' and replied, "Duh-huh. I don't know how she knows him, but I can take a pretty good guess at what they're doing together at this time of night."

I replied, "No, I know she has seen him in the classroom, but she never even looks at him. I mean; they seem to be strangers. And even if they are seeing each other, why are they dressed and sitting in the kitchen talking over coffee? Wouldn't they be in bed, or at least drinking some wine or something?"

"Shh, let's listen," I added.

"I thought he told us to just observe and get information. Why are you doing all of that flirting? You might screw things up if you get too close with him." Si scolded.

Connie got up, spun around and, leaning into Si's face said, "Look it, I'm doing my job. RJ won't have anything to worry about with me. It's you he should be worried about screwing things up. Why did you sign up for that class? Was that to 'infiltrate' as you call it, or were you just trying to keep an eye on me?"

Si, in a defensive tone, replied, "No, don't be silly. Dad thought that it would be a good idea if we both were keeping an eye on him. And why do you call him RJ; he's both of our father."

"I don't feel like he's been much of a father to me all these years."

"Give him time. You're here aren't you? Maybe you'll grow to see he's not such a bad guy. And besides, look at the up side of things; he owns this part of town. What better dad to have?"

"Yeh, he owns the underbelly of society; the pimps, prostitutes and pushers. What a birthright, eh?"

"Oh, don't be so negative. And don't forget, his business partner owns the unions; and they're not criminals – not technically anyway."

They both started to laugh at this.

After a few minutes, Connie continued, "Well I suppose someone's got to do it, right? I just hope he's not mixed up with the murders that have happened around here. I'd hate to be involved in something as gruesome as the hangings of those poor young women."

"Sis, they were hookers, hookers! They were the dregs of society, not some innocent young college girls."

"But they were someone's daughters and maybe even mothers!"

"Fine. And to answer you, it's no; dad's not involved in any of that. But don't be surprised to know that he probably does know who is. But that's not the business he's in, okay?"

"It may not mean much to you, but it makes me feel better to know that he doesn't go around killing people. Is that so horrible?"

"I suppose not, but there's something else that he and I are worried about right now; and that's your flirting with that college teacher you're working with. You're supposed to be getting in his head, not his bed!"

"What I do on my own time is my business; besides, why should you care who I sleep with?"

"Why would I care who you sleep with? We may have the same father, but it appears you inherited your mother's libido– much to your chagrin."

Just then she slapped him. As his head turned with the blow he faced the window where Slick and I were peering through. A look of horror came across his face. He stood up, pointed at us and screamed, "Who are you!"

At this Slick and I dropped to the ground below and ran for our lives, hoping not to be caught or recognized.

*   *   *

"And where was it that you and your sidekick had to go at this time of night?"

"Oh shit, she's awake."

"What was that?"

"Ah, ah, Slick and I were just over to see Sarge. You know, he hasn't been feeling well lately."

"Nice try. Don't you think I woke up when you tried sneaking off; and don't you think I called everyone I knew to see if they had seen you? Well?"

I know Joanie when she's mad, and she is pissed. I believe that this is one of those times that, as Slick says, 'the truth is reserved for'.

"All right, and I suppose you called my brother, Jeffrey, and my mom and Fr. Christopher, and..."

"Stop right there. You don't really think that I'm that stupid, do you?"

"I was kind of hoping."

At that she just gave me one of those looks, the one that says, 'Go ahead make me hit you'.

"Okay, here's the truth," I said, waiting to see or hear something – anything – from her; but not a word, nor a movement.

I continued, "Slick and I thought that we should do a little snooping around at the costume shop, you know, maybe get some clues or at least a hint of what this guy Norom has to do with anything. Maybe he knows something about your father's murder. After all, his shop is right across the street from your dad's."

She sat down and uncrossed her arms. That was a good sign.

"Okay, what did you find out?"

I sat next to her and, facing her now, began, "You will not believe what we saw and heard..." I went on to tell her the story.

When I had finished she looked puzzled and sat silently for what seemed like hours; but in reality it was only five to ten minutes. Then she got up, told me to follow her to the kitchen, put on the teapot to make tea, and sat at the table.

"Now what?" I asked.

"So this Connie that works with you at Canisius is this guy Norom's half sister. Is that right?"

"It appears so. What about it?"

"Hap, didn't you tell me that during the first day of class he kept looking at her and nodded several times, while she seemed to ignore him. And didn't you ask her about him when the two of you were in your office. What was it that she told you about him then?"

I interrupted her train of thought, "She didn't say much about him, but she never acted like she even knew him, let alone was related to him. Very odd."

"Very odd indeed. Even more odd is this mystery man, their father RJ. He seems to be a key player here. Who is he?"

"I don't know, but he does seem to be the one behind what they're up to. But what exactly are they up to?" I questioned.

"It might just be time for us to start our own spying. Let's go back to the letter and information you got from that journalist that was killed. Maybe that will lead us to this RJ person."

I could see Joanie's brain whirling away. I was too tired after our adventure to think about anything but sleep. We had our tea and went back to bed. Before I dozed off I could see her lying there still spinning.

"Hap. Wake up; you've had enough sleep. Get up, I want to show you something."

I'm not a morning person, never was. I like to sneak up on daylight; you know, get up very slowly. Open my eyes, look around, put one leg on the floor, and so on; nothing too quick, nice and slow; but not this morning.

"I'm on my way. What is so urgent? Couldn't this wait until I was better rested? You know, men don't grow as quickly as women. Why some men have experienced growing pains into their late twenties. Why, I've even read that..."

"You're thirty-four for God's sake! You're full grown already. The only growing you're going to do is to grow shorter and dumpier. Something to look forward to," she chided.

"Do I detect a note of sarcasm in your voice? Besides, *I'm* not looking forward to that," I stated emphatically.

"I wasn't talking about *you*; I was talking about *me*!"

The Allentown Murders

As I threw on my clothes, brushed my hair and teeth, then dragged myself into the kitchen, I could see she was already deep in notes. They were scattered all over the kitchen table and countertops.

"Okay, I give up. What is all of this – *stuff?*" I questioned.

"Open you eyes. Does any of this look even the tiniest bit familiar?" she replied.

"I don't know how you do it; you're always so pleasant," I remarked.

"Yeh, and I don't know *why* I'm always so pleasant!"

"I was being facetious. Never mind."

I looked at some of the papers lying on the table and said, "Oh Yeh, these are the papers that you were talking about last night, aren't they; the ones from the journalist, Bob Griffin. Right?"

"That's right, Sherlock; or should I say, Sherwood?"

We both laughed at the reference to one of the Buffalo detectives who had interviewed us.

"Now Hap, I want you to take a look at these over here. These are some notes and newspaper clippings about the murders of those three prostitutes last year in Allentown. It says that they were each hanged – *with a coated braided nylon cord; a very expensive rope used to hold a boat anchor!*"

"That is the same type that was used to murder your father, wasn't it?" I asked.

"Yes, it was. And there's more here. Look at this.

Buffalo News, Allentown, October 19, 1985.
Latest Murders Support Serial Killer Theory

Homicide detectives in the Buffalo Police Department are cautious to call the rash of murders of prostitutes, pimps and pushers in the Allentown area serial killings. They believe there are possibly two or more people involved. Given the similarities in the backgrounds of the victims and the manner in which they were murdered, the police say it's likely that the

179

killers selected these specific targets. There are no suspects at this time.

"But wait; there's more. Here's another article. This one's about some local union corruption. But how are these related? Listen to this one," she added.

Buffalo News, Allentown, November 6, 1985
Union Corruption Could Cost Workers Big

The police are looking into the alleged criminal activity of Reilly Seamus Fitzpatrick, a local teamsters union boss and suspected head of Buffalo's Southside Irish mob. His work as a union boss in the Allentown area has enabled the Southside gang to gain influence over this part of town, more recently controlled by the Westside Italian faction.

Fitzpatrick has most recently been indicted for fraud in a case now pending in federal court. He has been accused of bilking union members of nearly a half of a million dollars from money he invested for the workers from their pension funds.

He is also under investigation for the death of two leading union bosses in the Buffalo area. They were said to have had incriminating evidence that they were going to turn over to federal authorities proving Fitzpatrick's connection with the embezzlement of the funds. Both were found in a car at the bottom of the Niagara River early last week.

When asked for a comment about the deaths of Al Marone and Bud Korzak, Fitzpatrick glibly stated, "What's all the fuss about. They died of natural causes. I had nothing to do with it."

After he was reminded of the circumstances of their deaths he simply responded, "That's right, when you're sitting at the bottom of a river in a car you're naturally gonna die!" He laughed and walked away.

"Hap, here are several more just like this one. Maybe this guy Fitzpatrick is the guy who Connie and Si were referring to. His office is just around the corner from the costume shop."

"That might be true except for one thing," I said gloating over my astute observational powers.

"Oh, what have I missed that you, in your infinite powers of seeing the future, have divined?"

"Now *that* borderlines on sarcasm," I responded.

"*No shit!*" she said shaking her head.

"Well, in case you missed it, his middle name is Seamus, which does not start with the letter 'J', as in RJ."

"I hate to admit it but you're right," she said reluctantly.

Just as we were in the thick of things, the side door flung open and in walked Slick eating a piece of cold pizza.

"Right about what?" he said as if he had been a part of the conversation all along.

I looked at him and queried, "Cold pizza? I thought only dumpster-divers and college students ate cold pizza in the morning. And what are you doing up so early and standing in our kitchen?"

"Well, after last night I got to thinking. Oh, I forgot, it was a secret, right? Or did you confess?"

"She was awake when I got home. How about you?" I asked.

"Susie was awake, but she's used to me coming and going at all hours. She doesn't even ask anymore. Yep, I'm the king of my castle; what are you?" Slick said with a, well, you know.

"He's the king of *my* castle!" Joanie shot back.

I redirected, "I hate to interrupt, but going back to our previous discussion..."

"Right. Well, I got to thinking about what those two were talking about and it occurred to me that their dad, this RJ, might just be the one we're looking for," Slick said.

"That's about where we were when you came in," I replied.

"Oh, speaking of that. I heard you say that Hap was right. Right about what, may I ask?"

"Well, we found some articles talking about this guy name Fitzpatrick that is being investigated for some criminal activities, including murder in Allentown and we were thinking maybe he might have something to do with my father's murder."

I added, "Yeh, but this guy's name is Reilly *Seamus* Fitzpatrick, so that would make him an RS not an RJ."

We could see the gerbils spinning around in Slick's head as he scratched and made noises. The only thing missing was smoke coming from his ears.

"Not so fast Kimosabe. This guy just might be the one we're looking for."

Joanie seemed intrigued, "Oh; and how is that possible?"

"Go ahead, enlighten us; but don't try to convince us that Seamus really begins with a J, okay?"

"Well it does," he said knowingly.

Joanie was first to respond to this absurdity with, "Slick, I know we're two dummies, but not even you can convince us that 'Seamus' is spelled 'J-e-a-m-u-s'."

"Then sit down and be amazed, cause here I go. It's quite simple actually. Seamus is Gaelic for, Yeh, that's right, you got it, come on..."

"Stop already. Spit it out!" Joanie shouted.

"*James*! Yep, Seamus means James in English. Therefore, this guys first two initials are RJ."

"Slick you never cease to amaze me," Joanie said as she collapsed back in her chair.

"Now how about some breakfast? I think I've earned it, haven't I?" Slick said rubbing his hands together and pulling up a chair.

Shaking her head Joanie added, "Slick, how can you go from almost brilliant to worrying about your next meal?"

Slick just smiled and said, "*A man's got to know his limitations.*"

THIRTY-THREE
WEDNESDAY, JULY 9

"Joanie, it occurred to me that we've spent so much time on my new job and what I'm doing that we haven't talked much about your research project. That was the original reason we were coming to Buffalo, now wasn't it," I remarked.

"Yes it was, but with my dad's death and our investigation and your job and all, I guess I don't think much about my work, except for when I'm there."

"Well?"

"Well what?"

"Well tell me about it. Now's the perfect time – dinner's made, work is over, and Slick and Susie aren't here to interrupt. So tell me more about the research project you're heading up. Any new breakthroughs?"

"Fair enough, but let's eat first. I don't think that I could lay it all out for you on an empty stomach. Besides, whatever you made for dinner smells incredible. I wouldn't be able to keep my mind on the conversation smelling that."

"Oh just something I whipped up; some chicken Pozner, jasmine rice with Hap's world famous vegetable medley. Oh, and for dessert we are having vanilla mousse. How about that?"

"Let me get this straight. We're having grilled chicken breasts, jasmine rice – heavy on the butter, left over lima beans and broccoli, and ice cream sandwiches cut out to look like some animal. Is that about right?"

"Let's eat before it gets cold."

"Now that your fed and in a better mood..." I began.

"What's that supposed to mean? I'm always in a good mood. It's just that I don't often get to show it," she cut in.

"Right," was all I could muster.

"Let's go into the living room and get comfortable so I can give you some new details about the project I'm working on. Now remember, this is all confidential so don't tell anyone – especially Slick or Susie."

"My lips are sealed. So go ahead."

"Well, as you remember I was working on being able to alter the part of the brain that fosters addiction. What we've found is a way to virtually eliminate a person's addiction to many different things, including smoking and a variety of other drugs. What makes our research unique is that there are few side effects, at least from our current studies. Even better, the compound we developed is easily manufactured, cost is minimal and the raw materials are readily available – and abundant. But..."

"Yeh, you've already told me that much; but what?" I asked.

"Well, you know me. I'll be the first to admit that I'm a bit too honest," she replied.

"I don't know about that. Whenever I was confronted with some sort of moral dilemma my dad made it very simple for me. He would say there's no such thing as too honest. Honesty is a black or white issue; there are no grey areas. You're either honest or your not – with each decision in life that you make. So, with that in mind, How does this project call into question your honesty?"

"You know how I love to read, right? Well, it was sometime last year that I was reading this book I picked up on Native American medicine."

"I remember it. It's still sitting on your night stand by the bed."

"Right. I picked it up sometime this past March, you know, just to see if there was anything in there that might help me with my project."

I interrupted, "Was there?"

"Not exactly. But there was some mention of plant roots that helped with some related problems. Anyway, the bad news is the supposed addiction cure that we have come up with is available right in the ground we walk on at no cost."

"That's good, right?"

"Yes and no. It's good for people, which I'm elated about. It's bad for my company – and my research team, because we can't patent any of our findings, which means my company has spent millions coming up with something that nature provides."

"I have a feeling that that's not the only bad news. Am I right?"

"You are. When I wrote the report to my supervisor it went directly to the CEO who sent a message via my supervisor that this project must be ready for FDA approval and marketing by this fall."

"Basically to hell with your report, right?"

"No. My report no longer exists. My supervisor, along with some of the less honest; excuse me – some of the dishonest members of my team are rewriting it to come out the way they want it to be."

"And you?"

"Oh I'm still on the project, and still heading it up; at least in name. But I am not to disclose anything else of what I found out. I was warned that there would be dire consequences if I leaked any of this out."

"Wow. That's a lot to take in. Why didn't you tell me this back when it happened?"

"Because I know you. And besides it was right around the time I transferred to the Buffalo office to finish this thing out. And there's one more thing. It probably doesn't mean anything, but I found it very strange."

"Oh-Oh, that's usually when the bottom drops out. What is it?"

"It was also the time period when my father was murdered. Now don't go connecting any dots. I don't think for a minute that anyone from my company is nefarious enough to kill my father to scare me off."

"I wasn't thinking that; but obviously, you were. There is a great deal of money to be made or lost by your discovery. If I were in charge I think I might do anything to make sure the company didn't lose millions; wouldn't you?"

She snapped back, "No. You're either honest or your not, remember?"

"Rule number four – never pontificate unless you're the pontiff."

"What?"

"Never mind," I said. "So where does that leave you with this project?"

"In fairness to my supervisor, he directed me and my team to come up with an alternative to what we found; you know, something that is not found readily in nature, but will garner the same results – eliminating some of the possible side effects."

"Oh that's much better."

"In a way it is. Now I don't have to 'lie or die', and we still have until late fall of this year to come up with a new cure."

"I'm almost sorry I asked you to tell me about it."

"Why? We talk about your work. Oh, and by the way, Susie told me about that assistant you have – Connie what's her name."

"Here we go."

"Don't worry, I trust you; but just watch out. Especially after what you found out last night. She might just be looking for information on what you know about them. And that could put you in danger."

"You're right. I'm beginning to put some of the pieces of the puzzle together. But how could they know about the note and information we got from Griffin? And if it was sent to us upon his death; then who sent it?"

"Good questions. Just be cautious around her, okay?"

"And you be careful around your job. I don't think you can trust even your team members at this point."

The Allentown Murders

"Now, why don't we get back into that pile of newspaper clippings and notes? Don't forget, one of our prime objectives here is to find your dad's killer. Right?"

"Good idea."

THIRTY-FOUR
FRIDAY, JULY 11

"Connie, I think we're done for this week. Why don't you take off now? I know it's a bit early, but you've put in a good week's work, and I'm pretty worn out myself."

"Sure Hap. I don't mind being able to start the weekend early. I'm meeting a few friends at Mulligan's Brick Bar on Allen Street a little later for a few drinks. Would you like to join us?"

"No. I need to get home. I've got a meeting tonight with some people about a writing project. But thanks anyway; maybe some other time."

"I'll hold you to that. And maybe we can have those drinks alone," she said with a sly smile.

"Sure, that sounds great. Anyway, enjoy your weekend," I replied trying not to be unfriendly, or flirtatious.

"I hope it's better than last weekend."

Before I could stop myself I asked, "Oh, something happened last weekend?" After I said this I realized she was probably referring to when Slick and I almost got caught spying on her and Si.

"Yeh, I was visiting a friend when he saw some guys peering through a window at us."

Trying to blow it off I said, "Oh, probably just people passing by."

"No. They were looking at us through a window in the alley; and the window is on the second floor. So unless they were giants, they had to have climbed the wall."

I added, "Or they stood on garbage cans and pulled themselves up on the window ledge."

After I said this I cringed; I know why Joanie calls me *Nostra-dumb-ass!*

With a very peculiar look, Connie responded, "Yes, maybe that's how they got up to the window. Sounds like you've had some experience yourself."

Now I was beginning to sweat. "Only as a kid. You know, trying to spy on some other neighborhood kids. Playing games and such." I was rambling.

With a knowing smile she said, "Or watching the older girls getting dressed, eh?"

As embarrassing as this conversation was getting, she gave me an out. I replied, "You got me. You know us little boys. But I gave that up for Lent a few years back. Ha!"

"Well anytime you feel inclined to take it back up, just let me know and I'll give you the address to my window," she said with a very devious smile.

"Oh, look what time it is. I'd better be going or I'll be late," I lamely said.

"Late for what?"

" My own funeral, believe me – *my own funeral.*"

*   *   *

Slick and I had planned to meet Sarge and Fr. Christopher at McPartland's in South Buffalo after work for a few drinks. Since Susie and I ride together most days, I would drop her off and pick him up at the apartment they moved into when they could no longer stand living with Sarge. Joanie was planning on going over to visit her mom for the evening and Susie was just happy to have some alone time away from Slick; so it all worked out for everyone.

"Hap, Slick how the hell are you two sorry sons-of-a-sea cook?" Sarge said in his usual way of greeting us.

"Well, it looks as though the Lord's been smiling down upon you two lads. Tis a great joy to see you again, me boys," Fr. Christopher said in his Irish brogue. He's not actually from Ireland, although he is of Irish decent. He just likes to put on the accent whenever he feels the occasion warrants; or when he's dipped into the chalice at mass a little too much or visited a local establishment with someone like Sarge. We could tell that they had a head start on us by about an hour – which equates to two or three pints, depending on how much malarkey they've both been spreading.

"Fr. Christopher, Sarge good to see you both as well. I hope you two haven't been re-fighting the war again, or challenging those two old men at the other end of the bar to arm wrestling contests," I said with a smile.

Fr. Christopher got off of his stool, came over to me and gave me a handshake and a hug. Sarge just slapped me on the back and mussed Slick's hair saying, "How are you, junior?"

Slick hates that, so Sarge says it every chance he gets.

"Hello to you too, Hap. How's everyone. I haven't seen your mom around lately; she doing okay?"

"Oh Yeh, we're all fine. She's been doing some traveling lately, that's why you haven't seen her. I didn't see the old Studebaker out front; did you walk here, Sarge?"

"Yeh, the damn thing has been giving me trouble again. If it were a horse I'd have taken it out and shot it long ago!"

Slick jumped in, "Then why don't you get rid of it like I've been telling you for years?"

"What? Get rid of that antique? Some day it'll be yours and you're going to thank me for keeping it running all these years."

Fr. Christopher sat and shook his head. He knew Sarge, but didn't know how much he and Slick were alike. I decided it would be a good time to get down to some serious business.

"By the way, I've got the tab tonight. You two are going to earn it," I said.

"Why didn't you tell me sooner; I wouldn't have been nursing my beer up till now," Sarge replied.

Slick turned toward me as if to ask if that included him. I just shook my head yes.

"Fr. Christopher, Sarge, one of the reasons we're all back here in Buffalo is to find Mitch Taylor's killer. I know the police are investigating and we should probably stay out of the way. I know you're going to tell me how dangerous it could be. I also remember what happened when we came to find Devon's killer, and what we went through to track him down. But..."

Sarge interrupted, "Is this going to be a big *but*; cause if it is I need another pint."

Slick shot back at him, "Sarge, just listen for a change; would you? This is serious."

"You don't need to get all up in my shit just cause you're sober," Sarge said back to him.

"But you also need to remember that the police and everyone else wrote it off as an overdoes, when it was murder. Devon was our good friend and I wasn't about to let it go. Mitch Taylor was Joanie's dad and my father-in-law; and I'm not about to leave it to a stranger to figure out who killed him and why. I need your help; we need your help. What do you say?"

Fr. Christopher spoke up first, "Son, you know I've always been there for you. Your family and mine were tied together long before you were born, and I have made it my responsibility for the past twenty or more years now to see that you get the help you need. So what do you want us to do?"

We all looked over to Sarge who was arguing with the bartender about his beer having too much of a collar. He stopped when he saw us, looked over and said, "I'm in too."

Slick smiled and said, "Good."

I didn't want to put them in any danger, but I knew that I couldn't tell Sarge anything about Bob Griffin; at least not at this time.

Fr. Christopher I could tell, and will when I get a chance to talk with him alone. But for now they would be on a need-to-know basis.

"Let me start by sharing what we have from the detectives on the case and then Slick and I can fill you in on what we have found out ourselves. Okay?"

They both nodded in agreement. I told them what the two detectives had told Joanie and me, how Mitch was hanged with a braided nylon chord, and they suspected that the killers tried to make it look like a botched robbery to throw the police off. I told them everything I could about the way the shop looked after the murder and how the front door had not been tampered with.

"So the police didn't find it strange that Mitch had probably let these people into his shop in the middle of the night?" Sarge asked.

"Apparently not. They said he probably knew them from the neighborhood. Possibly some homeless men he used to help out, or maybe someone who appeared to be in trouble."

"And what about his partner, Toby? Where was he while all of this was going on?" Fr. Christopher asked.

"That's what I can't figure out either. From the looks of the place there was quite a scuffle. You would think that if Toby hadn't woken up when Mitch went downstairs to the shop, he would have heard all the racket going on when Mitch was being attacked," I responded, confused about that myself.

Part IV
The Convergence
[Hap Pozner]

THIRTY-FIVE
SUNDAY, JULY 13

"Hap, Slick. How the hell are you boys! I didn't think that we'd ever see the likes of you two again; but here you are – as big as life, and bold as balls on a brass bull. Welcome to 'The King of Clubs Bar'," Tripp said as he slapped me on the back.

"Yeh, well; we never expected to be in this place ever again, but we've come, believe it or not, because we need your help – and the help of your friends here," I said with a great deal of trepidation.

"Well, ain't it just like back in high school at St. Stephen's? Like the time you stuffed me in the locker when I was a Sophomore, or when you beat me at your trial in student court your senior year, or maybe like a few years back when you had the nerve to come here and get our leader, Jake, put in jail. Those were the good old days, right Hap? Now, what can we do for you?" Tripp said waxing nostalgic and a bit nasty.

Slick jumped in here, salvaging what was beginning to look like a very awkward moment, "The past is the past; but if you really want to reminisce, how about the time Hap and I bailed you and a few of these other guys out of jail; or the fact that you are now the leader of this band of miscreants; or possibly how we got this dump a new – and clean, I might add – front plate-glass window. We're here because who better to get to the bottom of who murdered Hap's father-in-law than you and your boys?"

194

Tripp pondered a moment and then, as a big grin stretched across his face, said, "Well, since you put it that way; how can we help?"

After a few hours of laying out the situation surrounding her father's murder and who we suspected, not to mention quite a few beers, I got down to how they can help solve the murder, "What we'd like you and a few of your boys to do is to infiltrate Fitzpatrick's operation and get as much Intel as possible on where and how the money flows. If we can follow the money, we can find Mitch Taylor's killer."

Slick added, "I've no doubt that Fitzpatrick already knows who you guys are, and that could work to our advantage."

Tripp questioned, "How's that? If the guy knows who we are and where we're from, wouldn't he look at us as trying to move into his territory?"

"At first, yes; but if you could convince him that you are impressed with his operation and want to form an alliance with him to your mutual benefit, he might just take the bait. Don't forget, we're dealing with a businessman; and a greedy one at that," I interjected.

Tripp suggested, "We go into Allentown, hangout with some of his boys, get a meeting set up with this Fitzpatrick person, then convince him that we're there to make some money for him and us; right? And the whole operation is to find out where and how the money flows and what his role is in the murder of your father-in-law."

I could feel things coming together. If they could pull this off, we could get the corroboration that we would need to bring our evidence to Holmes and Dobson. I was just surprised that Tripp would help. I guess, with all of his idiosyncrasies, Slick does have a knack for reading people.

"What say we meet in one week to see what you've found out," I said.

"*One week!* You've got to be kidding. How are we supposed to get in, gain his confidence and get the information you are asking for in just one week? You're just as crazy as you were in high school," Tripp complained.

He was right; how could we expect anyone to work that fast? But it had to be done that quickly. A lot depended on it.

Slick interrupted what was probably going to be an apology from me, "Look it; we wouldn't have come here to you if we thought you'd wimp out. 'Oh no, I can't do it; it's too dangerous, we're too scared; my chopper's not running...'"

As Slick ranted on, I could see Tripp and his boys begin to boil over. It looked like the end of the trail for him and me. Just when I was about to grab Slick and run for our lives, Tripp let out a big laugh.

Slapping Slick on the back once again, and this time spilling his beer all over his shirt, Tripp said, "You had me going there for a minute partner; but I got your point."

Turning to his handful of boys sitting with us and drinking, Tripp continued, "Hey, if we can't do this, who can? This is what we were made for. This is our destiny; this is who we are."

At this point I was beginning to believe he and Slick were long, lost brothers!

I added, "That's right. We came to you because you are the only ones who can pull this off; and whether it's one week or one day, I'm confident you can do it."

Tripp smiled and said, "Now don't go wild here. One week is short enough for what you want us to accomplish; but we'll get it done."

I turned to Slick and said, "Sometimes Slick you amaze me."

With a shit-eating grin on his face, he shot back, "Yeh, sometimes I amaze myself!"

THIRTY-SIX
WEDNESDAY, JULY 16

"I'll have a Genny Cream Ale," I said to the bartender at Mulligan's Brick Bar, wondering why I still drink that crap. But I guess it's an old habit picked up after many years drinking with Sarge.

"Are you sure?" he replied.

I laughed and said, "Of course, someone's got to keep them in business. Who knows, this stuff might outlive the both of us."

"From the taste of it, I think it already has," he said with a friendly laugh.

Just as he turned his back to pull the tap on my beer a voice from over my shoulder whispered in an ominous tone, "Be wary of your assistant. She and the lame shop owner are 'more kin and less than kind'."

As soon as his voice faded I felt his hand lift from my shoulder that was keeping me from turning around toward him. I swung around to see a man in a trench coat and hat walking briskly toward the front door and then out. I turned all the way around on my barstool to chase after him, but just as I was about to jump down to the floor Jim, the bartender, grabbed my other shoulder and, with a start, I turned back toward him.

"Hap, aren't you going to drink your beer before you leave. I know it's rot-gut, but you ordered it."

I looked back to the door to see the man gone. Who was he? Why did he quote Shakespeare to me? I knew Si and Connie were related, but how were they more related than I knew and how were they less kind than I thought. What did that mean?

Then it occurred to me. It must have been; it had to be – Fr. Christopher. He once did this same thing when Slick and I were in that bar on the Eastside looking for our friend, Devon's, murderer. He donned a disguise and came into the bar to watch our backs. Maybe it was him again, trying to caution me about something. But why not just call me or meet me and tell me straight out. There isn't any danger here for him? This didn't make any sense. I need to talk with Slick; he's a wiz at figuring this kind of stuff out. But for now...

"I know; I'm doing a study on how much of this stuff one can drink and still have a stomach!"

Jim and I both laughed.

"Hey, if you keep coming in here and drink it I may have to start joining you. There may be more to it than meets the eye."

It's strange that he would phrase it that way. 'More to it than meets the eye.' Exactly! There is more to Connie and Si than they are letting me know. Why is she my assistant, out of all of the students that had applied six months before? She came out of nowhere; someone had to place her there. Someone with some pull at the college. And why is Si in one of my classes? He owns a business in Allentown. If he needed any class, it wouldn't be a creative writing class. Not only that, but he asks the strangest questions in class, almost trying to probe into my personal life.

I've also noticed Connie acts strangely as well. While my vanity tells me that she flirts with me because I'm irresistible, reality tells me that she has a hidden agenda – and it has something to do with Joanie and her research. Mm...

"Hap, you ready for another?" Jim asked with a friendly grin.

"Sure, why not. By the way, that man that was standing next to me just a few minutes ago, does he come in here often?" I asked.

"Oh, thanks for reminding me; I almost forgot about it," he said hitting himself in the forehead.

"Forgot what?"

"That guy; the one you mentioned, was in earlier and left a note for you. He said he would be back, but just in case he missed you again he wanted to be sure you got this. I guess he must know your habits," he added.

"Thanks; and yes I'll have another pint. I have a feeling I'm going to need it."

It was addressed to me and dated July 16 – today. The handwriting looked eerily familiar. Filled with a sudden sense of curiosity I tore open the envelope and pulled out the single page that was inside. The writing was barely legible; it looked like it had been written in a hurry, or in a moving vehicle; a bus or a taxi perhaps. It read:

Dear Hap,

I can't reveal who I am just yet, but suffice it to say I am a friend. Don't make any attempt to find me out as it might cost the both of us our lives in the process.

I'm writing this as a warning about some pitfalls you'll encounter in your quest to find your father-in-law's murderer; things that I found out only too late.

Reilly and RJ are one and the same – they will stop at nothing to continue their bloody business.

Connie and Si are nothing more than two dupes for them, even though they are part of the same family.

Jimmy and Tony are the henchmen, fools at best and killers at worst.

Beware of them all; but most of all, the girl. She has been sent with evil intent. Her mission is to destroy you, your wife and, most of all, her research. Mitch Taylor's murder is an anecdotal note to the bigger picture. He stood in their way of gaining complete control of the Allentown area.

The key to this whole mystery can be found in the relationship between Reilly and RJ.

There's more you need to know. I will find you again soon and give you the evidence you will need to put them away.

Your brother-in-arms

How strange. That's exactly how that reporter signed his letters to me; but it couldn't be him – *he's dead!*

THIRTY-SEVEN
THURSDAY, JULY 17

"Hap, what in the world is this all about that we have to wait for everyone else to get here before you can tell me?" Joanie said sounding surprised at my stubbornness.

"This is too important to say twice," I replied.

"What? That makes no sense at all; not even for you!" she retorted.

"What I mean is...oh, wait; there's the doorbell. Good they're here."

As she moved to the front door she remarked, "Not Slick; he wouldn't bother ringing the bell, he'd just walk in."

And she was right; it was everyone else though. Fr. Christopher had picked Sarge up, as well as Susie. Slick decided he had to stay home for a little while longer. He was in the middle of a Road Runner cartoon and wouldn't leave 'till it was over.

"Well, I'm glad you all made it," I said as they came into the living room, "except for Slick I see."

Susie, in a disgusted tone said, "Yeh, he had to stay back to see if Wile E. Coyote gets tricked into falling off a cliff or some dumb thing. Speaking of which, Fr. Christopher was kind enough to pick us up since Sarge here was trying his best to break the land speed record for putting away Genny Cream Ale pounders."

"I'd take offense to that if she weren't almost a member of the family already," Sarge interjected.

"Okay Hap, what's this all about," Fr. Christopher asked rubbing his hands. He had a habit of doing that whenever he got excited about something.

"Let's wait just a few more minutes to see if Slick makes it here," I suggested.

Just as I was saying this, a voice coming from the back door rang out, "See if who makes it?"

It was Slick, and right on cue as usual.

"Let's all sit down. Would anyone like something to eat or drink?" I asked.

Almost as if it were choreographed they all said, *"NO!"*

Fr. Christopher spoke first, "I think it might be best if you start, Hap. What is it that has us all sitting here?"

"Right to the point; that's how I like it," Slick said with a smile.

I could see Susie look over at Joanie and roll her eyes.

I started, "Well, you're all here because I've learned a few things that effect us all. And I've also got a favor to ask of all of you."

They all nodded, as if to say of course we'll help.

"As you know Slick and I have been trying to find something, anything that will lead us to Mr. Taylor's killer. In the meantime I've found out that there are some people, and maybe the same people, who are trying to disrupt Joanie's research project over at Vericon Pharmaceuticals."

After Slick and I laid out all that we found out, I told them all about the reporter, Bob Griffin, and read them the letter he sent to me. I then told them about the strange meeting in the bar just yesterday, "...and these two men, Fitzpatrick and RJ, they seem to be somehow connected in a strange way. By the way, I got some help, from a certain friend who always seems to have my back, in finding out about those two guys."

As I turned toward Fr. Christopher and gave him a smile Slick chimed in with, "Hap, you know I always have your back. I'm the..."

The Allentown Murders

I knew this would be one of Slick's soliloquy's so I interrupted him saying, "Not you Slick; I'm referring to Fr. Christopher."

Looking again at him I added, "Thanks for being at the bar to give me some helpful clues. But you didn't have to wear a disguise; it's not like when we were looking for Devon's murderer. We weren't in any danger in Mulligan's."

With a puzzled expression on his face he stopped me, "Wait a minute Hap. As much as you know I'll always be there for you, I wasn't *there* for you; it wasn't me this time. The only information I have about this whole thing is what you've related to us all. You've kept us pretty much in the dark up until now. Whoever it was, you can thank God for his intervention; not me."

I was floored by this revelation. Just when I think that I have something figured out – I don't. If it wasn't Fr. Christopher, then who was it?

"All right, then I guess I'd better tell you about his warning and the letter he left. When he came up to me at Mulligan's he quoted Shakespeare from the play 'Hamlet', alluding to Fitzpatrick and RJ being more related than I imagined, whatever that meant; and in his letter he said to be especially wary of my assistant, Connie. She's Si's sister and RJ's daughter."

Joanie, with a knowing smirk on her face, cut in, "Ahem. Didn't I tell you that your assistant didn't succumb to your wanton good looks and irresistible charm? She was after something else. Well, didn't I Romeo?"

Susie spoke up, rescuing me from an almost certain embarrassing moment, "Okay, what do we know? The reporter, Bob Griffin, who finds out some very incriminating evidence linking this Reilly Fitzpatrick and RJ 'Somebody' to drug trafficking, prostitution and major embezzlement of union funds in the Allentown area, which, by the way, led to the deaths of several pimps, prostitutes and drug pushers, conveniently dies in a car wreck. Mr. Taylor is first beaten and shortly after murdered for reasons yet unknown. Your Connie *Dildo*..."

"That's *Dilworth*!" I interrupted, giving Susie an angry glare. She just smiled back and continued.

"Right, Dilworth. As I was saying, this Connie *Dilworth* was apparently placed in your office as your assistant to keep an eye on you and extract whatever information she could about your investigation and also Joanie's research project at work. Oh, I need to make a correction to your assessment Joanie. While this tramp's job might be to seduce Hap to get information, it looked to me that she was enjoying her job way too much."

I could feel the sweat rolling down the back of my neck at this point – as if I was guilty of anything but enjoying the attention.

Sarge saved me at this point saying, "Okay we get the picture about our lover-boy here, but what about this mysterious stranger?"

As we all talked, something seemed oddly familiar. Slick was quiet. I looked over to see that look of his when the chipmunks were busy at work in his head.

"I think I have it."

Susie moaned, "Oh no."

"No wait. I think I know who that stranger is. When you read the letter you got from him, it said, if you got it then he would already be dead; and he was. So who sent the stuff to you? He couldn't. That's right, it was this mysterious stranger; probably his accomplice, or at least his assistant or close friend."

Beaming, Sarge interjected, "That's my boy. Way to go Junior! Your mother always did say you had something. I just thought it was something you'd outgrow."

"Thanks *dad*; and don't call me Junior. You know I hate that."

I had to separate them. The others in the room have never seen what happens when the two of them get into an argument – it always ends up in a fistfight.

"Okay you two. Let's get back to business. I don't want you scaring the ladies," I said.

Susie leaned in toward the center of the circle we had formed around the room, all of us sitting, pondering the situation.

She queried, "There's just a few things we are missing; important things. You know, connections that we haven't made."

Joanie asked, "Like what?"

"Like what does the reporter's murder have to do with your dad's? And what does your dad's murder have to do with your research on drug addiction?"

Joanie spoke up, "Wait, how did you know about that?"

Just as she asked the question I could see she had already figured out the answer.

She demanded, "Well Hap, you didn't say anything; did you?"

Susie spoke while I squirmed, "I forced it out of him. You know how I can get anything out of anyone. Besides, Hap's easy."

Joanie shot her a look that could kill.

Susie turned beet red and sheepishly added, "I mean we ride together every day, and chat the whole way back and forth to and from work. Well, you have to expect something to slip into the conversation that might be, let's say, a bit too personal to be revealed in a normal, casual conversation."

That infuriated Joanie all the more, "Oh? And what other *personal* things have you and Susie been discussing? Or shouldn't I ask?"

Now the sweat was running down my brow as well, "Nothing else. I swear!"

Susie added, "No really; he never told me about anything personal that went on between the two of you – except for the project; and that isn't really..."

Joanie stopped her babbling, "*Stop!* I've heard *enough.*"

As if right on cue, Fr. Christopher got up and, trying to calm things, said, "Let's thank the Lord that we have good friends to aid us in our time of need. Hap, what about your dreams; you know, the little girl and the marionettes; and Devon's message? These are not messages from a mysterious stranger, but ones from God. He points the true way, but what do they mean?"

I breathed a sigh of relief at his remarks. He not only saved my ass, again, but he also brought up some things that may have a lot to do with all of this. But what are the connections?

Sarge got up and, walking toward the kitchen refrigerator, said, "I think I will take you up on your offer. You do have a cold Genny in here for me, don't you?"

We all smiled at this. I replied, "I always have at least one in there for you, Sarge."

He turned around, smiled, and then looked at Slick and said, "You know, he's always been my favorite."

Slick shook his head and muttered, "Sheesh. You see what I've had to live with."

Feeling things begin to once more slip away, Fr. Christopher said, "Okay. Any ideas? What are the connections? I'm sure there are some; there must be."

I interjected, "There are. I believe this is what is called 'the confluence' or 'convergence'. The point at which all the pieces begin to move into place to create the picture."

Looking puzzled, Joanie asked, "Okay Hap, I'll bite. What is the picture you're talking about? And how do these things all fit together? I'm sure I'm not the only one here who doesn't get it. Fill us in, oh master sleuth."

Shaking my head, "It's all quite elementary, my dear. This is one of those 'ah ha' moments; kind of like when the Good Witch, Glinda, talking to Dorothy in the *Wizard of Oz*, said '...you always had the power to go home. Just click your heels together, etc."

Letting out a moan of agony, Joanie said, "Now you're scaring me. You're beginning to sound like Slick!"

"Hey, I resemble that remark!" Slick said from the kitchen, now sitting with Sarge, opening his own bottle of Genny Cream Ale. Sarge slapped him on the back and said, "That's my boy." They clinked bottles and took a swig.

"Now here's the hard part. I should have said that I have a feeling I know how the pieces fit, but I need some more information in order to confirm my suspicions."

"Oh, now they're just suspicions. Whatever happened to the 'puzzle-master'?" Susie added.

"Well, let me put it this way. I think I know how everything ties together, but with a bit more evidence I will be able to prove it. And I wouldn't want to be pointing fingers at people, making wild accusations without solid evidence. Now here's how we can get the evidence. At Sarge's suggestion, Slick and I already met last week with some old friends from the Eastside who said they would help us out. We're meeting again tomorrow at McPartland's to see what they found out. Sarge, I'd like you and Fr. Christopher to meet us there to hear what they have.

But I'm also going to need each of you to find out some things for me in order to complete this puzzle. Are you game?"

I could see nods from everyone, including my beer-drinking buddies in the next room.

"All right then, Sarge; I'd like you to pay a visit to a Mr. Reilly Fitzpatrick. He's a union boss that has an office over the Teamsters' hall on Elmwood Avenue near Allen Street. I want you to pretend you're an enforcer, someone who can help keep his people on the street in line. You need to find out as much as you can about his operation.

Looking at Fr. Christopher, "And Fr. Christopher, I need you to see what you can find out about this RJ person; who he is, his connection to Fitzpatrick – anything at all."

"Joanie, I'd like you to find out as much as you can about the man who got us into this mess in the first place, Bob Griffin. He must have had someone he confided in. Find out."

Now I felt like a military commander barking out marching orders. It may be lonely at the top, but the view is, oh, so beautiful.

"Susie, I've got just the job for you. I want you to cozy up to my assistant; you know, come over and have lunch with her instead of me. Tell her you feel like the two of you got off on the wrong foot, and so on. Find out who she really is and what her interests are in Joanie and me. Also, what her connection is with RJ and Si, besides the obvious one."

Susie spoke up at this, *"You want me to do what!* I will not be nice to that home-wrecking bitch!"

Joanie, without thinking, blurted out, "It takes..."

Thankfully, I knew what was coming and salvaged our friendship by interrupting her and finishing the thought, "...a big person to work toward the greater good. I'm sure Joanie was about to say these very same words."

Looking skeptical, Susie responded, "Well, I suppose I can make the effort for you, Hap. That is, for all of us."

Sarge, seeing Slick without a job, said, "Hey, what about Junior over here. He needs his own covert operation."

"I was just coming to him. Slick, I have a very special job for you." At this he beamed.

"Sure, you name it buddy," he replied.

"I want you to see what you can get out of Toby."

He jumped out of his chair and complained, *"What!* You stick me with him? I'll tell you what I can get out of that sorry son-of-a-drag queen!"

"Calm down. I'm asking you to do this because I believe he knows much more than he told the police, or anyone, about Mr. Taylor's beating and murder. I think he witnessed both; but I can't prove it. This is vital to the whole case. Slick, I'm giving you the most important task here. Will you do it?"

I could see a look on his face that told me he was mulling over every word I said. The question was; did he buy it?

"Well, since you put it that way, how can I refuse?" he beamed. He bought it!

Slick then added, "But what about you?"

"I'll be working on Si. He might be the easiest one to get information out of since, I believe, he knows most of what's going on and he seems to have a grudge against his dad, RJ."

Just then Sarge stood up, pulled up his left sleeve, looked down at his wrist and announced, "Now everyone, synchronize your watches. I have exactly..."

I interrupted, "Sarge, excuse me, this isn't a military mission. But I do have a timeline for us. I'd like everyone to meet back here in two weeks, on Thursday, July 31 to discuss what we each found out. Then maybe we can take it all to the police."

Sarge added, "Good plan son. And we'll meet at O-Dark-30; synchronize."

Joanie chuckled at this and said, "How about at six p.m. for dinner."

Sarge grinned and said, "Now that's what I'm talking about. I'll drink to that." He went back to the refrigerator and took out another beer for himself and Slick. He looked around and then grabbed one for each of the rest of us.

THIRTY-EIGHT
FRIDAY, JULY 18

"Hap, do you think it was a good idea for us to all meet here at McPartland's in South Buffalo? Tripp and his boys are not the usual patrons. This *is* a family restaurant, you know," Sarge asked in a somewhat anxious tone.

Fr. Christopher was quick to reply, "The Good Lord loves all of his children. And don't forget Tripp was once one of us – he's a fine lad me-boys, a product of St. Stephen's after all."

Just as we were debating this, in walked Tripp and two of his buddies, all dressed in their leathers, tattoos and chains.

As they approached us one of the busboys dropped a tray of dirty dishes, startling a few families sitting at tables with their children.

Slick turned to Tripp and said, "Sit down, you're scaring the customers!"

I laughed at this and welcomed our guests, "Thanks for coming here, and thanks for whatever you have to tell us. I'm sure it will be valuable information."

Tripp joined me in laughter and replied, "Well buddy, I think we might just have what the doctor ordered."

Sarge gave him a stern look and interjected, "We don't do drugs here!"

Fr. Christopher added, "I'll drink to that!"

With that I felt the tension lift and we all had a good laugh.

"So what did you learn?" I anxiously asked.

Tripp went on to tell us about how Fitzpatrick had money coming in from all kinds of places: drug dealers, pimps, drug rehab clinics, kickbacks from contractors, protection money he collected from local businesses – not to mention the money he skimmed from the union pension fund.

"Wow! That's amazing," was all I could say at this revelation.

I added, "But where does Mitch Taylor fit into all of this?"

Tripp smiled and said, "That's the amazing part. You would think that with all of this money rolling in that Fitzpatrick would not want to bother with some small inconvenience created by one of the locals; but no, he wanted it all. That's what greed will do to a man."

Slick was mesmerized. He asked, "But how?"

Tripp continued, "It seems Taylor was giving Fitzpatrick a lot of heat about his shady dealings in Allentown, and he was spearheading the Community Group that was trying to bring his empire down."

Sarge cut in, "So that's what it was all about? Taylor was trying to clean up the area and shut Fitzpatrick down?"

Tripp replied, "Not exactly. Oh, he was trying to do all that; but what got to Fitzpatrick the most was that Taylor was on to his embezzling money from the union pension fund; that would not just cut off some of his income, it would get him killed. Do you know what a bunch of Teamsters would do to someone who is stealing their retirement money?"

Fr. Christopher asked, "So how did he get this information? And how was he going to use it?"

"Well, here's the best part," Trip said as he leaned in to us at the table where we sat, "He got it from Fitzpatrick's secretary! She provided the documents and the names of those involved in his scheme!"

I had to ask, "But why would his secretary turn on him? Did he jilt her or something?"

One of Tripp's boys finally spoke up, "No, in fact he had promised to take her with him when the time was right for him to get out of town and live the high life with all of his accumulated wealth. It seems he was having a fling on the side with some woman bank executive. And you know how women can…"

Before he could continue, Slick asked, "I'm sorry; who are you?"

He laughed and replied, "I'm called Bubba; I'm Jake's younger brother. You know, the guy you sent to prison."

Slick recoiled and timidly said, "Oh."

Tripp and his boys all laughed and then he said, "No hard feelings, right Bubba?"

Bubba laughed and said, "Naw; Jake was a snake anyway; even though we are brothers."

Slick, looking relieved added, "Good. I'd hate to have to kick your ass too."

Bubba stood up and, grabbing Slick across the table, pulled him so that they were nose to nose. Just when I thought this was going to get very ugly, Bubba and Slick both burst out laughing.

"Okay, so I must be stupid or something. What was that all about you two?" I said, totally confused.

Slick, now laughing at the rest of us, responded, "You know my nephew Greg, Clyde's son, right?"

I replied, "Yeh, so?"

Slick continued, "Well he has an older sister, Cynthia. She and Bubba are…" Turning to Bubba, "What exactly are you two?"

Bubba replied, "We're partners. We cohabitate…"

Before he could finish Fr. Christopher jumped in with, "And I would be more than happy to bring the two of you back to the Lord."

We all paused and turned from Fr. Christopher to Bubba and back again.

"And I would be willing to make an honest woman of her, if she would stop complaining about my friends," Bubba responded.

I laughed and added, "That'll never happen. Mine complains all the time about mine." Just as the words left my lips I realized what I had just said. Slick, Sarge and even Fr. Christopher gave me looks that had daggers in them.

Trying to recover, I said, "Present company excepted, of course."

After a few moments of unbearable silence, Slick questioned, "Oh; and what other friends do you have besides us?"

Beginning to feel a little warm, with a slight sweat noticeably breaking out on my forehead, I tried to explain, "I have other friends; you don't know them, but Joanie does and she doesn't like me hanging out with them. That's why you don't know them; because I never get to hang out with them."

As I rambled, I could see the others enjoying every minute of it.

Finally, Sarge stopped me with, "Cut the crap, Hap. I expect it from Junior here, but not from you."

He shook his head and continued, "Just when I liked you better than him," looking over at Slick.

"Thanks dad, I mean Sarge. You've always been a role model for me too."

Tripp, attempting to get me out of this situation, said, "Hey, I think we need a toast. To all the shit we got away with at St. Stephen's and all the shit we're piling up now."

Fr. Christopher added, "I'll drink to that – and there was a heap of shit I got away with back then as well!"

Everyone could see our heads jerk toward Fr. Christopher as he announced this. He just raised his pint and, with a devilish grin, drank it down.

THIRTY-NINE
SATURDAY, JULY 19

"Let me guess; you'll have a western on rye, coffee – cream, no sugar, and a piece of blueberry pie with a scoop of chocolate ice cream. Right?"

"George, I don't know how you do it? You must be a mind reader or something," I responded.

"You know we do make other things here; and some are even Greek," George shot back in a tone that screamed, 'I give up on you'.

"My philosophy is, 'when you find something that you really like, don't mess with it'. But to make you happy I'll add a glass of water with lemon. There, are you satisfied?" I said with a smile.

As he turned and walked to the kitchen to give the order to his wife, who did most of the cooking, I could here him mumble – *vlakas!*

I was 'in the zone' as they say; just about to pick up the second half of my sandwich, paying no mind to the world around me, when a strange-looking man came into the diner, walked right up to the booth where I sat, and sat on the bench directly across from me. He wore a brown trench coat with matching driving gloves and hat. On his face he had an enormous pair of dark sunglasses that covered not only his eyes, but part of his cheeks as well. They were the wraparound kind, like old people wear, or a welder might use.

214

I stopped mid-bite, put my sandwich back on the plate and looked up to see him grinning at me in a somewhat sinister way.

He spoke first, "Well, Hap; it's good to see you enjoying the many things that this part of town have to offer. I hope I didn't startle you. I am here as a friend, to help guide you along on your quest."

I was completely lost by his comments. I blurted, "Who the hell are you? I know now that you're not Fr. Christopher or anyone else I know, so what do you want with me?"

He just laughed at my exasperation.

I continued, "You were the stranger that came up to me at Mulligan's weren't you? And you left that note for me. Why are you following me?"

He looked around as if to see who might be eavesdropping on us and then, turning back to me said, "I don't think it wise for me to reveal who I am just yet, but I do have some information that might be of use to you."

"Go on," I said.

He leaned in toward me and, in a low voice said, "By now I've no doubt that you have made the connection between Reilly Fitzpatrick and RJ Sweeney. I'm also sure that you have a fairly good sense of their operation in the drug and prostitution business, as well as their involvement in several drug rehab clinics."

I interrupted, "Yeh, and I've also found out about their involvement as members of board of directors of several institutions, including the one that my wife works for."

He continued as if I had never interrupted him, "Mitch Taylor's death had nothing and everything to do with the shady goings-on in the Allentown area.

This had piqued my interest. I asked, "You lost me. How is that possible; to be both everything and nothing?"

He grinned and continued, "Mitch had done some investigating of his own. He knew that Reilly and RJ were very connected and held the strings to the whole underbelly that was destroying the Allentown area. He was about to expose them and their seedy operation when he was first beaten and then murdered.

They wanted to make it look like one of the recent string of murders that has plagued the area. This way no one would be looking for the evidence that Mitch had uncovered on this whole thing. Unfortunately for Mitch the only witness to either of these events was his partner, Toby. I say unfortunate because he isn't going to talk. They've made sure of that. He knows he's next if he breathes a word to anyone of what took place."

"But how do you know all of this? The only person who would have this information would be…" I began, but was interrupted.

"Stay focused. It doesn't matter at this point how I know; suffice it to say I have it from a good source."

"All right, but how can I prove any of what you've told me? I need someone who *will* talk," I added.

As if he ignored my plea, he continued, "I want to give you one more important piece that will help you connect all of the dots in this maze. You need to talk with a man named Ivan A. Job; he's the soon-to-be AWOL accountant and 'book cooker' for a one Reilly Fitzpatrick. You'll find him hiding in apartment 13 on the third floor of the Lenox Hotel on North Street."

He continued, "Knock twice, wait a few seconds and then knock once. Then tell him 'Bob' sent you. He'll let you in and you can see for yourself how Reilly has skimmed off the top of the union pension fund and made himself a very rich man. Ivan has enough on Reilly to send him away for life! Which also makes him a prime target, so be careful not to inadvertently lead anyone to him, if you know what I mean."

As he slid out of the booth and got to his feet to make his exit, he paused, turned back once again to face me and added, "Oh, I forgot to mention, I'm Bob."

With that he turned back to leave; I leaned forward, almost jumping over the table, grabbed the sleeve of his coat and pulled him back around.

"Wait. You don't mean Bob Griffin, the reporter?"

He smiled at this.

"But he's dead; I mean, you're dead, aren't you?"

The Allentown Murders

He just smiled, took my arm off of his coat sleeve, and said, "Have a nice day. This'll be the last time you see me *dead!*"

Then he turned and began to whistle the Beatles song, "Come Together", as he walked out the door.

FORTY
MONDAY, JULY 21

"Hi Hap. Hello Connie. How is everyone on this beautiful summer day in Buffalo?" Susie said as she bounced into my office.

"Well, you're in a good mood today. Is this the same person I drove in with this morning?" I asked.

"You know I'm not a morning person; and I just happened to have a terrific morning at work. So don't spoil it."

Turning to Connie she said, "Connie, I know that I've been less than nice to you since we met, so I'd like to make it up to you. I guess I was a bit protective of Hap. You'll have to forgive me, we did grow up together and for the longest time he had a tremendous crush on me. But that ended, years ago."

Susie shot me a look; I rolled my eyes. Connie, somewhat in disbelief, looked over to me, I smiled and nodded.

Connie responded to Susie, "Well, I certainly know how catty some women can get when they've been jilted and another woman comes along and steals the man's attention. I totally understand."

I could see Susie boiling over at this. I jumped in before it got ugly, "Listen, it's a beautiful day. I'm here with two incredibly beautiful women, and it's lunchtime. It would be far too distracting for me to get any work done with the two of you here, so how about this; I'll buy you both lunch and then why don't you go do some shopping – on me. This way the two of you won't keep me from my work here, and you will have a chance to make peace and maybe even bond a little. What do you say?"

Connie looked at me with suspicion and replied, "But Hap, if we eat and then shop I won't be back to work today. And I'm sure Susie here is needed back at the hospital, right dear?"

Susie responded, "As a matter of fact, I was planning on leaving early today anyway, so I cleared my schedule for this afternoon with my supervisor. I'm free."

I smiled coyly and said, "See Connie, she's free; and so are you. Go and enjoy the day – you know, 'carpe diem'."

"Well, that's very generous of you, of the both of you that is, but today's just Monday. I could see leaving early on a Friday, but..."

I interrupted, "Not to worry. I've already cleared it with your boss."

Looking puzzled, Connie said, "But you're my boss."

"Exactly. So you're both free to go have fun. Do I have to beg you to enjoy yourself?"

Susie smiled and, grabbing Connie by the arm, said, "Let's go dear, before he changes his mind. You know how fickle men are."

They both laughed as they left the office arm in arm. Susie never ceases to amaze me at how good she is at manipulation. But she did learn it from a pro – her mother!

*   *   *

"Well, what did you find out?" I asked impatiently.

Susie smiled, pulled up a chair and sat next to me and said, "You are not going to believe this. First of all, thank you for the wonderful lunch we had at the Cloister. Then we hit all of the shops on Elmwood, near Buffalo State. We each bought an early birthday present from you."

"Wait! I thought maybe you'd go to a fast-food place, or maybe a diner. What did I buy you for your 'not' birthdays? No, how much

219

did this all cost me? Better yet, don't tell me. I'll just say you're welcome and try to figure out a reasonable response I can give Joanie when she sees the credit card bill."

Out of nowhere Susie leapt from her chair and onto my lap, throwing her arms around me and kissing me. Unfortunately, it was at that exact moment that the office door opened and in walked Connie holding a bag from George's diner on Allen Street.

With a shocked look she stammered, "Oh, I, I didn't know you were busy. I thought that you probably didn't eat lunch so I picked something up for you at your favorite place. I guess you decided to have something else for lunch."

Susie got up off of my lap, straightened her skirt and blouse, then tossed her hair back into place and sat back in her chair.

"Oh, no, it's not what you think. That is, it's not what I think you think. I mean..."

Calm as ever Susie interrupted my rambling and stated, "Oh, that? You walked in just as I was showing Hap my gratitude for the expensive lunch and gift – for the both of us; you know."

Connie walked over and put the bag on my desk saying, "Well, I guess I'll just have to show him mine the next time we're alone. For now I'll leave you two to your devices. Tata sweetie. It was fun dining and shopping with you today. I especially enjoyed the girl-talk. Oh, and don't worry Hap, Susie didn't tell any tales out of school; it was mostly about in school. Ha, ha!"

I'm dead! That's all that kept running through my mind.

Fortunately, Connie left and Susie was a few feet away now.

"Hap, aren't you going to eat your lunch. The dear girl was kind enough to drive all the way to Allentown to pick it up for you. The least you could do is eat it."

"Sure, if you'll stay in your own chair. I wouldn't want a replay of what just happened. I suppose the good news is I'm less worried about how Joanie will react to the bill than I am about how she'll react if she finds out about this!"

Susie laughed and replied, "Hap, you worry too much. I'm not about to tell her about a little kiss of appreciation and how your assistant mistook it. And I'm sure she's not about to call your wife. So don't worry; it'll be our little secret."

Somehow I didn't find that very comforting.

"Okay Susie, what did you find out?" I said after a few moments pause, and a few bites of my western sandwich.

"All right, sit down and fasten your seat belt. This is going to blow you away!"

"*I am* sitting down; so tell me already!"

"It was during lunch, over the bottle of Champaign you bought for us, that she began to open up. She told me about her brother Si and his costume shop; she told me about her dad, RJ, and how she just met them both a few months ago. Then she began to tell me about the other businesses that they are involved in; or should I say, that RJ is involved in."

I put my sandwich down at this and asked, "Well, what is he involved in? I can almost guess, but I want you to confirm my hunches."

"He is the head of a prostitution ring in Allentown. Apparently, no hooker turns a trick without him getting a piece of the action, so to speak. He also controls the drug traffic in the area. But best of all, he and that union boss, Fitzpatrick own rehab clinics, are on boards at banks and other businesses, and even on the board of trustees here at Canisius!"

"I think I just lost my appetite. That explains how Connie got the assistant position here."

"Yeh, that's how I found out he was on the board – she told me he got her the position as your assistant. And here's why; because RJ wanted to watch your every move. He also wanted to put you in a compromised position so that he could force Joanie to abandon her research."

"Now you lost me. How would my having an affair with Connie make Joanie stop her work?"

"He would use that as his hole-card, so to speak, to get you to make her stop it or expose you and ruin your marriage."

I was still puzzled, "Okay, I can see how that would work, but why would I, or for that matter, Joanie's research concern him?"

"Don't you get it? He and Fitzgerald own drug rehabilitation clinics. Fitzpatrick is on the board at Vericon! He was able to find out about her work. It seems everyone knows about her project except your friends. She told me that Joanie had found a natural remedy which is readily available and it would not only kill Vericon's project, thus setting them back millions in research dollars that they have poured into the project, but it would also give drug addicts a means to get rid of their addiction without side effects, and change their craving so that they wouldn't need RJ & Fitzpatrick's drugs or rehabilitation. Now do you get it?"

"*WOW!*" was all I could say.

"There's more."

"More than that?" I asked.

I couldn't believe what else she might have found out.

"While I can't help with the connection to Mr. Taylor's murder, I can give you some other mind-blowing news."

Just then the door opened again and in walked Connie.

"Sorry to interrupt again, but I figured I'd given you enough time to report back on everything I told you during our little outing."

Susie blushed at this. My first thought was, how much did she overhear of our conversation and why did she come back in here? Was she just playing us for fools?

I stood up and asked, "Did you tell her all this to make us look like idiots or is this some little game of yours?"

She walked over and sat in the chair on the other side of my desk from me and began, "No. Please sit back down. I knew what this lunch and shopping thing was all about. I might be from the mid-west, but I'm not some naïve farm girl."

I felt foolish at this point. Here I was a mystery writer and college professor, thinking that I was some kind of brilliant detective.

"Look it, I apologize if I, we, made it look like we were trying to use you. We are desperate to find out some things that have hit home."

She smiled and replied, "I understand, and speaking of home, that's why I gave you the information I did. My home; my half-brother and wayward father are not nice people, especially my dad, I'm ashamed to say. I knew about some of the things that were going on, but when I was asked to seduce you to destroy your marriage and your wife's work I said enough."

"Basta." I mumbled.

She looked at me and asked, "What?"

I replied, "Basta. That means 'enough' in Italian. That's what my mother always used to say when my younger brother, Jeffrey, and I would argue."

Connie, looking confused, asked, "I thought you told me you were an only child?"

Susie looking at me asked, "You *didn't*, did you?"

I just shrugged.

Then turning to Connie, she said, "Honey, he does have a brother; although he seems to forget that most of the time."

Connie continued, "But there's more of a reason I had to let you know this. Si, while he's a bit of a jerk, has been trying to look out for me; and he is not that enamored of RJ either. Not since RJ pushed him down a flight of stairs. I've even seen him backhand Si and send him onto the floor once."

I looked at Susie as if to let her know that I had a bad feeling about what Connie was about to reveal to us. I was right.

"You may not recognize him, but RJ is Ronald J. Sweeney. The Ron Sweeney that once lived in South Buffalo, around the corner from you, Hap."

Susie and I looked at each other again. This time I saw the fear in her eyes. The same fear I saw years ago when she told me about Sweeney molesting her and threatening to do the same to her younger sister if she told on him. And I know she saw the same fear in my eyes that told of the beating I got from Ron Sweeney after Slick and I made those prank phone calls to his house, attempting to scare him.

Connie looked at the two of us and said, "You two look as if you've seen a ghost."

Susie responded, "We have."

After a short time; time enough to digest all of this information I asked Connie about how she ended up here with Ron Sweeney, and was she related to Hari, his wife.

"I never knew Hari, but we exchanged letters for a while. She was the one who convinced me to come here to stay with them. She seemed to be a loving wife and a kind person," she said.

"Yes, she was. Unfortunately, she didn't know what a horrible person she was stuck with all those years. I guess he left a trail of unwed mothers along the way, through every town he was run out of, from Texas to New York. Poor Hari stuck with him. I guess, from what you've said, she knew about these affairs he had," I added.

"She must have. She found me and before I could come here, she had finally left him; and then she died. So I didn't pursue meeting him. It was shortly after, when I graduated from college, that he must have found the letters I sent her and he contacted me. He asked me to come to Buffalo to stay with him and his son, my half-brother. So I agreed, and here I am."

"What about your mom?" Susie asked.

"Oh, my mom's fine. In fact, she married when I was about five years old. He was quite an interesting man. He died three years ago. He traveled a lot; and he drank a lot. I guess that happens to entertainers quite a bit. He was hit by a train; the train he was supposed to be on that was headed for Cleveland to do a show. Instead he had been drinking and staggered onto the tracks thinking he could stop the train so that he could get on and not miss his performance. I guess you could say that *that* was his greatest performance. If only he could've stopped the train."

I took a deep breath and said, "That must have been devastating to you and your mom."

"It was; more so to her. I did like him though. I'll never forget, at my first communion party he did a show for all my family and friends who came. It was my best remembrance of him. In fact, I have

224

a picture from that day, although I was crying in the picture. I wanted to wear my white gloves, but my mother couldn't find them. I have it here. He's in the background holding his marionettes. He was a *puppeteer!*"

She pulled an old picture out of her wallet and put it on my desk. Susie and I both leaned in to take a close look at it.

"Oh, that red box I'm staring at in the picture was put there by the photographer. He thought that the photo needed some more color to match the background, since I was all in white. These two puppets in the picture were my step-father's favorites; one a Jester and the other a Wizard," she added.

Susie and I stared, almost blindly at the photo for what seemed like eternity. Finally, Susie and I turned to each other and nodded. Connie looked unsure of what we were thinking and said, "I know it's not the best communion picture, but that's my family."

I spoke up, "No, it's fine. I'm sorry. You must think that we're both crazy."

Susie added, "You see Hap has been having these reoccurring nightmares where a little girl all dressed in white, with puppets just like the ones in your picture and a red box on the ground, is crying as she looks down at the box."

We could see a look of amazement on Connie's face.

"I thought that the little girl was someone else. I also thought that she was warning me of something; something to do with the costume shop that your brother owns. Now it all makes sense. You were the little girl in my dreams, and the puppets were your stepfather's. That box was the box that held the acetates and had the cord fashioned like a hangman's noose tied on it. All of it was pointing me toward one thing."

I paused to find the words, and then said, "The dream was leading me to you and the shop, and Si and to – *Ron Sweeney!*"

FORTY-ONE
THURSDAY, JULY 31

"Slick, what have you found out from Toby?" I asked as the six of us gathered around the kitchen table at our tiny upper flat apartment on Indian Church Road.

"Well, as usual, I was able to rise above my overpowering masculine demeanor and get in touch with my softer side, if you get my drift," Slick said, grinning.

"Oh my God; here we go," Susie bemoaned with a sigh.

Joanie stepped in, "Enough of the BS, Slick. Tell us what you've found out about my father's murder."

Slick, realizing how serious she was, said, "I'm sorry. I sometimes get carried away with myself. It wasn't as much of what he said; it was more of what he didn't say. I could tell he was terrified of these men and what might happen to him, especially with his protector gone. What I *did* get from the conversation was that he was there at both times. I have no doubt that he was there and saw Mr. Taylor being beaten by those thugs, and again when they returned to hang him. He had to have been a witness to them both; he knew too much to not have been there!"

I could see the fire in Joanie's eyes as Slick revealed this. She wanted to kill Toby and I couldn't blame her; but I knew I had to stop her.

226

"Joanie. Don't worry, Toby will get his due before this is all over; but for now, leave him to God."

"And then the police," Susie spoke out.

"Right," I added.

Joanie smiled at us and said, "As much as I'd like to kill him myself, I hope you know I wouldn't. In a way, I almost understand how he must have felt at the time, the poor pathetic creature."

Fr. Christopher chimed in, "As Hap said, it is for God to decide his penance, and his punishment; not us."

Seeing a lull in the conversation, Susie jumped up and grabbed Slick. She whispered something to him and he ran out of the room.

"Hold it everyone; I've got something important to say before we get too much further into our discussion. *Slick...Slick...SLICK!*"

"*WHAT?* You don't have to yell. I'm moving as fast as I can with a big cake in my hands. You wouldn't want me to drop it, now would you?"

Susie continued, "Well, I guess you can figure out the surprise we have is for Joanie and Hap. Today is their tenth wedding anniversary, so we thought it would be nice to celebrate it since we're all together."

I looked over at Joanie, who was about to cry, and then stood up and said, "That's great of you guys. I didn't think anyone would remember; and by Joanie's reaction, I guess you caught her by surprise as well. Why don't we take a break and have some cake and coffee (*looking over at Sarge*) or beer, and then get back to our discussion."

"Now where were we? Oh, Yeh. Let's hear from each of you as to what you have found out," I said.

Almost out of nowhere, Sarge, coming back from the frig with a bottle of Genny Cream Ale stated, "When I was in the Big One, WW II, we used to say..."

Just in time Fr. Christopher stopped him with, "I was in that one too; but weren't you stationed at Ft. Dix, New Jersey during the war? Now how about we stick to the present and make plans for the future."

I smiled at him, as if to say thank you. Not that I don't enjoy Sarge's tales of made-up heroism and battle strategies, but this was not the time for that.

"This is even too early for *you* to start drinking, Sarge!" Slick said watching him open his beer.

"I don't tell you that it's too early for you to say something stupid, do I?" Sarge shot back.

A bit flustered Sarge began, "I've infiltrated behind enemy lines; that is, I got a job as one of Jimmy's boys. I'm kind of in the background, you know, there to rough someone up if they need it. But I have been in the room with him and Reilly for one of their meetings. I learned that they have plans to go after a certain research leader at Vericon to convince her to lose her data on the drug addiction project. I'm guessing *that* someone is you, Joanie."

Joanie interjected, "Well, I guess everyone in the world knows about my research, so I might as well fill you all in."

She looked over at me and I gave her a nod.

She continued, "Where do I begin? About a year and a half ago I discovered a chemical compound, mostly made up of things that you might find growing wild in nature that had a curious effect on the behavior of our lab animals that we were using to test it. We first found that this new compound made them less rigidly tied to previous behavior patterns. As we watched these changes we postulated that maybe this might be just the right formula to change other behaviors, such as curbing the desire for certain cravings."

As I looked at the six of us around the table I could see that the others were all mesmerized by what Joanie was relating.

"One thing led to another and soon enough we began testing it for use as a means to inhibit that part of the brain that controls addictive behavior. As we moved to test groups we found that it worked very well in almost entirely eliminating addiction to many drugs out on the street without the painful withdrawal symptoms."

Fr. Christopher said, "Well, that's wonderful! So what was the problem? Wasn't Vericon thrilled with this discovery? And if Reilly and RJ are on the board there, wouldn't they be thrilled as well?"

I interjected, "They would if it weren't for their drug rehabilitation centers and drug ring operation. You see, up until this they controlled the entire cycle – they created the garbage and then took it out! The best part was, they got to repeat the same cycle with most of the same customers, while adding new ones all the time. Perfect, heh?"

Joanie went on, "It wasn't bad enough that we had come across something that might hurt their business, but it was the next step that led them and Vericon to want to kill the project. You see this new compound, like most drugs on the market today, don't come without a cost; and this was no exception. In fact, some of the side effects could be life threatening to the person using it. That's just one of the things we deal with in this business."

Slick, looking confused, questioned, "So Vericon thought that it was too risky?"

Joanie chuckled, "No, not at all. Big pharmaceutical companies don't look at the small picture like we tend to; they look at the greater good. And this had great potential. Remember, not everyone who would take this would be harmed or die from it. It would only be a small percent that would be adversely effected – collateral damage, if you will."

Susie spoke next, "So you were getting heat from both ends on this, but why from your company? I would've thought that they would be happy with your work."

"They were; that is, until I remembered something that I once read. In fact, I now think that I came up with much of this formula from that piece I read some years back. You see; most of what is in this compound is readily available in nature. As a matter of fact, Native American tribes discovered it hundreds of years ago and have used it successfully for all this time. That's what I read; it was in a book on Native American remedies. The things we added to the formula are the things that bring about the side effects. But we have no control over that, the Food and Drug Administration dictates that each new drug has certain kinds of additives – for safety reasons, they say. So the best cure for drug addiction is something we can all get our hands on and administer without the help of any doctor, nurse or pharmaceutical company. How's that!"

I added, "From seeing everyone's expression I think we all get it, but tell them how that sits with Vericon higher-ups."

"When I told my supervisor and he sent it upstairs they hit the roof. The company had just spent a year and a half and millions of dollars on a drug that they can't patent and get rich from. As you might guess, they didn't like it one bit. In fact, word came down almost immediately that my recent findings were to disappear and the drug we were working on was to be sent immediately for approval. I was kept on as team leader, but put in an advisory position. This way, still being an employee I was bound by my non-disclosure agreement. I can't tell anyone about this. I've even had threats made against me if any of this ever comes to light."

Slick let out a moan and said, "Wow, this is unbelievable. Sarge, would you get me a beer while you're up?"

"Sure Junior," Sarge said with a grin.

Susie chimed in, "Slick, is that all you can think about – a beer? After Joanie just poured out her heart!"

"I'm sorry, but that drained me. I need the beer to digest it all," Slick returned.

Looking over at Susie, and wanting to move on, I asked, "Susie, what can you tell us about Connie and what she's told you?"

She went on to relate to the group what she had learned, most of which I had been privy to as well. When she told the group about the photo of Connie as a little girl there was a noticeable gasp from the group.

Fr. Christopher posited, "So this was the omen foretelling of things to come; this is what led you to Allentown and the man who murdered your father-in-law."

"Now it all makes some sense. But what I can't understand is how you were able to see the future?" Sarge asked.

"It's a gift; pure and simple – it's a gift," I replied with a smile.

Next our attention turned to Fr. Christopher, who had been given the task of pumping Si for information.

"Si Norom, I found, is nothing more than a young man looking to please his father; to make him proud of who he has become. Unfortunately, his father could care less about his son. He sees him as a pawn, someone he sees as a means to an end. That end is expanding the wealth and power he believes he deserves."

He went on to relate how Sweeney had a hand in all of the murders that occurred in recent years and why he committed them.

I was the last to relate what I had found out and how I had been in contact with a stranger who appears to be leading me to find answers to the unanswered questions.

"Be careful, Hap. Sometimes what seems like a friend is someone who is trying to win over your confidence only to crush you at the end," Fr. Christopher reminded me.

"Oh, I'm well aware of that possibility. I'll heed President Reagan's advice, 'Trust, but verify.'"

"Did he say that in one of his cowboy movies?" Slick added, wearing his typical shit-eating grin.

"See what I have to live with?" Susie moaned.

"And that's why I gave him to you. He about drove me to drink!" Sarge added.

Slick shot back, "You *do* drink; and quite a lot, I might add!"

Sarge smiled and said, "See what I mean."

FORTY-TWO
FRIDAY, AUGUST 1

As I cautiously entered the union hall to meet with Reilly Fitzpatrick, I paused to question the wisdom in attending this meeting. I know it's not the best thing for me to be doing, but I need to find out about this Ivan character before I venture up to the Lenox Hotel. That may be a trap set by my mystery man, Bob. It's better to play it a little safe than to rush into things only to find out that you've been had. And if this stranger is telling me the truth it won't hurt to find out more before I talk with the accountant.

"Mr. Fitzpatrick, thank you for agreeing to meet with me. I'm in town partly to teach at Canisius College; but also to do research on my new book, 'The Allentown Murders'."

With a suspicious look he replied, "I know that already. I also know that you're the son-in-law of one of our beloved and highly esteemed community leaders, the late Mitch Taylor. Yes, that was indeed a tragic death, and so young. Well, anyway he's gone and nothing can bring him back, right? *So why are you trying?"*

His tone suddenly got much more aggressive. I was set back on my heels. At this point I wasn't sure what to expect from him or his two goons that were now flanking me as we sat in the dimly lit and very empty union hall just downstairs from his office. I didn't like what I was feeling right at this moment.

He then let out a laugh and said, "Had you going there for a minute, didn't I? No, I am sad to say Mitch Taylor is gone, but his spirit will live on; I'll see to that. I've even had our union kick in some money to perpetuate what he started here in the Allentown area. We're putting up a plaque in his honor right on the outside of his shop. But you're not here for all of that. What can I help you with?"

"I was hoping that you could give me some information...for my book, I mean. I'm sure you might have some inside knowledge about the other murders that have occurred here over the past few years. That's what I'm writing about."

"Oh, do you hear that boys? He thinks I know something about the murders? What do you think about that?"

Jimmy and Tony laughed and then Tony spoke up, "Gee boss, I thought that I killed those people. You mean to tell me that you did it?"

They laughed again, and at my expense. Mustering some courage to continue I said, "What I meant to say was, 'What can you tell me about a guy named Ivan A. Job?' His name came up as a possible suspect in a lot of what has been going on around Allentown."

I was hoping that they would bite and confirm that he worked for Fitzpatrick and that he might know something about the embezzlement of union funds, and about the murders – especially Mitch Taylor's.

The room became eerily quiet. The echoes from the laughter and discussion of only a minute ago were gone. All that remained was silence.

Breaking the excruciating minutes of nothingness Fitzpatrick suggested, "Boys, why don't you take Mr. Pozner out to the back room where I keep the books and let him take a look at whatever he wants."

Turning back to me, he then said, "Now Mr. Pozner, you can look, but you can't touch. In other words, what I'm letting you in on is strictly off the record. It seems you want the answer to your every question; and you want them now. But I'd like you to use what you learn tonight as a lesson in restraint."

I didn't like him referring to me as Mr. Pozner. That invariably signals that something bad is about to happen; and his remark about me learning a lesson in restraint tonight was a bit too ominous for my liking.

He got up, shook my hand and said goodbye. He then made his was out the door to a waiting car and chauffeur which whisked him away. Meanwhile, Tony and Jimmy led me to the backroom, closed and locked the door, spun me around and glared at me.

Jimmy shouted, "What do you know about Ivan; and where is that little rat-bastard?"

Tony added, "This is what happens to someone who gets too nosey!"

At that they both began to pound on me. I fought back as best I could, but to no avail. The one good thing about this beating I was taking was that it confirmed that Ivan *did* exist and that they were looking for him as well.

It was then that the cavalry came! A few loud booming noises came from outside the door that led to the back alley; and then with a loud crash it flew open and in came Sarge and Fr. Christopher screaming and swinging as they came.

Tony and Jimmy were caught completely off guard by this flurry of fists and, within a matter of minutes were subdued by my old friends. Seeing the situation, they both got up off of the floor, and, licking their wounds, ran off into the night. The three of us just laughed. It was more of a laugh of relief than of joy. We were all grateful that this encounter didn't end up with one or all of us lying in a pool of our own blood.

"They confirmed it. Ivan does exist; and he is the key to bringing down this whole evil empire of Fitzpatrick's," I stated.

Sarge added, "Then we need to pay this Mr. Job a visit right away. What do you say boys?"

Fr. Christopher chimed in using his sometime-Irish brogue, "It's a fine day that the good Lord has given us, me lads; a fine day indeed."

FORTY-THREE
TUESDAY, AUGUST 5

"Hap, I'm going to go over to Caz Park. I want to take a little walk," Joanie said, as if out of nowhere.

"What? We just got home from work; aren't you tired?" I replied; a bit surprised at her suggestion.

"I am tired, but I need to get some fresh air. Besides, this is the best time of year in Buffalo, weather-wise, that is," she added.

Not wanting to dampen her enthusiasm I suggested, "I'll come along with you to keep you company then."

"No Hap. I want to be alone, no offense. I need to sort some things out, and you need to relax. You had quite a harrowing experience only a few days ago. Don't worry, I can take care of myself."

"All right; I was just trying to be sociable," I remarked.

"I know; but I need to do this. I'll be back in about an hour," she said as she left the apartment.

"Hap, I'm back and I have someone with me I want you to meet."

I had been working on my book and completely forgot about the time or what Joanie was doing. It's a good thing she didn't need my help. But whom did she bring back with her?

"I'm coming right out; who's with you?" I asked as I left my desk.

When I got to the kitchen doorway, I was suddenly frozen in place by the sight of the man sitting next to Joanie at the table. He had a big grin on his face; a brown trench coat and fedora lay over the back of another chair, and a folder was on the table in front of him.

Joanie stood up and, putting her hands on her hips announced, "Hap come over here. I want you to meet Bob Griffin."

I smiled and greeted him with, "So your Bob Griffin, the reporter."

Joanie, looking confused at my not being surprised, said, "Yes, Bob Griffin, the reporter; the man who sent you those notes and news clippings; the mystery man that you met at Mulligan's and again at George's; the man that was burned beyond recognition in that car crash. Yeh, but how did you know?"

"Hello Mr. Pozner; or maybe I should call you by your first name, Hap. After all, we're not exactly strangers any longer, are we?" he said with a friendly smile.

"I suppose we aren't. It's a pleasure to finally meet you – that is, meet you as you. What I don't know is how you managed to fake your own death."

"Well, I didn't exactly fake my own death; at least not without the unwitting help of a one Reilly Fitzpatrick. But let me tell you all about it."

As we all sat at the kitchen table, he began his story.

"I picked up a hitchhiker at the foot of the Skyway downtown; after almost hitting him, I might add. It was just past midnight – early Saturday morning, May 3. I say I almost hit the poor guy; but it wasn't due to bad driving, as I thought then. Apparently someone had tampered with my steering.

Anyway, we were at the Catt-Rez gas station on Route 5 in Evangola, almost to the Chautauqua County line. I got out of the car and stretched my legs as I gassed up the Pinto, when all of a sudden it hit me."

He paused for a moment to reflect. We could see the pain in his eyes as he continued his story.

"This poor guy had over a thousand miles to go, and I was only a couple of miles from my destination. You could say it was one of those moments when fate takes you by the hand and guides you. I thought I would be charitable and help him out. But it didn't turn out that way; it did, however, save *my* life.

When the tank was full, I walked over to Jonah, who had gotten out to stretch his legs, smiled and said, 'It looks like this'll be the end of the ride for us cowboy'.

When I said this I could see he misunderstood my intent. He shook my hand, and, as he began to walk away, I grabbed his arm and handed him the keys. With a puzzled look on his face, he asked, 'Y'all changed your mind and want *me* to drive?'

I smiled, shook my head and replied, 'No, I'm giving you the car. You have a lot further to go than I do. I have a place just a few miles south of here.'"

He stopped to take a breath, then let out a sigh and continued with his story, "I could see his sad smile as he fought back the tears that had begun to well up in his eyes.

As he grabbed the keys, he also grabbed me and said, 'Thank you friend. I'll never forget this'.

I waved at my car as it faded out of sight around the curve headed south to wherever his final destination was. I was feeling good about my charitable act when I realized the added benefit. If Fitzpatrick or any of the others were to come looking for me, I would be gone – headed south! As far as they or anyone else for that matter knew, I had decided to leave the state!"

He looked up at us and smiled. Then he went on, "I found myself talking out loud as I started my trek toward my cottage just a few miles over the bridge ahead."

He stopped and, waxing philosophical, added, "Try as I might to be a 'do-gooder', my act of kindness was tainted with a bit of larceny in it. Oh well, '*Rome wasn't built in a day*', *now was it?*"

He caught himself with this last phrase; pausing as he realized that he was quoting someone else.

He looked again at us and, with a broad smile on his face, added, "As I just now said this, I was reminded of where I heard it recently; that's the connection between RJ and Fitzpatrick. They are one and the same person!"

Joanie and I both looked at him in amazement as he said this. I asked, "You mean to tell us that Fitzpatrick doesn't exist?"

He laughed and said, "I'm not sure which one doesn't exist, but I do know that there is only one of them that does."

Joanie said, "Please, continue with your story. I want to know the rest of the details of what happened."

He continued with his story, "I was startled back to reality when I heard a loud crash in the near distance, just around the curve where Routes 5 and 20 merge. In the darkness I could see a bright light, a flame reaching for the sky, at what appeared to be the bridge between Erie and Chautauqua Counties.

I began to walk faster; then run toward the bridge. As I rounded the curve, in sight of the old bridge spanning the Cattaraugus Creek, I could see it. There was a car lying upside down in the creek bed. It had apparently been driving too fast for the turn onto the bridge and broke through a guardrail sending it into the air and down to the creek below.

I crossed the bridge and ran down the 30-foot embankment to the burning car to see if anyone was still in it. As I approached the inferno, I stopped and gasped in horror; it was my Pinto!

The gas tank apparently had ruptured, causing the loud explosion I heard in the distance, as the tank we had just filled a few minutes ago ignited into flames.

'Jonah! Jonah!' I screamed; but all I could hear was my voice echo in the cold, dark night. The car was now totally engulfed in the hot, blinding tongues that licked the paint and rubber from the lifeless vessel. As I knelt down to see inside I could make out what appeared to be the burning body of the poor, lifeless remains of the man I was only trying to help.

'Jonah, in the belly of the whale,' was all that I could muster as I watched, helpless to do anything.

Sitting, now at the edge of the creek with my head in my hands, I prayed for him – and myself. Did I send him to his death intentionally? I thought about the steering problem and how I almost killed him downtown at the foot of the Skyway; and now, how I somehow finished the job.

'That's crazy! Don't overthink this thing,' I shouted at myself.

But someone did tamper with the steering on my car. They must have.

'They wanted me dead; well, now I am!' I told myself. I could feel an evil grin come across my face. Now I could continue my investigation and bring these criminals to justice.

'Jonah, I'm sorry for what has happened. You will never see the Atlantic or dip his toes in the Gulf, or feel the warm nights on those tropical beaches. This is your last beach,' I said to Jonah as I watched him burn.

'I never meant for any harm to come to you; but your death will help me find your killers and punish them. I promise you vengeance,' I continued as I stood and held a fist up to the black, night sky.

As I said these words I could hear sirens off in the distance. Someone must have heard the explosion or seen the flames and reported it. If I planned to remain dead, I knew I had better get away from there fast.

I found myself running, ducking behind buildings off the road as I made my way toward my cottage at Sunset Beach.

That poor son-of-a-bitch died in my place. But maybe his death won't be in vain. He was about my age, size and general features...and he was wearing my clothes!

He was a drifter. I didn't imagine that anyone would miss him or wonder whatever happened to Randolph Scott.

I hid out in the brush near my cottage and let the police get there before I showed up, so Kate's reaction to my death would look real to them. I hated to do that to her, but it was the only way anyone would believe her; she's not very good at putting on an act. Once they were gone I could show up, let her know I was alive and tell her what happened."

He stopped for a moment and began to mumble, "Maybe that's what Fitzpatrick had in mind for me all along. That's why he let me go, only to die in an accidental car crash somewhere.'"

He continued, "It was then that I decided to do a little of my own slight of hand. Fortunately, I was only a few miles away from my cottage and, with Kate's help, I could become a ghost and help put *RJ Fitzpatrick* and his thugs away for good; and I could do it with the help of my new best friend – *you Hap!*"

After he finished giving us the details of his demise and resurrection, we moved on to how he met Joanie in Cazenovia Park.

"I've been following her lately. I was afraid that they might try to kill her, or at least rough her up, especially after the attempt on you. I figured after all you 've done for me the least I could do would be to watch out for your wife. As you know, these are dangerous people we're dealing with. I couldn't take any chances, so I arranged to meet with her today in the park."

"I had a suspicion that you were still alive, especially when I found out that Fr. Christopher wasn't my mystery stranger," I said.

"Who is that?" Bob asked.

"I'll tell you all about him, and Sarge and the others later; but for right now, I'm curious as to what you have in that folder; and, even more curious as to why you decided to reveal yourself to us now. I guess my ego is a little bruised as well, since you didn't reveal your identity to me, but to Joanie."

They looked at each other and laughed. Joanie got up and came over to me, sitting opposite them at the table.

Kissing me on the head and mussing my hair she said, "Poor baby. You feel slighted. Oh, we're sorry." She laughed some more.

I spoke up, "I don't find it that amusing. Would someone please let me in on the joke here."

Bob looked over to Joanie, she smiled, and he began, "Well Hap, it was more a matter of circumstance than anything that I met with Joanie today instead of you. After our last meeting I talked to my snitch, Ivan, about how far Fitzpatrick and Sweeney were willing to go on this drug research thing. He told me that they had already been plotting to 'take care of' the person in charge of the project – Joanie. This was late last week. Fortunately, they were going to use a lower level contract hit man to do the job. That's where I came in. Through some contacts I had in my 'previous life' I took the contract to rough her up."

Just then Joanie took over, "That's when Bob first came to me. He told me about what was going on and said he would report through the chain that I would be compliant. This way no harm would come to me."

I interrupted, "And you didn't tell me because...? I thought that the wives were always the last to know; it seems that I'm always the one."

Chuckling at my remark Bob added, "I can attest to that. Just ask my ex-wife."

Joanie gave a look that told us she didn't find any of this humorous; so we pushed on.

Bob continued, "When we met today, it was at my request. I needed to make sure that there were no other contacts from Fitzpatrick or his thugs, and to bring you these."

He opened the folder sitting on the table in front of him. As he pulled out the contents I could see documents, spreadsheets and photos of some of the victims; not ones taken by the police, but ones taken right after the murders – these were taken by the murderers.

"As you can see, the person taking the photos was a rank amateur. Rule number one of crime scene photography is, don't put any part of yourself in the picture; and never, I mean never put anything in the picture that can help identify the perpetrator. Things like reflections in a mirror of the killer's face have a tendency to end up as evidence in court."

After Bob showed us all of the evidence, which included spreadsheets showing how Ivan had fudged the numbers for Fitzpatrick, he told us how he had been working with Mr. Taylor and how they almost had what they needed to blow this whole thing open. That's why Fitzpatrick had to eliminate the both of them. Bob was lucky; Mitch was not.

FORTY-FOUR
THURSDAY, AUGUST 14

"Mr. and Mrs. Pozner, we're sorry that it's taken months to wrap up this case; to conclude this chapter in you lives, what with the murder of your father and all. We're deeply sorry that it took this long," Detective Holmes said, as Joanie, Susie, Slick and I all sat in the outer lobby of the downtown headquarters of the Buffalo Police Department.

"And, if I may, we are very grateful for the trouble you all went through to assist us in uncovering the perpetrators. With the material evidence and witnesses you've provided we can now hand it all over to the D.A., who, last we talked, is ecstatic. He tells me that this might just turn out to be the biggest case he's seen since the trials stemming from the Magaddino crime family war that ran from the 1960s until a few years ago!" Detective Dobson added.

Holmes remarked, "Yeh, as a matter of fact there were many in the department that thought that the string of killings in Allentown were somehow related to that war. But hanging people is not their style."

Dobson added, "No; one bullet through the head is their MO. This was more of what a serial killer would do. Not just the hanging of the victim, but the fact that they all happened within a few blocks of each other."

Holmes continued, "Right. And all of the victims, except for Mitch Taylor, were snitches; and he was leading the way to run Fitzpatrick out of this part of town. So that made him a threat as well. We couldn't tell you before, but the fact that the victims were either gay or prostitutes really didn't come into play here."

"Nor did the fact that they were all junkies and owed money to their dealers," Dobson interjected.

"We, along with other law enforcement agencies, were collaborating to bring Fitzpatrick and his crime organization down. The information from these poor slobs was just a small part of the operation we were conducting. You dad was working with an investigative reporter named Bob Griffin, trying to get some solid evidence on Fitzpatrick. So you see, this case had many facets to it, with a lot of people working to shut down Fitzpatrick's operation. The notion that it was a serial killer was our first thought, but there were too many other things that pointed toward something else," Dobson added.

Susie commented, "After all of our work what will happen to Fitzpatrick and Sweeney?"

Slick added, "Yeh, what about Fitzpatrick and Sweeney?"

Dobson replied, "Well, Mr. and Mrs. Graham..."

Susie interrupted, "I'm Susie Brennan. Mr. Graham here hasn't seen fit to commit himself to much of anything so far."

Slick added, "And you can call me Slick; Mr. Graham was my grandfather's name."

Looking puzzled at his remark Dobson commented, "That's unusual; most people would say 'that's my father's name'."

Slick replied wearing his shit-eating grin, "Naw, my dad's Sarge; just Sarge."

"Okay...as I was about to say, Slick, Reilly Fitzpatrick and RJ Sweeney are one and the same. Sweeney created Fitzpatrick so that he could run his operation without his checkered past coming back to haunt him. We have a file two inches thick on Sweeney; but Fitzpatrick, since he really never existed, was off the radar," she continued.

The Allentown Murders

Holmes spoke up, "The bad news is they both disappeared; that is, Sweeney has fled the country."

"Just great; after all of our work, not to mention the help of Bob Griffin, only for Sweeney to slip through your hands. My father is dead and you let him get away," Joanie remarked.

Holmes and Dobson looked at each other and hung their heads, knowing Joanie was right.

Dobson said, "We are truly sorry. We didn't get the bad guy this time. Unfortunately, in our line of work that happens much more than we would like; but we're not through."

When she said this our ears perked up. Joanie remarked, "What can you do at this point? How will you find him?"

Holmes replied, "Since he is wanted for murder, embezzlement and other assorted felonies we can get the Feds involved. With them working for us he can run, but he can't hide. We *will* find him and bring him to justice! And, on another note, we have rounded up the top men in his crime ring; and those low-level criminals that we didn't, have scattered to places far from here."

Dobson, seeing Joanie's grave disappointment, got up and walked over to where Joanie and I were sitting, and, putting an arm across Joanie's shoulder, added, "I know this is not what you had hoped for, nor any of us for that matter, but the wheels of justice sometimes turn very slowly; but I promise you we will not let your dad's murder get buried in the cold case files in the basement."

"We'll stay in touch with you and keep you up-to-date as we try to locate him. But the good news is that when a criminal this slippery gets away with as much money as he did they always leave a trail. All we have to do is follow the money and we'll find him," Holmes said.

"Not to mention his two, very disappointed, henchmen – Jimmy and Tony. Don't forget, he burned them pretty bad. I'm sure they will be more than willing to help us find Sweeney, especially if we cut a deal with them," Dobson concluded.

Hearing this I could see Joanie and the others perk up a bit. I remarked, "That's all any of us can ask of you. Thanks for all of your help."

Holmes asked, "Call us any time, you hear? So, what are your plans now?"

Joanie answered, "I've got some unfinished business at work to complete. I think I found the answer to a sticking point because of all of this. I guess you could say my father taught me one last important lesson in life."

I could see the confused look on everyone's face; but Joanie had a knowing smile on her face, so none of us wanted to ask her to explain – at least not now. She needed to enjoy the moment.

"And I guess I'll be looking for a new graduate assistant," I laughed.

Joanie turned to me and said, "No you won't. I think the one you have is just fine."

I gave her a warm smile back. It's good to know she trusts me that much; and, hey, Connie did help us in the end. Maybe it'll all work out okay.

Susie, in her usual never happy way, stated, "Well, I for one want to go home. I'm missing the best part of the tanning season back in Wilmington."

We all laughed at this.

I turned to Slick and asked, "Well Slick, you've been pretty quiet through all of this, which is not at all like you; what are your plans?"

Out of nowhere he blurted, "Um, um, I, I guess I plan to ask Susie to marry me."

We were all stunned.

Thinking that this would make Susie happy, we turned toward her as she got up from her chair and walked over to Slick, who got up thinking she wanted to kiss him, or at least give him a hug.

When she reached Slick she hauled off and smacked him in the face saying, "What kind of proposal was that? You propose to me through Hap? You weren't even addressing me; and in the lobby of the Buffalo Police Station to boot! Oh, and where's the ring, huh?"

As she rambled on, Joanie and I said our goodbyes to Detectives Holmes and Dobson; I grabbed Slick by the arm and pulled him out the door, while Joanie put her arm around Susie, trying to calm her down.

"So I guess that means yes," Slick confided as we took in the warm summer sunshine in downtown Buffalo.

FORTY-FIVE
WEDNESDAY, AUGUST 20

"Well?"

"Well, what?" Joanie replied.

"You know, that thing about the lesson from your dad."

"Oh that thing. What about it?" she responded.

Beginning to get a little annoyed at her evasive tactic, I remarked, "Okay, if you don't want to talk about it I can respect that. I'm sure that there are many things that I probably won't want to discuss in the future. I'm good with that."

I thought that this might get her to talk; but she proved once again that she's too smart for the 'bait and switch' move.

"Hap, did you really think you could extort a response out of me? Please!"

"All right, so I'm not Slick," I replied.

"Honey, Slick's not even that slick!" she said with a grin.

We sat there in our tiny apartment kitchen eating breakfast, getting ready to leave for work – in silence.

Finally, after finishing her cereal, Joanie looked up at me and commented, "It's killing you, isn't it?"

"What? I haven't a clue as to what you're referring," I said nonchalantly.

"Okay, since I'm going in today to clean things up, I might just as well let you be the first to know, " she said in a patronizing tone.

"Look it, if you don't want to tell me, you don't have to," I responded.

"Oh, don't pout; I was planning on telling you anyway. I just like to make you work for it," she said with a laugh.

She continued, "I'm going to the third floor at Vericon today to hand in my resignation. What I learned from my dad was you have to stand for something; and I'm standing for helping people that need help badly, not for some corporate clones that think only of the bottom line."

"Good for you; and by the way, I approve. Although I don't know if that really mattered anyway," I responded.

"Now don't play hurt. This is a big moment for me and I need your support more than ever," she added.

"Okay, but what is it that you're going to do?"

Joanie's face became intense as she stated, "I'm going to publish my real findings; the one that goes all the way back in Native American medical history to their discovery of the treatment of chronic addictive behavior; the natural remedy. I'm going to send it to newspapers, magazines, journals, radio, television and any other medium that I can think of that will spread the word."

"So I guess this makes us a one income couple again," was all that I could get out.

"No. More like a one income family!" she said with a grin.

It took me a few seconds to filter what she just said and finally, after a short delay, I lit up, "You mean you're..."

She nodded and just said, "What do you think?"

FORTY-SIX
SUNDAY, AUGUST 31

"Do we really have to go, Hap? You know how I hate parties at Sarge's. It always ends up in a fight," Joanie moaned, as we got ready.

Shaking my head at her complaint, I responded, "You know we have to. Besides, your mom and mine and my brother, not to mention Fr. Christopher, will all be there. Oh, I almost forgot, Karen, Susie's mom will be there too. And you know I invited Bob Griffin and his assistant turned girlfriend, Kate, as well. I'm sure there will be enough of us to keep Sarge and Slick from trying to kill each other."

"All right. But if they start, we leave. Got it," she commanded.

"I wouldn't have it any other way; and, look on the bright side, Slick and Susie will announce their 'real' engagement and wedding date, we can announce the coming of our new family member, and who knows, maybe Sarge will announce his opening a new chapter of Alcoholics Anonymous!" I said with a laugh.

"And that's why you're a fiction writer; because you think the impossible and try to get us to believe it's possible. And by the way, I don't want you to make a big thing about the pregnancy; the focus tonight needs to be on Susie and Slick's engagement," Joanie said in a stern voice.

She continued, "Just keep them apart; got it!"

The Allentown Murders

"Sheesh. You'd think that they were bitter enemies or something. That's just their way of showing affection to one another. It's sort of a bonding ritual with them. But okay, I'll do my best."

*   *   *

"Sarge, I want to thank you for having this party," I said in an attempt to mingle with the big group that milled around Sarge's modest ranch house.

Sarge replied, "Well, Hap, we have a lot to be thankful for tonight; for me it's that Tops Supermarket got in a new shipment from the Genesee Brewing Company. That's why I was able to stock up my Genny Cream Ale supply enough to have this party. Ha!"

Overhearing this, Slick commented, "I guess that puts my news in second place. Oh well, here we go. Susie, I think we'd better make our announcement while Sarge is still conscious. I'm sure he's going to want to hear this. Can I have everyone's attention please? Susie and I have an announcement."

Looking over at Susie, Slick gives her the nod to make it.

"Well; he's finally done it. After many years of waiting and wondering, I might add, Slick has finally asked me to marry him. That's right he proposed right in front of our best friends, God and the Buffalo Police Department, not to mention a few druggies and hookers! We've set the date for May 1st next year..."

Slick interrupted, "In the Spring; this way she can wear white."

Everyone stopped at this; the women gasped, while the men chuckled under their breath.

Susie shot Slick a few daggers and continued, "...and you're all invited, of course. As you might expect Joanie will be my maid-of-honor and Hap is going to be my best man...I mean Slick's best man."

You could see a noticeable blush race across Susie's face at this faux pas. It made me wonder if she didn't still have a slight crush on me.

There I go again; Joanie would just tell me that I'm making something out of nothing. But, I wonder, mm.

After all the slaps on the back and hugs – and crying, which was mostly done by the girls, we toasted the couple.

Making their entrance at a most opportune moment, Bob and Kate arrived. They both still looked a bit worse for wear from their encounters with Sweeney and his men not that long ago.

Slick came over to greet them, took one look at them and asked, "Who won?"

Pushing him away from the couple, I said, "Don't pay him any mind; none of us do. You'll learn to love him from a distance."

They laughed and I took them around and introduced them to those at the party that they hadn't met.

The party seemed to be going smoothly; too smoothly, for this group, I thought.

It was then that Susie stood up, raised her glass high, and hitting it with a spoon to get everyone's attention, announced, "We have another thing to celebrate tonight, as well."

Thinking she was going to toast the resolution to Mitch Taylor's murder, we were all shocked at what she said next.

Continuing, Susie added, "I want to toast the soon-to-be new addition to the Pozner family. Hap and Joanie are expecting a baby!"

Turning to Joanie, Susie hugged her and said, "I'm so jealous. Congratulations."

As she hugged Joanie, she turned her head toward me, standing right next to them, smiled and winked at me. I felt a cold chill run up my neck.

Joanie looked over to me as Susie made her way around the room hugging everyone as if it were she that was pregnant. Joanie, gritting her teeth now, questioned, "How did she know?"

I responded, "How should I know. I didn't tell her."

But like any good lawyer Joanie pushed me further, "Okay. Who *did* you tell?"

Trying to get out of answering her, I replied, "Maybe your mother said something. You know how she blabs."

"Hap, I'm going to give you one more chance to answer my question; and *only* one more!"

Over my short, but fairly happy, life I've learned a few things; one of which is, I hate to admit, from Slick's philosophy – 'the truth is sacred. It should be reserved for only those times when there's no other explanation possible, and, at all costs, used sparingly'. This is definitely one of those times.

"Well I might have mentioned it to Slick a few days ago, you know, when we were out with Sarge and Fr. Christopher having a few pints down at McPartland's."

"I imagine Sarge and Fr. Christopher couldn't help but overhear your telling Slick, now could they?"

"Now that you mention it, that's probably how they knew. Mm, didn't think of that. Thanks!"

Joanie glared and said, "I'll deal with you later."

As she stormed away I mumbled, "I see what they mean about pregnant women."

Once again everyone was chattering about this news. Hugs, handshakes, and toasts went on for quite a while. At this point I could see Sarge had cornered Fr. Christopher over by the cooler Sarge had in the living room. He does this at gatherings so he doesn't have to walk all the way to the frig to get another beer.

I walked over to them, thinking Fr. Christopher might need to be rescued.

Sarge let out a loud belch and said, "Hap, I'd shake your hand if I weren't holding a beer in each; and I'd even give you a hug if it wouldn't make me look like, well, you know. Oh, what the hell! It's taken me a long time to become an '80s kind of guy, but hey, *Rome wasn't built in a day, now was it?*"

I stopped, almost frozen in fear for a brief moment, then, realizing it was all over, for now anyway, let out a laugh.

Then he hugged me, spilling beer from each bottle down my back. Some men should never hug; he's one of them.

Fr. Christopher, in a curious tone, asked, "Hap, when are you going to tell everyone here about the results of the investigation?"

"I wasn't sure if this was the right time or place to address the issue, but I guess everyone's itching to find out. I know I would be."

I walked over to Joanie, Susie and Slick and told them it might be good to take care of this bit of business, especially since the others all had a hand in helping us in one way or another; that is, except for Mrs. Brennan.

"It seems like this party's been about announcements, celebrating one thing or another. I think it's time to get everyone up to speed on where we are with Mr. Taylor's murder."

We all had a chance to add additional pieces to this puzzle. Slick and I had invited Tripp and Bubba, along with Slick's niece, Cynthia, to come to the party. Tripp and Bubba filled everyone in on what they had discovered about Fitzpatrick, and Mitch Taylor's murder.

When all was related I could sense everyone except Fr. Christopher was satisfied. He seemed to have some concerns. I can always tell because he rubs his hands together, just as he does when he is excited about something.

Fr. Christopher asked, "Hap, there is one thing that I would like to know the answer to that has puzzled me all along. Those colored pieces of acetate in the red box; what was their significance?"

Slick and I just shot each other a knowing glance.

I explained, "That is one important clue to the whole mystery; in fact, if I would have figured out what they were in my dream I would have had the answer to the big question, 'who dun it'. The colored acetates were what Ron Sweeney used on his black and white TV in order to make the picture appear to be in color – granted, one color; but a color none-the-less. Remember there weren't any color TV's at that time; at least not in South Buffalo."

I continued, "Now I think it's time we tell the rest of you all about what we found out and how."

The Allentown Murders

After the six of us related our part of the story, Fr. Christopher reminded us of a time, not that long ago, "It seems the last time we were all together like this was just after your friend Devon was murdered. I remember it like it was just yesterday and not years ago."

At his mention of Devon, Slick remembered my haunting dreams where Devon was warning me of something, and said, "Hap, tell them about how you dreamed Devon spoke to you, and what he said."

I could see a spark light up in his eyes as he said this. I also saw the curious looks from everyone else, so I replied, "Okay. Now let me see. I had these reoccurring dreams where Devon kept repeating these same phrases over and over."

I went on to relate the dreams, and his warnings.

Katherine, Joanie's mom asked, "What do you think they mean?"

"It's funny. When I was having them, and before we found Mr. Taylor's killer, I couldn't figure it out. But now; now I understand what Devon was telling me when he said to start at the beginning, just like we did when we were looking for *his* killer. We started with the drugs; remember the drugs that were on the bed next to his body when you found him, Slick. Well, this was about the drugs as well. This time it wasn't drugs literally near Mr. Taylor's body, it was about the drug traffic he was trying to stop in the Allentown area. That's how I see the connection; and, as my mom here can attest, we both have this sixth sense about some things. Right mom?"

With a big smile she simply replied, "I knew you were going to say that, Hap." We all laughed.

FORTY-SEVEN
FRIDAY, SEPTEMBER 5

"It's been six months Hap; I want to go home – *PLEASE!*"

"Joanie, I've never seen you act like this. What's wrong?" I asked.

She insisted, "I want to get back to our house, our nest; in the place we now call home. That's what's wrong. What don't you get?"

I mumbled, "This must be one of those pregnant women things again."

"What was that? I heard you; and it's not one of those things. I just want to be in my own house," she ranted.

"All right, all right. I get it; and your timing couldn't be better. The new semester is just about to start and you want to go back to Wilmington. That gives me about a week and a half to get out of our lease, turn off the power and phone to the apartment, inform Canisius College that I won't be staying for the fall semester like planned, contact my supervisor at UNC-Wilmington so he can schedule classes for me, pack, say goodbye to everyone and, let's see, what have I forgotten? Oh Yeh, drive 800 miles back to North Carolina. Not a problem."

She smiled, kissed me on the cheek and replied, "Thanks; I knew you could handle it. I'll see you when you get home from work."

As she left the room I shouted back at her, "That was sarcasm; I was being *sarcastic!*"

But she was already in the bedroom, lying down, to take a nap.

*   *   *

"Joanie, I'm home. Susie and Slick are with me. I thought it might be a good idea for you to let them in on our plan change, since it affects them as well."

As Susie sat down at the kitchen table, Slick made his way to the refrigerator to find a snack. I went into the bedroom where Joanie was still where I left her in the morning.

"Are you all right? Have you been in bed all day today?" I asked.

She laughed and replied, "Yeh, that's all I do all day while you're at work; lay around, watch TV and eat bonbons. No, you dummy. I got up shortly after you left this morning, packed clothes and cleaned the apartment; after which I went to the store to pick up a few things and then I laid back down for about a half hour. Is that okay with you?"

I smiled and said, "Sure; that's fine."

She smacked me on my arm and moaned, "Oh."

"Are Susie and Slick out in our kitchen?" she asked after hearing the noise they were making.

"Yeh, Susie and I stopped by Sarge's and picked Slick up. That's what I was telling you when I came in here."

"Why did you bring them here, now?" she asked impatiently.

"I think we need to talk to them about our change of plans, don't you?" I queried.

"I guess you're right – for once," she shot back.

"Susie, Slick I wasn't expecting company. Hap should have told me."

"You mean he should have warned you," Slick quipped.

"So we probably need to talk. It was wonderful of you to come back to Buffalo in May to help us find my dad's killer..."

Susie interrupted, "We even left our jobs and found new ones; but isn't that what friends do for each other."

I could see this was not going to go well.

I interjected, "So I thought, with Joanie being 'in the family way' that it might be better if she were back home in Wilmington; you know, in her own house, on the Ponderosa, so to speak."

Joanie smiled at me and spoke, "Thanks Hap. No, it was really me. I am the one who wanted to get back home. In fact, I asked Hap to leave his job here so that we could go back now. I've been packing and cleaning all day trying to help get things ready."

We both looked at Susie and Slick to see what their reaction would be. We knew that they weren't going to take it well, but we had to do this for *us*. Besides, they still had family in town and they, no doubt, would follow us back in no time.

Susie smiled and said, "Great. When do we leave?"

We were all dumbfounded, even Slick.

"You can't just quit your job like that," Slick shot back at her.

"Of course I can. Besides I'm getting a bit tired of spending so much time at Sarge's and having to deal with his, his – you know – *his ways*. Well, aren't you? I can easily get a transfer back to New Hanover Regional in Wilmington, and you can get back to your office and research vessel. Anyway, I want to be married at the beach and it will take six to eight months for Joanie and I to plan everything."

I could see by Joanie's expression that she hadn't been consulted on this decision yet; but I knew she wouldn't have it any other way – their our best friends, for better or for worse.

Joanie smiled and said, "It's settled then. We leave the 15th of this month. That gives us 10 days to take care of any loose ends here and head home."

I could see that dim bulb light up in Slick's head once again. He said, "Hey, this reminds me of when Lucy, Ricky, Fred and Ethel packed up and headed out to California..."

The three of us all moaned, "*Oh, no. Not again!*"

FORTY-EIGHT
WEDNESDAY, APRIL 15, 1987

"Devon, I, that is we, all miss you. It's been ten years, but I still come here every chance I get to talk to you; even on days like today with the rain and the cold. Ha! But what am I complaining about; at least I'm still alive. I'm beginning to sound like some people when they talk about a couple where one of them just died of something – like a sudden stroke or heart attack. Everyone comments on how the surviving spouse is so upset and depressed; they feel so bad for him or her. They seem to forget that the other person is *DEAD!*"

"Devon, I wrote a poem for you. It's sort of a sardonic look at death. Anyway, I call it:

I'm Sad I Missed Your Funeral –

I'm sad I missed your funeral,
You need not come to mine.
But if you feel you have to,
I think that would be fine.

You needn't come sit Shiva,
I partied during yours.

259

We seem to live much longer now,
The outcome of more cures.

I missed the morning paper,
That echoed your demise.
I'll follow better next time,
Though I doubt you will arise.

Don't sit and mourn in grief for me,
I'm happy, you will see.
Since you've gone on before I do,
Please save a place for me.

I hope you like it...what now? Even at a cemetery I can't find peace."

I could hear footsteps coming up the path behind me. Who is it now? I wish that if someone is going to bother you they at least wouldn't try to sneak up on you as if they really don't want to disturb you. But I suppose it's time for me to snap back to reality; the sound bringing me back from an almost hypnotic state. I guess it's because I have the gift my mother does; she has a 'mindful connection with the spirits of lost loved ones', as she calls it.

Without turning, I query, "Is that my good friend Slick that I hear attempting to sneak up on me as I communicate with our dear friend Devon?"

"How did you do that? Ever since we were kids you've been able to, not only hear someone trying to surprise you, but you know who it is?"

"It's a gift; what can I say? Besides, it doesn't take a clairvoyant to detect the sound of sneakers making a sucking sound as they're lifted from the muddy path that leads from the parking lot. Oh, by the way, I think I would invest in a new pair; your left one seems to be separating at the seam."

"That's what I mean! How did you know that?"

With a playful laugh I respond, "Rather than explaining the obvious, why don't you walk back toward the car and this time listen to yourself as you trudge along."

Slick takes a few steps trying to hear what I detected, but without much luck. He continues on and suddenly spins around shouting, "Ah, ha! I got it. When I lift my left sneaker the mud pulls it apart at the rip and makes a flopping sound as it comes back together. Right?"

"Exactly. Now to the question of how I knew it was you."

"Yeah, how *did* you know?" Slick asked.

"Elementary, my dear homeless..."

Slick interrupted, "Now wait a minute. I have a home. I live with you, don't you remember!"

"Right, how could I forget? Which reminds me you were going to look for your own place when we returned from our trip to Allentown, weren't you?"

"Yeah, we are. Quite frankly, Susie and I are getting a bit tired of all the chores you and Joanie have us doing around the house. We never did any of this at any of our places!"

I added, "Which might be one of the factors that led to your being evicted so often. Did that ever occur to you?"

Slick snidely quipped, "People are just too fussy now-a-days. Just too fussy."

I remembered what we were discussing before this digression and said, "Where was I before I was so *rudely* interrupted? Oh Yeh; besides the very cheap sneakers, I could tell it was you by your gait."

"My what? I didn't go through any gate. What are you talking about? Remember who you're talking to."

"Sorry, I forgot. No, I said gait, like the manner in which you take your steps – how you walk."

"Well why didn't you just say that. So you can tell who is walking toward you, even if they're trying to sneak up on you. You're telling me that you could tell if it were me or Susie or Joanie."

"That's right."

"So if Joanie were coming up behind you, you would know that it was her without a doubt."

"Yes."

"Okay, I'll bite. How would you know that it was Joanie and not Susie, or anyone else for that matter?"

"That's easy. If it were Joanie she'd be telling me what to do as she came toward me. She can't help herself."

At that we both began laughing.

"All right, but how did you know it was my left sneaker and not my right?"

"I didn't; but I had a 50/50 chance of guessing it right, didn't I?"

Slick got serious for a moment, "As I was getting closer I could hear you talking, as if to Devon. Was I hearing things or were you talking to him?"

"Slick, as you know, ever since he was murdered I've been coming here almost every week. I know we found his killer and brought him to justice, but I have this gnawing feeling that there was more to it than what we found out. I mean, whenever I come to talk to him I get this feeling that he is not at rest. He's trying to tell me something. I don't think that Jake was behind the murder. Oh, he definitely did the killing, but I feel that Devon is trying to tell me that there is someone else; someone very sinister behind his death."

"Oh, no. I know that look. And somehow I'm going to get dragged into this. No; we're *all* going to get dragged into this, aren't we?"

With a resolute look, I respond, "You know I rely on you, and Susie and Joanie. You all have skills that keep me from missing things."

Shaking his head Slick says, "Well, where do we begin?"

"I'm not sure; but I have a feeling something will come to us to guide us to where we need to be. A sign, or a clue will emerge...and soon, I believe."

"Now you're scaring me. But, as usual, I know that no one or nothing is going to stop you. It's that AC/DC you got."

"Do you mean A.D.D.?" I asked.

262

"No between you and Devon I believe it's called AC/DC," he smugly replied.

"Bad joke. But if he were here he'd probably have something to say to you as he laughed at your poor attempt at humor."

After a brief moment of silence I sighed and announced, "Well, I guess we'll be off on a new adventure soon!"

"Hey what are we doing here anyway; your wife and new baby girl are in the hospital. Why aren't you there with them and Susie? They sent me out to look for you."

I replied, "I told Joanie that I was just going out for a minute to get some air, but I really felt a need to come here. Maybe to tell Devon about my new baby, maybe to see if things were settled with him."

"Hap, he's dead. It doesn't get much more settled. Now let's get back to the girls. By the way, I had a couple of great ideas for a name for her. Do you want to hear them now or wait until we're with Joanie and Susie?"

"No."

"No to which choice I gave you?" Slick replied.

"No to both," I stated.

In true Slick fashion, he ignored me and went on anyway, "Okay, I'll tell you now. I was thinking, since today is the day taxes are due that you could name her..."

I interrupted, "If you're going to say Texas or something stupid like that you can stop right there!"

He grinned and replied, "Of course not. I'm not an idiot, you know. No, I was thinking maybe something like Austin or Dallas, a city in Texas. Get it – taxes, Texas. Pretty good, eh?"

"Well, it's better than I thought you might come up with; but we've already come up with a name. You know that today is also the day that Devon was murdered. Well, we thought it might be a nice tribute to him to name her after him – Devon. After all, I might not be here today if it weren't for him, or at least the dreams where he warned me of danger."

Slick smiled, "I couldn't have given her a better name if I tried. Now let's get back to your family. By the way, where is your car, I didn't see it when I came in here?"

"I left it at the hospital. I walked here. It's not that far, just a straight shot up 17th Street to Market and a few blocks down."

"Well, I'll drive you back.

I just smiled and said, "Let's go; we don't want to keep our three girls waiting, now do we?"

*   *   *

ABOUT THE AUTHOR

Michael is the author of three prior works of fiction: *Where the Road Begins (2011), Murder at Ravenswood Hall (2012)* (the prequel to this novel) and *The Almost Definitive Collection, vol. 1 (2013).*

His non-fiction works include a journal writing program called, *Journaling with Character*, which incorporates character education trails for elementary, middle and high school students, and a book on leadership titled, *Leadership: IQ vs. EQ.*

All of his books can be purchased from your local bookstore, at all online book sources, as well as from his website. eBooks of all of his works are also available. You can visit his website at: **http://www.mjmaccalupo.com.**

He has been a guest on several radio and morning television programs in Buffalo, NY, Wilmington and Raleigh, NC including: (morning television) *Winging It! Buffalo Style* with Victoria Hong, Allie Hartwick, Joe Arena and Lauren Hall, *A.M. Buffalo* with Linda Pellegrino, and WNED (radio) with Mike Desmond in Buffalo; WHQR (radio) with Jemila Ericson in Wilmington, NC, WPTF (radio) with Brian Freeman in Raleigh, NC.

His writing has also been reviewed in *Encore Magazine, The Wilmington Star News* and *The Buffalo News.*

He lives in beautiful Wilmington, NC with his wife, Gigi, and Swiss Mountain dog, Bravo; and now has four grandchildren to enjoy. He divides his time between writing, spending time with his family and riding his H-D Road King Classic motorcycle.

www.ingramcontent.com/pod-product-compliance
Lightning Source LLC
Chambersburg PA
CBHW021231250626
47155CB00008B/2957